# Voodoo Dreams

## by

## Alana Lorens

**Voodoo Dreams**

Cover Art by *Kim Mendoza*

The Wild Rose Press, Inc.
PO Box 708
Adams Basin, NY 14410-0708
Visit us at www.thewildrosepress.com

Publishing History
First Faery Rose Edition, 2013
Print ISBN 978-1-62830-045-1
Digital ISBN 978-1-62830-046-8

Published in the United States of America

**Brianna snatched a triangle-folded paper from** her bag and dropped it onto the table between them. It sat there, looking fairly harmless. Evan studied it from the top, from the side, not seeing any sort of wire or other device that could cause a shock.

"It stung me. Like a jolt of electricity."

"You said you 'saw' something. Was that when you touched it?"

"Look, it clearly wasn't real. I don't want to think about it."

Frustrated, he took matters into his own hands, literally. He reached for it, ready to draw back when it zapped him. But it didn't. He cocked an eyebrow at her.

"Just throw it in the trash," she said.

In the trash? No way. Not after this whole freaky scene. "Something's going on here. If it's a real threat or danger, we'll call the police. They can handle it."

He spread the white sheet flat.

Thickly-inked black letters jumped out at him.

*WHAT YOU SEEK IS WITHIN YOUR GRASP.*
*YOU MUST PASS THROUGH DANGER*
*WHERE SAND BECOMES WATER*
*AND THE GREATEST PERIL IS TO BE ALONE.*
*THE PRIZED POSSESSION OF YOUR ENEMY*
*IS YOUR KEY TO THE CITIES OF THE DEAD.*
*FIND THERE THE BLOOD-RED FLOWER.*
*MAKE YOUR SACRIFICE*
*TO SHOW YOUR PURITY OF HEART.*
*THEN WILL YOUR DEBT BE SATISFIED.*

"What kind of bizarro weirdness is this? Where did you get it?"

Mystified, he read it again. But the words made no more sense the second time. Or the third.

## Dedication

For all those who embrace the magical...

Chapter One

The plane's sudden dip brought Brianna Ward fully awake. Her fingernails dug into the arms of her seat. She didn't like flying. Never had. But she cherished efficiency. The fastest way from Pittsburgh to New Orleans was by air, so that's how she went. Even if the cost was nearly prohibitive.

True, she hadn't put in a lot of thought. In fact, all she'd invested was a phone call to her travel agent.

"I want out of town, and I want out now!" she'd said. "What's happening that's fun?"

It turned out to be the week before Mardi Gras. That sounded fun, right?

"I've gone to Mardi Gras three times," her agent said. "You'll have a blast. Let me see what I can arrange."

Seventy-two hours later, Brianna was on her way to the Big Easy, set for five days of fun and frolic. Thanks to a last-minute cancellation, she'd lucked into a room at a nice B-and-B in the Garden District, instead of the airport chain hotel. The excursion would be rough on her wallet, but she'd earned it, and she meant to enjoy every minute.

The small child in the seat in front of her tossed her stuffed animal back over the seat for the fourth time. Eyes sparkling with mischief, she peered through the narrow crack between the seats. Irritated at first,

Brianna was quickly won over by the child's delightful and contagious giggle. Smiling, she tossed the animal back, dismissing the mother's apologies.

The pilot's calm voice came over the speakers, warning everyone they might experience more turbulence, but his intention was to fly above the storms over Georgia. She'd survived the last three weeks; she would survive this. She laid her head back on the hard cushion and closed her eyes.

Better to sleep now. When she got to New Orleans, she intended to have the adventure of her life.

****

The prior three weeks had probably been the worst of Brianna's five-year career as a corporate attorney in the Steel City. She'd lost a huge case for Artotech, one of Brannigan and Strauss's largest corporate clients. The three-week jury trial had been a disaster from the get-go, bolstering her long-held opinion that the only thing worth believing in was Murphy's Law.

Everything else always turned out to be a lie, one way or another.

She'd prepared for months, reviewed a dozen experts' reports, organizing and tagging hundreds of documents, all over the objections of a belligerent company representative who kept complaining that he didn't want a woman lawyer.

Even as she'd selected each juror, Brianna set out to impress them. She started the trial in her navy blue suit, with a conservative white blouse, the trial attorney's most "sincere" uniform. She still lacked connection with them, even the women, who usually took in her petite figure and dark pixie-cut hair and subliminally considered her like a daughter or little sister. As she'd felt them slipping, she wore more colorful outfits, until the last day of trial found her in a brightly-flowered silk dress with a white jacket. It was one of her favorites, and she'd been told many times it made her appealing.

It hadn't helped. The twelve men and women didn't understand the subtleties of a non-competition clause in the Artotech contract, and they'd let the former employee continue his business, a direct theft of Artotech's procedures.

The disappointing verdict burned her clear through, and the happy contortions of opposing counsel Frank Dellenbach, of Givens, Dellenbach and Spicer, had just been poisonous icing on the cake. The whole Pittsburgh bar knew the sharp rivalry between the two firms. This case was surely a feather in Dellenbach's cap. The smug bastard had gone so far as to offer to buy her a drink to celebrate. Pig.

But now she was as far away from facts and briefs and Pittsburgh and Artotech and Frank Dellenbach as she could be.

The captain's voice announced their impending arrival at Louis Armstrong Airport, adding it was sixty-five degrees and clear—a far cry from the twenty-two degrees and six inches of snow she'd left behind.

She pulled the lever to set her seat upright, relieved to see the ground in sight, at least. Five days. The Insight Guides and Frommer's guidebooks were tucked into her purse, from which she'd selected nine tourist spots or restaurants and bars recommended for good food and some of New Orleans' best music, both jazz and zydeco. She preferred planning things in as much detail as she could. Anything she had control over was one less thing that could go wrong. Or hurt her.

*You mean like the Artotech trial?* nagged her conscience.

"Shut up," she mumbled, drawing the attention of the man sitting next to her.

"Pardon me?" he asked. The man was about her age, in his early thirties, she guessed. His collar-length light brown hair was rumpled—he must have been sleeping, too. Now he held a John Grisham book and studied her with bright blue eyes from behind gold wire-rimmed glasses.

"Nothing. Sorry. Talking to myself."

"That can be a sign of something dangerous," he said.

"Dangerous?" She had to laugh. "Right, that's me."

"Sometimes the cutest things are the most deadly. You know those tree frogs from the rain forest? The blue and yellow ones? Poison."

As soon as the words came out of his mouth, she could see where this was going. A fine example of the "what happens at Mardi Gras, stays at Mardi Gras" syndrome. Well, she wasn't looking for a date, thanks.

"Poison," she said with a little nod. "I'll keep that in mind." She turned her attention pointedly back to the window, dismissing him.

"Are you visiting New Orleans for business or pleasure?" he persisted.

"Business." She hoped that would shut him up.

"Can't imagine much business goes on these last few days before the holiday."

The skepticism in his voice put her back up and almost engaged her again, ego stinging from the implication that she'd lied.

4

Well, she had.

He wasn't bad-looking, and she could have whiled away the remaining time on the flight in conversation with him. After all, he could at least read, and seemed like a nice guy. But, her mind still tangled in legal musings, she hadn't yet found the sweet spot of "getaway" she desired. Maybe later in the weekend, but not now. And *not* if he was comparing her to poison. Talk about backhanded flattery!

She was about to deliver a magnificent retort when the pilot broke in again, announcing their impending landing. The flight attendants started their runs up and down the skinny aisle, collecting cups and papers. Everyone began to pack their personal belongings away and retrieve their under seat baggage, ready to run for it when the door opened. She managed to ignore her neighbor in the noise and confusion until it came time for their row to exit.

"Hope you get a lot of work done," he said, amusement sparkling in his eye.

*Hope you take a flying leap.*

She smiled and let the others in front of her sweep him away, hoping to discourage the man. He was reading John Grisham, for heaven's sake. Probably some wannabe-hotshot lawyer who wouldn't know one end of a case file from the other.

It was seven o'clock, p.m., New Orleans time, when Brianna finally extricated herself from the plane. She headed immediately for the baggage carousel to collect her luggage, hoping taxis were still running. Surely this late in the week before the big day, they would be available any time. From what she'd read, Bourbon Street never slept.

Disappointment awaited at the carousel. She watched for the small yellow silk flower she'd attached to the suitcase handle, scanning the noisily-rotating batch of luggage as bags were claimed and hauled away into the music and lights of the city, but she never saw it. As the better part of an hour went by, it was clear her luggage did not intend to appear at all.

Her indignant inquiry yielded only a drawled, "Let me check on that for you, ma'am," and the disappearance of the female attendant.

Brianna fumed by the counter. This was not in her plans. How could she run her life with any semblance of order when plans kept falling through?

"Not to worry," a friendly voice said behind her. "Your bags will turn up very soon."

Expecting Mr. Flirtypants, Brianna turned to find an attractive, tall man in a gauzy ecru-colored cargo shirt and khaki pants watching her, his luminous dark eyes set in a face the color of creamed coffee. "Hopefully," Brianna said, her voice tight with irritation.

"Oh, they will," he said with a wide grin. His teeth seemed very white in contrast to his skin and were perfectly-spaced. "You must have faith."

Faith. She'd rather have a supervisor. She tried not to grimace.

"Are you here for Carnival?" he asked. He wore several strands of sparkling beads, gold and royal blue, about eighteen inches long. She idly wondered what he had to show to get them.

Intuition tweeted a small alarm he might be too friendly. The crime statistics she'd read set her nerve on edge, though she hadn't let them influence her final choice. Dire warnings of crime and danger here, particularly after Hurricane Katrina displaced a percentage of the more affluent population. Was he trying to trick her into letting her guard down? What was he after?

He continued to smile.

Feeling pressured to be polite by this complete stranger's concern, she replied, "Yes." She wasn't giving away any secrets; thousands of tourists descended on the city during this celebration. It would be more unusual if she weren't there for the fete.

He spoke with the faintest hint of an accent, slightly British, or maybe from the islands. His clothes were sophisticated, expensive. He didn't look like a criminal.

"That explains it."

"Explains what?"

"No beads." He gestured to her shirt, then behind her to others waiting for departures. Several wore multiple strings of shiny colored beads. "They're a trophy, you know." Suddenly he took off one of his own gold strands and placed it around her neck. "There. Now you're officially part of Mardi Gras."

Startled, she pulled back, and his hand tangled in her hair. She yelped, and an immediate look of apology came over his face. He frowned at his heavy gold ring with a large ruby in the center, several strands of her hair caught in its elaborate setting.

"Are you hurt? I'm so sorry. I should have this repaired." He looked over her shoulder. "Are those your bags?"

Her eyes watering from the momentary pinch, she glanced behind as a set of matched brown luggage passed by on the carousel; attractive, but not hers. He waited with an expression of ultimate patience, as though he expected her to say more.

Where was that baggage check clerk?

Rattled, she reminded herself not everyone was an axe murderer, even here. Perhaps he was just trying to help. Southern hospitality, and all that.

"Yes, I'm fine. It's—um, it's kind of you to share your beads," she added, patting them with the fingers of her right hand, hoping he didn't require some sort of payment.

His continued presence unnerved her, but she couldn't decide why. If anything, he seemed to exude calm. His nails were well-manicured, in contrast to her own. His smile was warm like the southern sun. Something in his eyes was almost hypnotic. She found her suspicions fading the longer she looked in them.

She tore her gaze away at last and checked her watch. The later it got, the more she worried about getting to that bed and breakfast. She knew nothing about the city. That's why she'd decided not to rent a car. The streetcars would get her where she had to go once she'd checked in. But if she didn't get there…

"You're from the north?"

"Yes," she said, thinking it was obvious, since the flight origination information was still posted on the board over the conveyor.

"It's cold there still, isn't it?" he asked, leaning an elbow on the counter.

She nodded. "Snow and ice everywhere."

"You'll enjoy our city, then. It's a tropical paradise." He let his attention wander about the baggage area, then returned it to her. "Are you traveling alone?"

*None of your damned business.*

She tapped a foot, the situation becoming uncomfortable. A security guard passed by, glanced at them, and moved on. She nearly spoke to him, but let it go.

He smiled, adding, "I just wondered if we should be asking after someone else's bags as well."

She shook her head.

"Ah, looking for love at Carnival, perhaps?" He beamed and waved in the direction that the attendant had disappeared. Blood rose hot in her cheeks at the thought of "looking for love," like she was some sort of mad husband hunter. Her first instinct was to leave.

But without her bag, she was stuck. Next time, carry-ons only, she promised herself. She'd noticed so many of her fellow passengers stashing several small bags instead of one large one. This must be why.

As if summoned, the smiling attendant reappeared, her uniform crisp and clean, not a hair out of place. Her soft Southern accent almost made her words feel like an apology. "Your luggage will be out shortly, ma'am. It was sent to a different conveyor. Please wait over there." The woman pointed to the far side of the carousel.

Brianna turned to her companion, hoping he'd be satisfied and move on. "You were right."

"Copper is never wrong," he said mysteriously.

"Copper? That's your name?" she asked, realizing how it fit him, both for the color of his skin and also for the inner fire of his eyes.

He nodded. "Copper Delacroix. My mother has a bent for the mystical."

A dark shadow in his expression tugged at Brianna's curiosity, but she dismissed the thought. Mystical? If she couldn't see it, hear it, or touch it, she didn't believe in it.

Her eyes focused on the moving belt. If her luggage appeared, she'd believe that. When it happened. An awkward silence fell between them, and she finally offered her name as apology. "I'm Brianna Ward. You've been very kind."

"It is my pleasure, Miss Ward." He waited nearby until her two bags showed up. He reached for the large one before she could grab it.

"Thanks, I can get it," she said, and moved to the carousel to drag it off the conveyor. She shouldered the second one by its strap, anxious to be on her way. "You've been very generous. I'm all set now. Good night."

He didn't argue, but bowed slightly and stepped back. "I'm sure you'll have an interesting visit here."

"I sure hope so." She adjusted her grip on the handle of the suitcase and headed for the exit, with a murmured farewell to the man called Copper, ready for her adventure to begin.

Chapter Two

Evan Farrell traveled often enough, post 9/11, to know how little to carry for the best escape vector from the small airplane seat. Three hours he'd been trapped there waiting for his vacation to begin. The only part of the trip that had been even barely tolerable was the woman in the seat next to him She was attractive and she'd smelled good, too. Nothing fancy or stinky, just appealing. Some sort of homey scent, vanilla or cinnamon or something.

He'd tried to start a conversation; after all, they would be in a magical city during a magical time. They could have had some laughs.

But she'd made it clear she wasn't interested.

He could swear something about her attitude, the set of her jaw, was familiar. But she dismissed him so fast, he didn't have time to ponder it. Frankly, he didn't care. He was in New Orleans in the days counting down to Mardi Gras. He meant to have a good time.

Passing by the baggage claim area, he spotted the woman talking to a tall black man. Maybe that explained why she'd been so short with him—she was meeting someone.

But his police-officer past noted their body language. She stood stiffly, like she didn't want to speak to him, and she kept looking over her shoulder at the moving carousel, which held very few bags. The man, on the other hand, seemed confident, kept smiling, but he didn't move in closer. *So, not together.*

Evan continued to the rental car counter, picking up the sweet ride he'd reserved three months before. Always a shortage of cars during Mardi Gras week, that's what he'd read on the Internet, so he'd made plans ahead of time. For several years, he'd wanted to experience the wild debauchery and abandon of this particular time and place, certainly while he was unencumbered by any sort of wife or family. But his junior position as an associate at his law firm had kept him from first choice of vacation dates, at least until now.

Rank has its privileges, just like they said.

He headed back, keys in hand. The woman had claimed her luggage and waited outside at the curb. The black man remained by the carousel, his eyes focused on her. *Huh. That's odd.* Evan studied the woman, who attempted to flag down several cabs, but they rushed by her.

*It's nearly nine o'clock. Maybe you should offer her a ride.*

Evan hushed the Boy Scout inside him. He was a lawyer now. Didn't that excuse him from having to do good deeds? Besides, she'd dissed him pretty well, without knowing the first thing about him. Let her find her own ride.

Walking past without another glance, he made his way out to the rental lot, where he claimed his vehicle and tossed his suitcase in the back seat. He set his cell phone on the dashboard, the GPS guiding him to the Garden District, two blocks off St. Charles, to a bed and breakfast recommended by one of the firm's secretaries, who'd stayed a few years before. The lights blazed as he pulled up, the front door decorated by a wreath lit with green, purple and gold LEDs. Jazz music spilled from most of the well-restored Victorian houses on the block.

"Now that's what I'm talking about," he said, a grin sneaking onto his lips. "Party time, here we come."

He retrieved his bags, sure to lock the car, then walked up to knock on the door.

A smiling blonde woman near her half-century mark, wearing purple stirrup pants and a gold and green peasant-style blouse opened the door. "You must be Mr. Farrell," the woman said, waving him in with a purple-finger-nailed hand. "I'm Terri Worley. We were beginning to wonder if you'd make it."

"Couldn't keep me away," Evan said, stepping inside.

The living room, dining area and what he could see of the kitchen were decked out in the same Mardi Gras colors, all brightly lit like the inside of a disco bar. Several people nodded in greeting as his hostess closed the door. "Hey," he said, the party atmosphere buoying his spirits even higher.

"We can do introductions later," she said. "I'm sure you want to get washed up after your trip." She handed him a key. "Your room's the second on the left at the top of the stairs, and just past there's the bathroom. You take your time, now."

"Thanks."

Evan bounded up the stairs like a puppy exploring his new home, peeking into a couple of the open doors as he passed, another habit left over from his five years on the Pittsburgh force before law school. *All clear.*

Counting off, he found the room assigned to him, done up all tropical in blues and greens and frilly bedspreads that were too ornate. He dug into his suitcase for his "ready-to-celebrate" outfit, a bright Hawaiian print shirt and some crazy hat he'd bought on impulse at the airport in Pittsburgh before he left. Once he put it on, he took one look in the mirror and laughed.

"Who's that guy? Someone about to have a wild time!"

He pointed at his reflection, gestured like he was shooting up the place, and then laughed at his own antics. *Man, you've been working too hard. The boss has you squirreled away studying interrogatories and briefs way too many hours per week. For sure.*

He extricated a small bottle of rum from an interior pocket of his suitcase and drank a gulp straight from the bottle, not his usual style, but he was ready to kick off his night of revelry as soon as possible. It burned all the way down and gave him a quick jolt. Prepared now to tackle the city, he checked his wallet, set the red hat at a jaunty angle and headed for the steps.

Chapter Three

Brianna set her larger bag down on the curb and waited for a taxi to the Garden District. Several passed in the next ten minutes, but none responded to her anxious waves. Frustration bubbled up like a thick, hot fountain, especially when Copper exited the building, raised a hand, and a cab glided to a stop in front of him. The driver came around to open the door, deferent as though Copper were some sort of royalty.

How did he do that? "I can't believe it," she groused.

Just before he climbed in, he noticed her standing there. "Do you need a ride?" he asked.

Her first impulse was to refuse. Then she thought about how late it was, and getting later. How desperate was she?

Not desperate enough to get into a cab with a stranger in New Orleans.

When she hesitated, he chuckled, his face bright under the fluorescent lights of the airport deck. "I'll take the next one."

Two more taxis whizzed by without slowing down. She sighed, defeated. "If you're sure."

"Of course. I want you to feel welcome in our great city." He opened the door for her and even helped the gold-toothed cab driver load her bags in the trunk.

"Thank you, that's very kind." She took inventory

of the bags she'd brought, then sat in the back of the cab. Copper leaned down to speak to the driver through the open back door.

"Take the lady where she needs to go," he said, the quiet sound of command behind Copper's words, definitely an order from a superior. Maybe she was reading into it. Or maybe she was just tired after a long week. No, a long month. Heck, a long several months.

"Where to, darlin'?"

She gave the driver the address. He pulled away smoothly from the curb, blending into the traffic leaving the airport. The city view took her attention as they rode in on the freeway, a network of bridges ahead, on the left, the huge Superdome and the skyscrapers of downtown lit against the night sky.

The cab drove out St. Charles, quickly leaving office buildings behind as the avenue became lined with huge, Victorian-style homes. It was too dark to see much detail, but she noted bay windows, turrets and broad porticos so different from the narrow row houses that constituted much of Pittsburgh. She could hardly wait to see them by daylight.

"Why does everyone have green and purple decorations?" she asked.

"Those be the colors of Mardi Gras, miss. Purple for justice, green for faith, and gold for power," he replied. "Now here's your place."

Brianna's bed and breakfast looked much like the others on the block, hung with blinking strings of lights in the festival colors. The holiday decor made her feel welcome. The driver set her bags on the curb, and she paid him, glad to have arrived at last. When he drove away, she hauled her suitcases to the door and knocked.

The front of the home was beautifully restored, the big front window topped with inlaid stained glass in diamonds of gold, royal blue and a soft pink. Through the window she noticed a large ficus tree in the front room, decorated like a Christmas tree with strings of lights in the Mardi Gras colors.

The door opened, releasing a burst of accordion-laced zydeco music. A festive group of faces turned to see who'd arrived, and a woman dressed in purple and gold invited her in. "Here's our last little duck, so late! Come in, come in—I'm Terri Worley."

Brianna smiled tiredly. "The airline lost my bags."

Terri put an arm around Brianna's shoulders, drawing her inside. "You poor child. I understand completely. I just hate the places. Of course, since I've come to New Orleans, I've never wanted to fly out again."

Brianna noticed Terri pronounced the city's name as "N'awlins" not New Or-leens, as Brianna learned at school. Just another example of how experience in the real world was nothing like a classroom. She wanted to thank her hostess for her warm welcome, but Terri really never stopped talking long enough.

Brightly-colored beads like the ones Copper had given her adorned every available flat surface room in the tan-walled room, in bowls, on plates, hung from the corners of the pictures on the wall. Terri noticed her gaze.

"You'll have plenty of those by the time next Tuesday passes," she said.

"Well I'm not the kind to—you know. Be demonstrative in public." Brianna wasn't a big fan of jewelry. The idea of lifting her shirt for a handful of cheap beads really didn't appeal to her.

A dark-haired man in T-shirt and shorts snickered, and Terri gave him a look. "Now, Hank, don't you start," she scolded gently.

To Brianna, she said, "The Krewes in the parades throw these to the spectators. Without the need to get naked. I promise." She smiled knowingly. "But these are just ordinary beads. I'm sure you'll have the opportunity to get something really special by Mardi Gras Day."

Ordinary? Brianna marveled at the rainbow of colors and different sizes represented. What on earth were the special ones like?

"Have you eaten?" Terri asked. "Can I get you something? Coffee? A cold beverage?"

"No, thanks."

The day was definitely catching up with her, especially the extra hour she'd lost coming west. What she really wanted was a few minutes to herself. It must have showed.

"You look exhausted. Hank, take her bag up and show her the room." Terri leaned closer and added, "It's our best one. How lucky for you the other couple cancelled."

Hank left the brown sofa and strolled over to pick up Brianna's bag.

"I can do that," Brianna said hastily.

Terri sparkled. "Nonsense! Hank's my husband. He knows this keeps jambalaya on his table. Right, baby?"

"Whatevah you say, sweet pea," Hank said, with a quick peck on Terri's cheek.

"Breakfast is from about seven to about nine,"

Terri said, "but we're flexible. This weekend we've got six guests for Mardi Gras. Not everyone gets going at the same time. The kitchen's through these doors here—"

Footsteps bounded down the stairs. Hank ducked aside, stepping in front of Brianna in case the runner fell. "Slow down there, son," he said. "No need to trample the other guests."

"Negligence is not my style, buddy. Not to worry."

Brianna peered around Hank's arm, that voice sounded familiar. Sure enough, it was the John Grisham reader from the plane. He was show-stopping in a very loud Hawaiian-style shirt in blues and a tight pair of black jeans. But what really grabbed her attention was the brilliant red derby with alien antennae on it.

When he saw her, he broke into a smile. "Hello! You again? Must be fate."

A little overwhelmed by his sudden appearance, she could only shrug. "Must be. I'm Brianna Ward." She gave him a firm handshake, noticing his eyes were just the color of summer asters. Since he wore glasses, they weren't contacts—they were natural.

"Evan Farrell," he replied. "No need to be formal. Call me Evan."

Terri beamed like she'd just won the lottery. "I hoped you two would hit it off."

"Could be." Evan winked at Brianna, openly appraising her.

She, in turn, found herself admiring his casual attitude and the hint of mischief in his outlandish outfit. Maybe she'd underestimated him on the plane. That kind of slightly delirious distraction was just what she needed. Something completely different. No lawyers, no papers, no filings. Just fun.

Terri went on in a flood of introductions, gesturing at several people in the kitchen congregating under the shiny foil ornament hanging over the table, which was decorated with purple, green and gold candles. She finished with, "Both of you are from Pittsburgh, too. Isn't that a hoot?"

Interesting. Pittsburgh was a hub for several airlines—he could have been from anywhere. Or even coming home to New Orleans. She looked him over again, her heartbeat quickening. Evan could be more than a casual holiday acquaintance. The thought gave her a little thrill of anticipation. She didn't really need any complications, but when she imagined him for a moment on the cover of a magazine, dressed in an expensive suit, instead of this weird get-up, she imagined him delicious.

"A hoot," Evan agreed, his initial enthusiasm fading under the group's attention.

Terri went bubbling on. "What a coincidence. Both of you from Pittsburgh, both of you lawyers..." She trailed off as they both reacted to her revelation.

Brianna froze, sure the expression of horror on Evan's face mirrored her own. A lawyer? The last person she'd wanted to meet! So much for that warm glow.

Evan stared over the top of his glasses, his relaxed posture stiffening. "A Pittsburgh attorney. Certainly is a coincidence."

Her initial disappointment seemed magnified in his tone. She could tell he disliked her and fidgeted with her suitcase strap. The Worleys hovered, Terri's chagrin that her matchmaking plans had gone awry clear on her face.

"What firm?" Evan persisted.

She blurted out, "Brannigan and Strauss."

"Givens, Dellenbach and Spicer," he said, words clipped short.

Brianna was so shocked she actually shuddered. This man worked for that pig Frank Dellenbach? She'd barely escaped from her humiliating Artotech defeat, just to find a member of the enemy camp at her lodgings? Unreal. A nightmare, even.

A thought of finding a chain hotel room in another neighborhood flitted through her mind, but she guessed there wouldn't be a thing left to rent now for the next five days. She was stuck.

"Brianna... Artotech?" Evan asked, recognition dawning. His smile acquired sardonic underpinnings. "Damn skippy! I thought you looked familiar. I saw you at court last week with Frank. Liked the flowered dress, by the way."

Stung by his sarcastic tone, Brianna wanted to protest, but couldn't come up with a sharp enough retort to stab him. "I—"

He looked as if he enjoyed her discomfiture. "Got a date with a drink downtown, y'all, so please forgive me if I rush off. Nice to meet you, Brianna."

He opened the door and stepped out, a quick glance over his shoulder for her before he disappeared into the darkness outside.

"That boy's going to get himself killed," one of the other women murmured, breaking the awkward silence.

An older man with a paunch and a buttoned-up shirt, standing close enough to be her husband, chided her. "No, honey love, he's got a car. He'll just waste a lot of time finding a place to park down in the Quarter."

Terri finally said, "Hank, why don't you see Brianna to her room?"

He seemed relieved to escape. "Oh, sure. This way."

"Thank you," Brianna said, grateful to end further discussion. A cowboy-themed couple emerged from the kitchen holding purple plastic cups they raised as she went up. "Happy Mardi Gras!" the tall man said with a wink and a drawl.

"You bet," she said, unsure of the proper protocol. Disarmed by the conversation with Evan, she wasn't at all her usual glib self.

Hank showed her the third room on the right, handed her a key, then set her bag down on a large chair near the dresser. "Bath's down the hall at the end. If you need anything, c'mon down," he said with a big dumb smile, and lumbered out.

The silence was welcome. After her evening, she wanted to de-stress in privacy. The room was wonderful, clean and neat, with a dark green bedspread on the tall four-poster double bed, and filmy curtains delicately edged in lace. A molded decoration in the form of garlands of roses lined each wall near the ceiling, which was itself delicately painted with roses. Admiring the artistic restoration, she gave silent thanks for a wonderful travel agent.

Yeah, what a talent. She'd located the only place where Mr. I-work-for-a-Pig was staying.

She forced the uncharitable thought from her mind, resolved to pay attention to the good things. The window was open—in February!—and music filtered in, something about a "Mardi Gras Mambo." The catchy, happy rhythm threatened to remove the black cloud hovering over her. The neighbors on their back deck congregated, laughing and obviously celebrating the arrival of the weekend.

The weekend. Hurrah. Five days with no deadlines, just time to relax and get away. It was Heaven.

Or could be except for that jerk Farrell.

She felt his presence like the grit of travel on her face, and decided the first order of business was to wash it off, so she'd feel human again. A clean white towel and cloth were set out on the foot of her bed, so she gathered them and headed down the hall for a grateful encounter with warm water and lemon-scented soap.

She washed her face once, then just kept washing. Every time she thought she was finished, that face appeared before her eyes again.

So unfair!

The grumbling came from deep within her. She stared at her reflection in the mirror. What the hell was wrong with her? She'd actually thought he was good-looking. She'd even entertained the notion of something beyond these five days with him—though she hadn't intended to act on it yet, just letting her mind free itself in anticipation of vacation mode, you know...

But the handsome stranger had turned out to be a wolf inside that sheep's derby.

Fate obviously had a very dark sense of humor.

She took a quick glance out the door, saw the hall was clear and skittered across to her room, closing the door behind her, shutting out the embarrassment of the encounter.

*That comment about her dress—who the hell did he*

*think he was?*

Still burning, she needed something to do. It sounded like the party had kicked off again downstairs, the roar of the basketball game competing with occasional exclamations and raucous laughter. But she really wasn't in the mood.

Unpack. That was at least something.

She emptied her suitcases into the drawers of the white rattan dresser, a little surprised at how much she'd brought with her. In that mad last-minute rush, she'd clearly chosen more than just a few outfits and a good pair of walking shoes, probably three times what she'd actually need. At least she'd be prepared for any occasion, right?

It was small satisfaction.

Once that was done, she had nothing else to do. But she was sure she wanted to remain upstairs, not risking further embarrassment. Instead, she spent several minutes doing stretches, priming her muscles' recovery from the cramped flight, then stretched out on the bed with a paperback by Mary Higgins Clark.

She let the mystery tingle her into relaxation, her cares distracted by the action of the tale. It didn't take long before the tension faded. The exhaustion of the last three weeks gradually overcame her, and she slipped away into sleep.

## Chapter Four

The Friday morning light shone through the insubstantial curtains onto Brianna's face. Bleary-eyed, half-conscious, she glared at the window. The pristine white mini-blinds were pulled up to the top; all she would have had to do was let them down.

Too late now.

She pulled a soft pillow over her head, feeling like she'd hardly rested. Perhaps because she slept in a strange place, but more likely because Copper Delacroix had haunted her dreams.

As she tried to remember their content, they faded into smoke. She couldn't think of a reason why he should have been on her mind. Ridiculous. Copper had only helped her get where she needed to be. It was Evan Farrell who'd acted the consummate ass, not him.

Her eyes closed, she tried to force herself back to sleep, but after a few minutes, she surrendered to the inevitable. It wasn't going to happen. She sat up, realizing she'd fallen asleep in her traveling clothes, and her blouse was hopelessly wrinkled.

She crawled out of bed and grabbed a hanger from the closet. A steamy shower would do her—and her blouse—a world of good. She opened her door slightly and peeked down the hall, seeing the bathroom door was closed.

*Take a number...*

Listening intently, she waited until she heard the door open, and another door close. Another peek showed her the bathroom was free. Clutching her jeans, her blouse and green polo shirt, she hurried down the hall. When she'd finished, feeling refreshed and ready to tackle the city, she wrapped her hair in her towel, leaving the drying to her room, out of courtesy for other guests. Eight adults sharing one bathroom was a traffic jam waiting to happen.

She hung the blouse on the door to her closet and checked her watch. Nearly eight a.m. She'd planned to be on the streetcar by now, heading to the French Quarter. Late! A quick blow-dry of her short, wispy hair would have to do while she reviewed her first day's plan she'd made on the plane.

First, coffee.

Lots of blessed coffee.

Then, pick up a public transportation pass at the New Orleans Tourist Authority. The French Quarter in all its splendor was penciled in for the rest of the day with highlights marked in her tourist guide. She intended to be on Canal Street for the parade of the Krewe of Hermes by eight p.m., and perhaps catch some jazz later in the evening at Preservation Hall.

*But not if I'm late already!*

Downstairs, her hostess presided over the morning table. The other guests were already enjoying a variety of breakfast foods, including a spectacular Danish cake decorated in the now-familiar colors of gold, green and purple. Brianna poured her coffee from the pot on the sideboard and carried it to the table. She hadn't planned a sit-down breakfast, especially since she was late, but the bowl of fresh fruit seemed to be calling her name.

Five more minutes wouldn't hurt anything, especially when she'd been so anti-social last night.

"Good morning," Terri said. "Did you sleep well?"

Brianna gave a polite smile, seeing no reason to provide the truth. She wasn't under oath, after all. "Yes, thank you. It's a lovely place." She chose a shiny navel orange and began to peel it.

"Let me present you to our other guests, now that it's a little calmer. This is Brianna Ward, from Pittsburgh," Terri said to the others.

The introductions continued with the Nielssons, first-time Mardi Gras participants from Wisconsin, who watched everything, wide-eyed, as if they expected fairies or gypsies to materialize out of mid-air, and the McCurdys, festival veterans from Texas, who lounged at breakfast in faux cowboy gear.

Mr. Farrell, however, was nowhere to be found.

"Is this your first Mardi Gras?" Terri asked.

Brianna nodded, her mouth full of juicy citrus tartness. "I'm pleased the city is back in business. We were certainly shocked at the pictures of damage after Hurricane Katrina."

A ghost passed over Terri's face for a moment, but she took a deep breath. "It's been years since that storm, but every time we've got rough winds or hard rains, I have to confess, I flash back. It was horrible."

The woman from Wisconsin made sympathetic noises. "Coming from the airport, we saw many buildings still in ruins."

"Yes. The Ninth Ward took the worst, but anyone without insurance or money to rebuild was hit hard. Many just left the city, never to return." Terri stared into her cup for several long seconds, then cleared her throat with a determined change of subject. "But we're back to letting the good times roll, once again."

Brianna took a long sip of her coffee, finding it very strong and black. She stared at the cup a moment, wondering if she'd taken espresso by accident. When she set her cup down, a dark film lined the inside of it.

Terri grinned at the expression on her face.

"Chicory," she said. "It's an old French tradition from war times. When they didn't have enough coffee to go around, they'd grind up chicory and add it to the coffee to stretch their supplies. We don't need to do that anymore, but over the years, it's just become part of the local culture. Chicory adds a certain unusual flavor that's just the city's own. If you go to Café du Monde down in the French Quarter—and I hope you do, because it's one of those universal New Orleans experiences—you must get some of their café au lait with beignets. It's a little piece of paradise right here on earth, I swear."

"Chicory. I've never heard of that before."

"Try some of the king cake," the cowgirl suggested, handing her the platter with the tri-colored Danish.

"It's a Mardi Gras tradition, this cake. They come with different fillings, but all are decorated in Mardi Gras colors. Be careful while you're eating it, though, because there's a tiny plastic baby inside each cake. Whoever gets the baby is supposed to buy the next king cake, for any celebration until next Mardi Gras, at least for the locals," Terri explained. "But for you out-of-towners, we say it gives you a little extra bit of luck during your visit."

Brianna took a piece of the sweet cake, and

examined it closely before she took a bite. It was stuffed with cherries and a cream cheese filling and...sure enough, a naked little plastic baby. "I guess I found it," she said with a hesitant smile.

"Luck for you," the Wisconsin woman said, looking a little envious.

"Don't worry, Mrs. Nielssen, we'll have another tomorrow," Terri said. "Some more grits? We don't add cheese to ours here. We eat them Southern style."

Mrs. Nielssen nodded and picked up a conversation that must have begun before Brianna arrived. "Now what were you saying about the dress balls, Terri?"

"There's a masked ball at the Spanish Plaza, down by the Riverwalk, that's free and open to the public. Most of the other events are for Krewes only, sponsored for their members. Hank and I went to the Orpheus ball several years ago, when he was part of that Krewe. But on Monday night—that's Lundi Gras, in N'awlins talk—you can dance under the stars as the King of Rex lands at the dock by barge. He's welcomed by the mayor, and given his twenty-four hours to rule the city." She smiled. "It's very romantic."

Not inclined for romance at the moment, Brianna returned to her cup, savoring the dark aroma as she sipped again, better prepared this time. It didn't taste bad. Though she usually drank her coffee black, some cream might help cut the hammer effect. It would take some getting used to. Especially that sludge along the sides and bottom of the cup.

"What are your plans today, Brianna?" Terri asked.

There. A topic that didn't require a lot of thought—or emotional investment. "I'm going to the French Quarter. I figured it would be less visited before the weekend."

"Laws, yes," Terri said. "You definitely don't want to be down there Monday and Tuesday. So crowded. Besides, the parades all come along St. Charles, right down the street here. No need to put yourself in that crush."

Speaking of things to avoid…

*If I hurry, maybe I can get out the front door before Evan Farrell comes downstairs.*

"All right, I'd better get going then. Thank you for the advice." Brianna grabbed the large canvas bag she'd bought at the Pittsburgh airport, already loaded with her guide books and usual traveling items.

"Have a great day!" Terri called as she headed for the door.

She nearly made a clean getaway.

Before she could pass the foot of the stairs, Evan started down. He raised a hand to catch her attention. "Brianna? Can we talk?"

"Sorry, I'm late," she said, not even turning to acknowledge him, still burning about the comment on her dress.

*Yes, I know it's stupid. But I don't care.*

A shiver of frustration ran through her, picking up her pace. She practically ran the three blocks to St. Charles Avenue, where streetcars ran from the west side of the city to downtown for a dollar and a quarter each way. Just as other travelers had done since the 1830s, riding these historical and picturesque cars through the streets under a canopy of broad live oak branches, added a special dimension to the aspect of this vacation as getaway from her normal world.

She needed a chance to let go. Not only because of

the Dellenbach antics, though finding one of his cronies practically across the hall certainly dampened her outlook. Her daily *modus operandi* dictated that she lived with a fist clenched around all the loose ends of her day, hopefully choking the life out of them. Control of everything—her life, her job, her cases—this was how she functioned best.

Growing up in Homestead, a town devastated by the closing of the Pittsburgh steel plants in the 1970s and 1980s, her parents struggled to raise four children when the good money was suddenly gone. Her father had died of an unexpected heart attack before Brianna had left junior high school. Her mother Nona had always believed his heart was broken by the betrayal of his employers and the loss of his job that had provided for his family.

Nona held on long enough to get Brianna, her baby, off to college, before succumbing to the deep depression that consumed her after her husband's death. Brianna had been amazed at the speed of her mother's decline and passing. Nothing any of the siblings could do slowed it. Nona's insurance money helped pay Brianna's way through law school.

The gift had been dearly bought; Brianna had resolved she would never depend on anyone else's goodwill to provide for her.

Five days, she had. Five days to let go of all that held her in tight and to release some of that long-trapped torment, freeing her for another round.

Maybe she'd take some chances. Something completely out of the ordinary.

*I got the baby from the cake—I've got a lucky charm already. Time to use it.*

Chapter Five

Hurrying the last several yards to St. Charles, she crossed the very classic-appearing southern boulevard with its magnolias and airy tangles of Spanish moss hanging from the trees overhead, seeking a stop along the median strip's two parallel streetcar tracks. She caught a glimpse of one stopping three or four blocks toward downtown; she'd missed it.

With a muttered curse, it was all she could do to pull back the foot she was about to stamp. When exactly was this luck going to kick in?

"This time of morning, they're by every five minutes."

Impossible.

Copper Delacroix stood about twelve feet away, a soft leather case hanging by a brown strap over his shoulder, a newspaper open in his hands. His shirt was light, an off-white weave, and his tapered black slacks were perfectly creased. The distance between them seemed calculated, as though he meant to show he wasn't crowding her personal space.

*Now who's being paranoid...*

"Well. Good morning," Brianna said, noting in the leaf-dappled sunlight, Copper was a handsome man. "What a surprise to see you here."

Copper's lips relaxed into a wide grin. "The Garden District is a haven for genteel living. I had no idea we were traveling to the same neighborhood, or we could have ridden together."

She had no quick response, and silence fell between them. Others joined them at the streetcar stop, and morning traffic continued lazily along St. Charles on either side of the median strip, what the guides called the "neutral ground." She chewed her lip and looked up the street, hoping the next car would come quickly to end the awkwardness.

"Your unhappiness would fade if you let people inside the walls you build."

Startled, she turned back to him. "What?"

"A pretty lady like you shouldn't be unhappy. I couldn't help noticing."

She just stared. Would everyone in town jump on the "criticize-Brianna" bandwagon?

He studied her a long moment, then gave that mysterious, Mona-Lisa smile again, gesturing behind her. "Here, the streetcar's come."

*Where had that been a moment ago? Nowhere.* But sure enough, the green streetcar—named Desire?—came to a smooth stop before her.

Copper stepped aside to allow Brianna and the others to board first. Brianna fed her fare into the box, then took one of the wooden slat seats, feeling she'd returned to a different era.

The windows weren't tiny portals like those of their city buses in Pittsburgh, but were nearly three feet tall, with a green shade which could be pulled down if the sun got too bright. This morning, the windows were, for the most part, open, allowing spring-like air to circulate through the car's interior. After the last passenger boarded, the streetcar rattled and rumbled off to the next stop, wheels squeaking, continuing toward downtown as the driver called off the stops in what was obviously a well-practiced sing-song.

"Jackson Avenue!" he cried, as Copper slid into the seat in front of Brianna.

She must have been gawking like a child in a candy factory, because he seemed delighted at her touristy fascination.

"N'awlins is a beautiful city," he said.

"It certainly is." She admired the blooming flowers in front of the majestic Victorian homes they passed. Lavender azaleas, tulip trees in pale pink and white, and even a rainbow of bedded flowers, still going strong in February. Every home seemed to cultivate its own haven of greenery.

When she remarked on this observation, Copper nodded.

"You have no idea," he said. "Most of these homes have courtyard gardens in the back, beautiful landscaped settings with antique roses, stone fountains and more. There's a tour you can take downtown to reveal all these secrets to you." He paused, then just the corners of his mouth twitched upward. "If you like discovering secrets."

The closer they got to downtown, the car became crowded. Copper yielded his seat to an elderly man, then slid in next to Brianna, sitting very close. Her bag sat between them; he handed it to her, and she set it on her lap. All too aware of his proximity, and his musky aftershave, Brianna concentrated on the passing scene.

The architecture was stunning. Huge old stone mansions held court next to Doric-columned Greek Revival houses, surrounded by Victorians and Queen

Annes, delicate "gingerbread" trim brilliant in the morning sun.

The Garden District and areas west of Canal Street had been settled by Americans, while Creoles, European by birth and descent, had tried to keep to themselves in the French Quarter. First the Spanish, then the French, with a healthy dose of Italians and others, had settled in the old city, the atmosphere changing as political machinations on a national scale, beyond the immigrants' control, ruled the ownership of Louisiana. But New Orleans had always been a place of luxury, and the exotic aura still prevailed, as it did in the man sitting next to her.

His speech cultured and softly accented, he continued to point out details of interest on their journey into the city. But she noticed his attention repeatedly drawn to the folded newspaper in his lap that bore pictures of debutantes and information about the parades.

"It's a big hush-hush thing, isn't it?" she asked, pointing to the article about the Mardi Gras events. "I mean, no one knows the identity of the King of Rex, not till the last minute?"

His mouth set into firm, disapproving lines, and emotion burned in his eyes. "By tradition, the name of the King is supposed to be secret."

She'd been an interrogator long enough to suspect something behind that look. She had to ask. "You know who it is?"

Pinned down, he smiled for a brief moment, then it faded. "Copper knows many things." He stared out the window, jaw set in a hard line. His lips moved, and as the moments passed, he finally whispered, "Copper knows those who cross him will suffer..."

Belatedly realizing she was hanging on his words, he snapped back to the present, and his sunny expression returned. "I discovered the identity of the King by chance. It wouldn't be fair to ruin the surprise for others."

Brianna knew none of the players, so it didn't matter to her. Copper's grudges were certainly none of her business. His words, now—those were a bit troubling.

Copper abruptly rose from his seat as they traveled around Lee Circle with its tall statue of General Robert E. Lee, hero of the Confederacy. They crossed into the business district, which looked more like the Avenue of the Americas, like any other big city with its office warrens, filled to the brims with tiny cubicles for the clerical workers there. "My stop," he said with an apologetic nod. "Enjoy your day in the Vieux Carré, my lady."

"Thank you for your tour. And the beads, last night," she said, feeling she should be gracious, at least.

Copper bowed slightly, and took Brianna's hand, kissing it lightly, then giving it a squeeze. "You are most welcome. I will be interested to learn what you think of the city."

He joined those exiting the streetcar at Julia Street, leaving her a little surprised at the old-school farewell—when was the last time someone had kissed her hand? If ever?

An odd bird, this Copper. Odd, too, that he'd appeared at her streetcar stop. She hadn't told where she was staying. Just a coincidence, right?

She watched him walk away, almost wishing he

would have come with her, to share his insights on the city, rather than leaving her to depend on the cold, hard facts of her guidebook.

Though he had certainly implied they would meet again. Would he play some part in her weekend visit...an adventure, to use his word? *Ridiculous.* Letting her imagination run loose served no purpose, no purpose at all. Time to buckle down and get back to her plan.

****

Brianna walked several blocks from the modern city of New Orleans, tall, wide buildings piercing the sky with their multiple stories, east to the French Quarter, noting that the much-older structures returned to two and three-storied buildings, squeezed close together like a crowd of people waiting for a spectacle to occur.

Balconies bounded with iron railings overflowed with tropical plants and ferns, and many of the courtyards she passed as she continued on into the Quarter were shut off from the public with iron gates. But to classify them simply as "iron gates" didn't do justice to their uniquely crafted art, like the fence on Royal Street molded and painted to resemble a row of cornstalks, complete with yellow ears peeking out from their husks. The balconies of the Royal Café, three stories high, were set off in a leafy-patterned ironwork which stretched to the next building on St. Peter Street. Brianna could just imagine sitting on one of these balconies of an evening, listening to the sounds of the Vieux Carré, as the French Quarter was called—the "Old Square."

Music came at her from all sides. A gospel singer's

warm voice caressing an old spiritual came from the open door on the corner, saxophone and trumpet notes floating to her from more distant musicians she couldn't see. Before her, a shabbily-dressed man and woman played folk guitar in the middle of the street, which was blocked off to traffic. Their black mutt, wearing huge sunglasses, was tied to a chair, patiently waiting for his owners to move to more comfortable territory in the shade.

The buildings were worn Southern belles beyond their prime, their painted faces chipping away, but the streets were packed with them, each adding her own layer of atmosphere to the mélange. Brianna walked the streets, laid out in straight lines, exploring boutiques, souvenir shops, art galleries and more of the small specialty shops which followed, one after another.

A couple of times, a hint of unease stung her, as she felt someone on her heels, but she'd turn around to find the crowd interested in its own pursuits. It could have been Copper, she supposed, but she'd have noticed him, even in a crowd.

*And he'd better not be stalking me.*

She turned back to her guidebooks. Each home seemed to have a history, from the haunted LaLaurie mansion to the Merieult House, whose mistress was reported to have had such beautiful blonde hair that Napoleon had offered her riches, even a castle, if she would allow him to present it to a sultan who desired a wig of such hair. Madame Merieult had refused.

Good for her! Brianna thought. *The only one you can count on to look out for you is yourself.*

After perusing fresh fruits and hot pepper sauces by the row at the French Market, Brianna came at last to the crowded sidewalk café at Café du Monde, and wiggled her way into a seat near the front, just across the street from Jackson Square, where fringed-top carriages lined up to take tourists on a guided journey of the area.

Three hours into her safari, she was worn out.

The Quarter was only a square mile, but there was so much to see. Spending time sitting in a courtroom sapped the stamina she'd had when she was younger. Still on the down side of thirty, she shouldn't be ready for a walking stick and oxfords just yet. *I promise, more time at the gym when I get back.*

She treated herself to a cup of the strange coffee, mixed half and half with hot milk, and what the guidebook said was *de rigueur*, some beignets, squares of fried dough thickly drenched in powdered sugar, which she discerned to be heavenly.

Between sips of coffee and listening to the chicly-dressed mother behind her flipping out every time powdered sugar fell on her daughter's new blouse, Brianna watched the street performers on the sidewalk in front of the Square. A man of indeterminate age, dressed in a gaudy red and white clown costume, twisted multi-hued narrow balloons into animals, flowers and other shapes for passing children. A half-filled bucket before him received donations from the recipients. How did he live on such a capricious income?

As he bantered with the parents of the children waiting for their balloons, she hypothesized who he might be, under that makeup. No pressures, no preparations, just working the street, meeting people for a minute or two, and then sending them on their way. A real fantasy life, if an unpredictable one. The first half of that appealed to her; the second terrified her.

Her life was tied up in deadlines and demands, unhappy clients who returned again and again, their problems never solved. Observing the shining faces of the children who happily waved their air-filled pets, she vicariously shared their joy.

*What if I could make people that happy at the end of my day's work?*

The lawyer's life suited her, with its reliance on what could be proven by hard fact. She'd been a top student in her law class, driven to succeed by the guilt that her schooling had been paid by the proceeds of her mother's death. Her work was dispassionate, numbers on paper, everything reducible to a bottom line. Memos from superiors complimented her professionalism, and she saved each one and filed it for later inspiration.

The emotions she'd locked away inside were comfortably kept hidden, while she argued black and white issues. Clients left her office "satisfied," not "happy." It was a reflection of her own state of mind: happiness was not in her field of expectation.

But she'd been content this morning, delving into the little shops, finding brightly-colored *objets d'art* or delicate earrings that pleased her. Here at the open-air table, birds twittered in the trees overhead, the unaccustomed sunshine warm on her northern shoulders.

A sigh completed her sense of release, letting go of the tension. She'd held off the sting of loneliness all morning, diverting herself with the nooks and crannies of the Quarter. Copper's words about her "walls" nagged at her. Perhaps she distanced herself from people. So what?

The family at the table behind her moved out and another moved in just as quickly, this group speaking some Asian language, perhaps Japanese. Two small girls, dressed for vacation instead of a beauty pageant. Much more realistic.

She dipped her finger in some discarded powdered sugar and licked it, savoring its sweetness. She had more to see, but it was comfortable here, and she nearly felt relaxed. A few more minutes, then she'd head down to the waterfront. Maybe take the ferry over to Algiers.

The soulful strains of a jazz saxophone captured Brianna's ear. An old black man in a shabby dark suit, a red carnation in his lapel, played his instrument on the sidewalk before the café, the worn red velvet lining of his instrument case awaiting the jingle of silver. His gray hair curled tightly against his skull and his rheumy eyes spoke of years of life's experience.

He turned to serenade the coffee drinkers, pouring all his heart into the notes as they floated from the brass horn in his wrinkled hands. The jazzman's bliss and his suffering added depth to his music, as his tempo changed, slower, then faster, wrapping around Brianna's heartstrings.

Someone cleared his throat behind her, and she pulled herself back to the present, preparing to move her chair or whatever was necessary to accommodate. But when she lifted her gaze, she found Evan Farrell, looking contrite, carrying two cups of coffee.

"Is this seat taken?" he asked, gesturing to the seat opposite Brianna.

"This whole table isn't taken," she snapped, gathering her things and rising to her feet. "Enjoy."

He set the cups down and reached for her arm. "No, wait! Please. I'd like a chance to talk to you," he said. "Brought you coffee."

She eyed her empty cup on the table, nearly popped off a tart answer, then reconsidered. Coffee sounded good, and he did look awfully sincere...*must be those baby blues.* "Fine. But I doubt we have much to discuss."

"Good enough for me," he said, and he sat down before she could change her mind.

## Chapter Six

Relieved she'd stay, Evan joined Brianna, leaning forward, elbows on the table as he held his white foam cup and sipped carefully. He'd rehearsed what he wanted to say since he got out of bed that morning, regretting his off-the-cuff comments the previous night.

If Terri Worley hadn't sprung this little match-making endeavor on him that way, he might have handled things more like a gentleman. What had he been thinking? The shock on Brianna's face as she realized he was a GDS lawyer. Hadn't he even made some snarky comment about her dress? Her *dress?* Like he knew one style from another. *Man.* His brain had obviously traveled to another dimension.

At least this morning Terri had tattled where Brianna was going, so he could try to follow her and make it up. He wasn't even sure if—or why—he wanted to.

He could chalk it up to professional courtesy—it was rude to treat another lawyer so shabbily. Or he could admit he found the idea of spending time with an attractive, intelligent companion appealing. Especially one who wouldn't just fade back into the New Orleans crowds after next Tuesday.

"Well?" Brianna asked. Her face hadn't softened.

"Good coffee," he said.

Would she really listen? Or would she just let him

inside the perimeter far enough so she could slam the door and cut him in half? His bosses had lucked out with that Artotech win, and they knew it. She was tough as well as pretty. Exactly the kind of woman his mother would have loved him to bring home.

And he was talking to her like he was a tongue-tied idiot.

"Good coffee. Mm-hmm."

Suddenly unsatisfied with his prepared apology, Evan juggled his stash of words, trying to find the right combination to win her over.

"Actually, I liked the dress," he said at last.

"Excuse me?" She eyed him over the top of the cup, then slowly set it on the table, as if she needed her hands free in case she had to slap him.

But she was still listening.

He might have disliked Brianna Ward solely from the description Frank Dellenbach had given of a driven, hormone-ridden witch, but Evan had seen her in action, passionate as she argued her client's case, eyes sparkling as she wooed the jury. He'd sure been won over, and he'd wished he knew her better.

He'd blown his best opportunity, sitting next to her on the plane, but he hadn't recognized her then. Who would have guessed she'd be traveling to New Orleans the same time he was? And she certainly hadn't been very friendly. His book was a better companion.

"The dress. I really did think you looked pretty in it. I was in court the day you wore it."

"I see." A lightning flash of interest zipped through her eyes.

Evan sighed. "Please forgive me for last night. My brain was elsewhere. Really, I mean, partying way ahead of me. You were the last person I expected to see. Even on the plane, you looked so different, dressed for comfort, not court, you know." He shrugged. "I came here determined just to have fun and get the practice of law as far from my mind as possible."

A real smile escaped from her closed face. Her dark eyes seemed surprised. "Funny. That was my plan, too."

"So you probably would have preferred I was a zookeeper or a fast food server or—almost anything else."

"Almost," she agreed.

"Sorry." He meant it. For a split second, he wished he was an accountant. Then he wiped that from his mind with a shudder. *Way too much math.*

She studied him while they sipped their coffee. "How can someone like you work for Frank Dellenbach? You seem nearly human."

He had to laugh. "Thank you. I think."

"No, it's a compliment," she assured him, leaning forward. *Now that was a good body language sign. As long as there wasn't a weapon in her hand.* "Most of the guys in that firm, I'd cross the street to avoid. And I'm sure they'd do me the same honor."

"What? No way!" He considered the reputation of his colleagues. "Okay, that's probably fair. You're right, I'm not like them. Actually, I'm discovering I don't like lawyers very much."

Pathetic, right? Would she see it as a ploy for sympathy, some poor-me statement? He was second-guessing himself already.

But he truly meant it.

He didn't like the practice of law. It wasn't at all

what he'd expected. He'd envisioned attorneys as shining knights on white horses, charging in to save people in their hour of need, righting wrongs, slaying dragons, and sharing good outcomes with clients with whom he felt a genuine connection.

But what he'd found at GDS was a devotion to the bottom line, a willingness to take any case to make money for the firm, regardless of the client or how just their cause.

As a former police officer, Evan had started in the firm's thriving criminal defense practice, until he'd realized that many of their "frequent flyers" belonged to the local organized crime and drug cartels. Unable to stomach the smug attitudes of the not-so-alleged criminals, he'd transferred to the civil side, mostly large corporate accounts where the real client was the black line of profit.

He'd yet to find the client who was a real person, who needed Evan's help to save his life, to make it better. If he had that person to believe in him, then it would justify the work he was doing.

"After five years in the force, I should have known better before I chose to study law," he said. "It hasn't been what I thought."

He went on to talk about law school at Duquesne University, first at night, then full-time his second and third years. Her eyes softened, seemed to connect with sympathy, as he shared his dreams.

Worried he'd bored her, he trailed off, a little embarrassed, but to his surprise, she agreed.

"It was all I could do to get through George Washington Law right out of college. I can't imagine doing it along with a regular job." She stirred her cooling coffee. "If you wanted the white hat, why didn't you join the DA's office?"

"I interned there. But three months in, I met Frank. I got the hard sell."

"It's a great group of guys, kid," the heavy-browed attorney had confided as they lifted weights at the gym one evening, now two years before. "The cases? You name it, we do it. But there isn't a partner in the place without a Beemer or a Lexus."

The thought of a good income to cover his student loans was certainly attractive, but financial security apparently came at the cost of his conscience. He didn't like that. Not at all.

"Sounds like you've got to get your priorities straight," she said, setting her empty cup on the table. "The game is about money and taking care of yourself. If that's not what you're looking for, maybe you need to check out Legal Aid or something."

Disappointed by her mercenary attitude, Evan looked away. A carriage loaded with passengers across the street at Jackson Square. The driver joked with the family, a man and woman and three children, the kids fascinated with the nattily-decorated horse's mane. He settled them in and snapped the reins for the ride to commence. The father checked his children's seats, bringing Evan a sting of jealousy, *Now that's something I'd like. Talk about someone depending on you...*

In the silence, she picked up her purse, putting the strap over her shoulder. Apparently she'd stayed long enough.

"People are waiting," she explained, gesturing to the anxious faces searching for empty tables.

He didn't want to let her escape just yet, hoping

47

she'd come to know him as a person, not just a GDS schlub. "Want to take a walk?"

She looked surprised and stood up quickly. "Well, I had plans for this afternoon. But I guess there's no reason to do them alone." She maneuvered between the crowded tables onto the square.

"Lead on," he said, following her. He'd go wherever she wanted, as long as he got to show her all the attorneys in his firm weren't cold, heartless bastards.

Chapter Seven

A short walk took them across the Riverfront streetcar tracks to the water, up the steps to the wooden platform called Moonwalk, named for former mayor Maurice "Moon" Landrieu, who'd lobbied in the 1970s to secure this space for tourists and locals all to enjoy.

Brianna's first glimpse of the Mississippi was breathtaking. The sun reflected off the water, creating sparkles in the eddies left by the ships that passed through the half-mile expanse that reached to the other side, where the town of Algiers was dwarfed by its big-city neighbor.

The river water was indeed muddy, as she'd always read, in shades of every tawny color she could imagine, brown and tan and even gold, where the light caught the surface just right. Vessels of all sizes and types greeted the eye, tiny tugs, a Navy gunboat, barges, cargo ships, and along the dock awaited paddle-wheeled steamboats like elegant layered wedding cakes. The air echoed with the haunting sounds of boat's horns.

She sat cross-legged on a bench, fascinated by the view. Evan stood behind her, his glasses darkening in the bright sun. Pittsburgh had its rivers and history of shipping, but this place was the stuff of legend. Mark Twain's stories had defined this river in Brianna's mind as a place of escape—she'd never forget Huck Finn making his last bid to avoid the civilizing influences of

49

the widow who wanted to care for him. It was a perfect place to be.

Evan said, "We could do this at home, you know. Down at the Point."

She looked up over her shoulder, surprised he'd had parallel thoughts. "But it's not the Mississippi."

He just grinned.

A huge orange ore freighter slowly cruised past, engines straining. Sea birds circled overhead, calling out to each other. Brianna let go of her everyday life, taking in this new experience. "I never have the time," she confessed in a near-whisper. "I'm always rushing to the next case, the next brief, another deposition."

He came around the far side of the bench to join her. "Sometimes I feel like I'm barreling through my life without even experiencing it."

Joined in a silent conspiracy to indulge in more "wasteful" time, the two sat and absorbed the slow pace of life on the waterfront, watching tourists travel the ferry across to Algiers. A young, black trumpet player set up in the center of the platform, playing requests from passersby as well as improvising tunes in the New Orleans jazz tradition. He coaxed notes from his instrument Brianna wouldn't have believed possible. She dropped several dollars in his hat, rewarded by a smile and a bow, the player never missing a note.

"All that?" Evan asked. "Just for a song?"

Brianna blushed, then shrugged it off. "Sure. Music is art, right?"

"What would a guy have to do to get real lucky? Say, a twenty's worth?" The light of mischief shone in his eyes.

"Mr. Farrell, really. Solicitation must be a crime

even here in New Orleans."

"My apologies, ma'am." The tawny-haired attorney bowed as he walked by her side. "I'll try to behave myself in your presence."

She tried to erase the smile he brought to her lips. Remember she didn't like him! Why was he still here? She'd accepted his apology. He had better options, if he wanted to drink and be merry. What else did he want from her?

She could have dismissed him, maybe should have. But something in his lively-puppy step convinced her to let him tag along. When he wasn't being such a jerk, he was quite charming.

They continued past the huge blue glassed-in Aquarium of the Americas, toward the Riverwalk shopping complex. The fountain at the center of the beautifully-tiled Plaza de Espana, the Spanish Plaza, shot some thirty feet in the air, its glittering waters entertaining a score of children who scurried around its circumference, tossing in pennies.

Brianna hesitated a moment, caught by the beauty of the sun lighting the cascading spray, and impulsively dug in her pocket for change to make a wish. She wasn't even sure what to wish for—but she wanted to be open to whatever possibilities existed.

*No change. Damn.*

"Need a quarter?"

Brianna turned to find him smiling at her, hand extended, full of silver coins. "Oh, I shouldn't—"

"Go ahead." He took her hand and gently turned it over, pouring the dozen-plus coins into her palm. "If it's my money, and your toss, then the effort should yield luck for both of us, right? Hey, we're lawyers on vacation. The phrase itself is an oxymoron. Let's live a little."

One thing to let him buy her a cup of coffee. But wasn't throwing their luck in together a bit risky?

Her mouth open to object, she read in the lines of his face that he intended to insist. Fine. It's probably all a bunch of malarkey anyway. Might as well play the lottery. Avoid stepping on a crack. Knock on wood. No more point in believing in superstition than luck. Neither one got her anywhere.

"If you say so."

She squeezed the coins tightly in her hand, then wished for emotion, for magic, for adventure, for escape—for love, even?—to overtake her in the next four days in New Orleans. When she'd put all of herself she could into the silver bits, she threw the handful high into the air over the fountain, watching each flash before it splashed into the pool like silvery rain.

Ready to make some self-deprecating remark about the futility of such wishes, she swiveled on the balls of her feet to look at Evan. He seemed absorbed in the process, his gaze following the progress of the coins into their watery bed. His hands clenched in front of him, as though he had wished along with her.

When he realized she was watching, he shifted his weight from one leg to the other and adjusted his glasses in a transparent attempt to be casual. An embarrassed grin came to his face, slowly, like a Cheshire Cat smile.

"What? I guess I'm just a gambler at heart. Hedging my bets, that's all." He added, "Come on, counselor, it can't hurt to pitch a coin for luck, can it?"

His flippant words didn't comport with the

intensity she'd caught in his eyes. *How odd.* Which one was the real Evan Farrell?

"I suppose not," she said, as off-handedly as she could. After all, she'd welcomed frivolity, along with some deep-hidden hope. Who could believe it possible to find love in four days? Who defined 'love' anyway?

As arguments piled up in her head, her mother's voice scolded her.

*Not everything comes from your cold logic, Bri. If you don't open your heart once in a while, you'll never have happy days like I had with your father...*

Ugh. Move on.

She glanced over at those blue eyes that tugged at her heart. Like picking at an old scab, knowing it could be painful but unable to stop herself, she had to test his commitment.

"So, I'm sure you've got other plans for the day, more fascinating alcoholic pursuits to be found. You've done your duty, made your apology. Accepted."

He looked startled, then a bit insulted.

"I—ah, well, no, not really. But I don't mean to intrude. If you'd rather be alone, that's fine."

Her first instinct was to snap back that she didn't need him. She didn't say it, though. Something contrary inside her still wanted to put the burden of choice on him. Her eyes scanned the horizon. *Ah. Perfect.* "Riverwalk is right up here," she said, pointing ahead.

"Shopping?" Evan glanced longingly at Harrah's giant casino across the street. "Now that we've started gambling, maybe we could move on to serious cash opportunities."

*Just as I thought.*

"Like I said, I'm sure you'd rather invest your

time—and your liver—in other activities." She shouldered her purse strap.

His eyes flickered with self-deprecating amusement. "No problem. I can waste my money at the roulette wheel down on the river in West Virginia any weekend I choose, woman. How often do I get to spend an afternoon with a lawyer as pretty as you without carrying a stack of statute books and legal arguments?"

She chewed her lip a moment, discounting his blatant flattery. Maybe he really meant what he said. In her heart of hearts, she felt a small warmth for Evan starting to grow. He might just be a stand-up guy, even if he shared an office with pigs.

Besides, what could happen in a shopping mall?

Chapter Eight

As they walked along the waterfront, Evan couldn't help thinking of the glass.

Not the one he usually thought of as half-full, but the window glass in the buildings around them, from the aquarium to the skyscrapers to the Riverwalk mall itself. After Katrina had blasted through the area, it would all have had to be replaced. He remembered news reports about moving zoo animals and what aquarium residents, who survived the power outages, to other areas of the country while repairs were made.

What a huge expense, and all to be paid from insurance purses stretched much too thin to cover all the losses. His mind automatically kicked into damage and liability assessment mode and whose percentage of fault would cause the greater part of reparations to come from their insurance company's deep pocket. A few moments later, he pinched himself as a reminder he was supposed to be on vacation.

*Leave that behind, will you?*

He caught Brianna's sidewise glance and his cheeks heated up.

"What was that for?" she asked, a grin hiding to pounce on him.

"Just…" *Might as well be honest. She'll understand.* "I'd hate to be their insurance carrier."

Her eyes widened. "You keep reading my mind."

"Not at all. Law school just twists the way you look at everything."

"Gives you focus, you mean."

Was she teasing him? Maybe. "Right, that's what I meant."

She laughed softly, not in a cruel way, and the flush that came to her cheeks was very appealing. It was an opening, one of the first he'd gotten from her. *That, and an opportunity for shopping.*

He sighed, thinking of a dozen things he'd rather be doing. Perhaps once they'd finished here, he could persuade Brianna to move on to something more interesting.

At this point, though, he'd conceded control. So he followed her to the third level, to the Mardi Gras Masquerade shop, where they stepped into a purple, green and gold world of unreality and mystery. Racks of gaudy necklaces hung in rows, ones with golden babies, some two yards long, others made of pearls an inch or more in diameter. He tested some strands in his hand; they had to weigh a quarter-pound or more.

*How could you throw these from a float without putting out someone's eye?*

The unbidden legal query annoyed him. "Do people really wear this stuff?" he asked, holding up a gold-spangled vest.

"I suppose they do. It's supposed to be a masked event, isn't it?" She peered at him through a purple painted jester's face, her dark eyes bright with excitement.

"Even in the street? There weren't many in the bar last night all duded up."

"Terri said it's something that builds through till

56

Fat Tuesday. Maybe next week everyone plays dress up."

She put the mask back and moved on down the costume row, her fingers caressing long strings of feathers and frills. He couldn't help picturing her in some of those outfits, tearing himself away from the thoughts of those more in the showgirl vein.

*As if, Farrell. As if.*

But the masks, hats and costumes were just the thing to disguise oneself from the world and become a king, a princess or a jester for a night. "Do you have a costume?"

She shook her head, eyeing a glittering tiara on the top shelf. "I didn't think that far ahead. I really only decided to come on a whim." She traced a delicate edging of soft pink feathers on a mask with one fingertip. "Not that I could have found anything like this in Pittsburgh."

"But you will?"

"I suppose so." His interest in a long black cape with a tall collar, almost vampire-style, drew her attention, and she added a tart comment. "That bloodsucker look would suit most of the guys in your firm."

His hand dropped from the costume as if it had been on fire. Nothing in the universe could have persuaded him to wear it after that. Dress-up was for kids, anyway, right? Who needed it?

Terri Worley was clearly steeped in the spirit of the holiday, and Hank seemed like a party kind of guy. Perhaps all the natives carried on the traditions of the past. That didn't mean he was required to wrap himself in spangles and beads.

*Dignity, yeah, that's what I have to protect me. Dignity.*

She took a deep breath, as if settling an issue. "I'm taking this one."

She picked up a jeweled turquoise mask and marched to the counter with it, waiting for the customer before her to finish paying for his set of ostentatious pink pearls, a string that had to hang thirty-six inches long.

Evan pondered the mask, sizing up his chances with Brianna if he played along. The cape had been cool, in a way—men always looked dashing and dangerous if they had a cape to flip. *Think of Darth Vader, or Batman, or even Superman...* Snidely Whiplash came to mind and he tried to dismiss that one.

*No, thanks.*

If push came to shove, he'd bet old Hank had a spare Evan could borrow. Desperation drove men to crazy things, especially where women were involved. He sidled up to wait at Brianna's elbow. She put her purse on the counter, digging in it for her wallet, then gasped and yanked her hand out as if she'd been bitten by a snake.

"What?' he asked. "What's the matter?"

The clerk stared at them both, curiosity written on her face. "Ma'am?" came her southern drawl, concern there, too.

"It's...it's nothing," Brianna said. She dug in her wallet, then handed the woman her credit card.

Her reaction told him whatever happened, it was far from "nothing." Brianna trembled as she leaned against the counter, her face pale. Her fingers shook when the clerk returned it. She just dropped the card in, careful not to put her hand inside the purse at all.

*What was in there?*

"Come on," she said. She lurched for the door, almost running into the silver frame as she passed through.

"Brianna! Wait." He shouldered past several shoppers to catch up, then took her elbow to steady her. She didn't pull away, but shuddered. "What the hell just happened?"

"I-I saw s-something. But it wasn't real. I-I know it wasn't."

He walked her over to a bench, afraid she was going to collapse. "What was in your purse?"

"It s-stung me." She seemed baffled.

*That makes two of us.* "What was it?"

He knew better than to grab a woman's purse. Those contents were often a private rabbit warren of personal belongings. But if something dangerous was in there, it needed to come out.

"I don't know." She set the purse on the bench next to her. Instead of opening it, she just stared with wide eyes.

"You look scared. Are you okay?"

"Yes, I'm fine," she said. The words sounded automatic. She kept staring at the purse.

"Let's get you some water." He took her arm lightly. "The food court's down the hall."

She went with him without protest, which told him something was surely wrong. He found a shop to sell them water instead of the daiquiri bar, which he belatedly thought might actually do her more good. He came back to the table with two bottles of water and opened hers before he sat down. The look in her eyes was still one of shock.

"Drink that," he said, when she didn't move to do it of her own accord. She did so, almost on autopilot. His cop sense of something being "wrong" overwhelmed him. "Brianna, may I check your bag?"

Hesitating, she frowned. "No."

His fingers drummed a staccato rhythm on the table. Whatever it was had painted a shadow over the morning. If she was in trouble, he needed to know now. "Then get it out here."

She took a long drink of water, which seemed to have a positive effect. She reached into her bag, drawing back sharply once. Then she snatched a paper folded into a shape of a triangle and dropped it onto the table between them. It sat there, looking fairly harmless. He studied it from the top, from the side, not seeing any sort of wire or other device that could cause a shock.

"I know, it just looks like paper. But I'd swear it stung me. Like a jolt of electricity."

That had been the reaction he'd observed, all right. "Is that yours?" When she shot him a quizzical look, he said, "It's in your bag."

"I haven't seen it before." She drank more of the water, the color returning to her face.

"You said you 'saw' something. Was that when you touched it?"

She nodded slowly.

"What did you see?"

Her eyes closed and she shook her head. "I said it wasn't real. I don't want to think about it."

Frustrated she was so recalcitrant, he took matters into his own hands, literally. He reached for the strange triangle, ready to draw back when it zapped him. But it didn't. Even when he picked it up. He cocked an eyebrow at her.

"Don't ask me!" She slammed the plastic bottle on the table, spraying water over them both. He shook a few drops off the paper.

"Calm down. We should at least see what it says."

"Just throw it in the trash."

*In the trash? I don't think so. Not after this whole scene. Something's going on here. If there's a threat or danger of some kind, we'll report it to the police and move on.* He grabbed napkins from a nearby table and wiped the table dry before spreading the white sheet flat.

Thickly-inked black letters jumped out at him.

*WHAT YOU SEEK IS WITHIN YOUR GRASP.*
*YOU MUST PASS THROUGH DANGER*
*WHERE SAND BECOMES WATER*
*AND THE GREATEST PERIL IS TO BE ALONE.*
*THE PRIZED POSSESSION OF YOUR ENEMY*
*IS YOUR KEY TO THE CITIES OF THE DEAD.*
*FIND THERE THE BLOOD-RED FLOWER.*
*MAKE YOUR SACRIFICE*
*TO SHOW YOUR PURITY OF HEART.*
*THEN WILL YOUR DEBT BE SATISFIED.*

"What the hell kind of crap is this? Where did you get it?" Mystified, he read it again, and she did, too. But the words didn't make any more sense.

"You're sure you haven't seen this before?" he asked.

"Never." Her face edged toward shocked pallor once again.

He believed her.

"When did the note get in your bag? Have you had it with you? Where have you been?"

She looked away, lost in thought. "I've had it with me all day, mostly on my shoulder." The purse had no zipper or other closure. Anyone could have dropped something in, depending on how she held it. She was damned lucky someone hadn't just snatched the thing as they passed by.

"What about at Café du Monde? Did you set it on a chair?"

"No, there I had it on my lap. I didn't want someone to be able to get my purse—" She stopped, a stricken look in her eye. Of course that's exactly what had happened. *But apparently not at the Café.*

He hadn't noticed anyone close enough since they'd been together, so it must have been before that. He was going to ask her another question when the young black janitor who'd been sweeping the area next to their table stopped to stare at the paper. Evan put on his best cop-interrogator face.

"What do you think?" Evan asked him. "Any idea what that means?"

The young man straightened his green apron, his eyes flicking to Evan, then to Brianna. "Where'd you get that?"

"Found it," he said casually. He picked the most obviously mysterious clause of the verse. "What does "Cities of the Dead" mean?

"It's the cemetery," the young man said, then he licked dry lips. "We're too close to sea level here, so everyone is buried in tombs. They look like cities."

"I see. And what's a 'blood-red flower'?"

The young man shook his head. "You got me,

man." The boy's fingers clenched tight on the handle of the push broom.

"Really? No clue at all?"

"Nuh-uh." The kid took a step back.

Evan leaned forward, his voice like thunder. "Look, pal, if you know what's going on, you'd better tell us."

"Don't know, man. Crazy shit happens, okay? Just leave me alone." Something of a frightened rabbit looked back at Evan from the kid's eyes, and he backed away, applying the broom's bristles to the floor with increased intent. Still sweeping, he continued moving as far from them as he could, as fast as he could.

"Odd," Brianna said, gingerly picking up the paper to study it.

"The whole damn thing is odd. Maybe you were right. We should toss it. Unless you intend to press charges."

"Press charges? For what? And against whom?" Brianna examined both sides of the paper, then held it up to the light. "Besides, I'm kind of intrigued now. Don't you want to figure out what it means?"

"What it means? It means you're as loony as whoever wrote it, if you don't pitch it." Evan finished off his water and tossed the empty bottle in the recycling bin along with hers. "There's more to this, Brianna. You saw that kid's face."

"That means there's more to the story, doesn't it?" Seeming much more like herself, Brianna folded the note and put it in an outside pocket of her purse with the bag that held her mask. "I think we've had enough shopping."

He agreed wholeheartedly. "Damn skippy."

They went out the opposite end of the mall, coming to the British Plaza, where a tall statue of Winston Churchill graced a small common area in front of the Hilton. She walked along, lost in thought. Gradually, his inner alarms calmed to a dull roar. His gaze darted around the plaza, trying to pinpoint if anyone took an inordinate interest in this pair of out-of-town visitors. But no one did.

Maybe just a practical joke, some kid trying to pull one over on an unsuspecting tourist.

Maybe the tourist agency in town had come up with a new campaign, trying to make the festival more mysterious, spooky and delightful so everyone would rush back home and tell all their friends what a great experience it was.

Maybe it *was* a threat. But she didn't seem to take it seriously. Until she did, anything he did would just be overreacting, wouldn't it?

But if it was a threat, the time for action was now.

His distracted silence must have gotten to her, because she tapped him lightly on the arm.

"Evan, don't get all wrapped up about this. We're fine. I mean, *I'm* fine," she added hastily, blushing. "I-I'll puzzle it out tonight when I'm trying to go to sleep. It'll be better than a mystery novel."

It wasn't the right answer. He snorted in disgust. "Fine." Ready to launch into a diatribe about how ridiculous he thought she was, he was derailed when his stomach growled loudly.

Her turn to raise an eyebrow, then a smile. "Hungry?" she asked.

"Wouldn't do much good to say no, now, would it?" He grinned, embarrassed, and looked around. "Hey there's Mulate's. It's supposed to have great Cajun food." He turned to look over his shoulder at her. "Do you like Cajun?"

"Sure." She glanced at her cell. "It's almost two. No wonder I'm feeling light-headed. Nothing but those beignets since breakfast, and it's already warm."

Her sunny smile barely covered a note of uncertainty. Light-headed, was it? *I don't think it's her diet at all. Something about that damned paper. And now she wants to track down the crazy message in there.*

*Guess that means I know where the rest of my night's going to be spent—right next to her, before she gets herself in trouble.*

*Damn skippy.*

## Chapter Nine

Cajun food sounded great. She hurried after Evan, not wanting to be alone.

*But not because of that silly note...*

She was made of stronger stuff than that.

More because of the vision she'd had when she first touched the paper, when it burned her fingers. Unbidden, a vision of the mysterious man named Copper appeared in her head. Dressed all in black, he was costumed, with unusual gold symbols painted across the front of the blousy shirt. A red turban was wrapped around his head, and he carried a black candle. Most shocking, jagged streaks of red and white paint crossed his face. His eyes were open, staring into hers.

Thinking about it sent shivers of fear reverberating through her spine, and she missed a step.

*What an odd thing.*

It must be some sort of dehydration or hallucination or something. Surely the cultured man she'd encountered would have no need to dress that way, even for Mardi Gras festivities.

But she found herself intrigued, especially so soon on the heels of her wish at the fountain. She'd wished for adventure, hadn't she? Here it was, literally shoved into her hand.

*What you seek...*

What was she looking for in New Orleans? Escape

from her responsibilities. So was this a promise of solace before it was time to return to the frozen north lands? Or was it tied to her wish at the fountain? Was it love that was within her grasp?

Then a dangerous journey to a place where "sand became water." Where was that? The beach? The river? She couldn't imagine there was a lot of sand there. Mud, maybe. Not sand.

Then something about an enemy's "possession" that needed to go to the Cities of the Dead. The janitor had claimed that meant a cemetery. With a red flower. And then a sacrifice.

Okay, maybe that last part wasn't so fascinating.

Back to "good reason not to be alone."

Evan definitely didn't see it as an adventure, though. He'd seemed genuinely concerned about her. That was sweet.

The smell of hot gumbo and fried shrimp assailed her as they walked into the restaurant, and she decided they'd made the right choice.

Mulate's was a large open room, with tables situated at an excellent angle to see the musicians setting up on the stage at the far end. The band warmed up as Evan and Brianna were seated, a fiddle player tuning up with the help of the accordionist as the drummer tested his percussion and extras.

She snuck a peek over the menu at Evan. She hadn't expected to be spending the day with him after their meeting the night before. But today had been remarkably pleasant. Until she'd found the note.

Evan drank the tall beer the waiter brought with a definite sullen flatness to his face. Even the dark, spicy soup that tantalized her tongue didn't seem to perk up his mood, nor did the band's lively music.

She leaned close to him. "Look, you're off the hook for this note. I don't expect you to do anything about it. I'll probably just ruminate over it for the night and then throw it away." When he didn't answer, she added, "What harm can it do, hmm?"

"I guess that's the sixty-four-thousand dollar question, isn't it? Without any indication who put it in your purse, there's a lot of doubt as to the impact. I told you I used to be a police officer. I take some of that language as a potential threat, not the innocent riddle you want it to be."

A fire blazed in his eyes, and she wondered how much of that was due to his annoyance that she didn't just do what he said, and how much came from the possibility that he really cared.

*Cops, they're always coming from the paranoid side.*

"Well, I disagree. Can we move on?"

His face remained closed, and she decided she didn't intend to play his game. Instead, she struck up an easy conversation with two women leaving the next table, both bejeweled with beads, who were from Youngstown, Ohio, hardly an hour from her hometown.

"Going to the parade?" one asked Brianna.

She nodded.

"If you want a good spot, you should be out on the street by five o'clock. It starts at the uptown end of St. Charles about six-thirty, and it takes a while to work its way down here."

"Thanks," Brianna said, checking her phone. She still had plenty of time.

"Maybe we'll see you there," she said. "Enjoy."

After they'd gone, Evan turned to her. "Brianna, I'm sure you think this isn't any of my business. But I saw your reaction when you touched that note. *Something* happened. I wish you'd tell me what."

He watched her intently, waiting for an explanation. But she didn't have one. At least one that didn't sound crazy.

"I'm going to say it once more. I think you should report that letter to the police."

Brianna struggled to determine what might reassure him and finally patted his hand, finding his fingers warm. For a second she imagined them holding hers.

"Evan, who would I tell them it came from? Who would they look for? Right now, it's just a riddle. No more." She waited for him to agree, but he didn't. "If I remember something helpful, I'll let you know. If you want me to."

The man was a bulldog—he wouldn't let go. "Can we go over your day once more? Just for my peace of mind."

"Fine. Then we'll move on," she said. "I left Terri's in the morning about eight, took the streetcar downtown and walked all over the French Quarter, then I met you."

A sneaking suspicion buzzed through her mind, along with the memory of the feeling of being stalked. Could Evan himself have planted the note, with some intention of making himself indispensable to her? "You were following me this morning, weren't you?"

She eyed him, thinking that would have been a huge mistake on his part.

As if he'd read her mind, he bristled. "It wasn't me.

I did track you down, but I didn't see you until the café. Believe me, I've got much more colorful ways of getting your attention."

"Like that hat last night?"

His cheeks turned red, and Brianna grinned. "Yeah, I thought so, too."

He cleared his throat. "You could have met hundreds of people in the shops and bars."

"I wasn't in a bar," she snapped, noting his teasing smile too late. She didn't like him scoring points off her.

He returned to her recitation. "On the streetcar, did anyone get close enough to put that in your purse?"

She remembered how Copper had slid in next to her when the streetcar filled up. He'd handed her the purse when he sat down. Could he have done it? His running commentary had directed her attention outside the streetcar to passing landmarks. It was possible.

But why would he?

Their waiter came to gather their empty plates. "So what's on the agenda for the evening?" he asked.

Brianna seized the opportunity to change the subject. "See the parade, Hermes, I think," she said. "Isn't that the one rolling downtown at dusk?"

"Definitely hit Bourbon Street," Evan said simultaneously.

The waiter confirmed that Hermes was in fact the parade people would be watching, then gave Evan a wink. "The Blue Penguin has two drinks for one till seven p.m. My brother works over there. Ask for Rene—tell him Charlie sent you."

He set the check in a black case, on the table and she reached for it. Evan got it first.

"You don't have to do that," she said. "At least let me pay for mine."

"The least I can do for a fellow litigator." He smirked as he tucked a couple of bills inside the black case, then walked her to the door.

Brianna got her bearings. She had to head up Canal Street to find a spot to observe the parade. It wasn't yet five o'clock, but she could take her time, see the sights along the way. "Thank you for lunch."

"You're welcome."

They stood on the front step, an island of awkward silence as the city sang in its many voices around them.

Brianna had no intention of trying to convince him to see the parade with her if he was hell bent on getting blitzed downtown. For herself, she couldn't imagine dulling these new experiences with alcohol. Why come all this way to live the magic lollapalooza and spectacle of Mardi Gras and spend the night sitting on a bar stool? That, you could do back on East Carson Street any night of the week.

"So…what are you going to do?" he asked.

"I'm going to Canal Street. Terri suggested I should catch one of the big parades down here. The rest we can see on the neutral ground by their house. Go on, now. I'm a big girl, counselor. Don't you worry about me."

She smiled, a little thrill of independence zigzagging through her at the thought of spending the night on her own in a new city. Who could say what might happen? "You be sure to take care of yourself."

His jaw tightened. "I'm perfectly aware of the risks." He looked left, looked right, sounding reluctant to separate from her. But even she could see he'd backed himself into a corner. "See you back at the house?"

"Sure. Have a great night."

"You, too." He hesitated, then turned and walked off toward the party district on Bourbon Street. They could have walked together, but in his current mood, Brianna was just as glad to have him move on. She had Copper's necklace in her purse, and she put it on. *The first of many, if she was lucky.* All she had to do was wait.

## Chapter Ten

She followed the crowd of people back to Canal Street, the ample sidewalks already starting to populate with a crowd high on adrenaline or alcohol—or both.

Women in black leather and red feathers stood next to men in three-piece suits of green, gold and purple, and people in hats of all description. Her mask waited in her purse, but she felt more secure, at least for now, keeping her field of vision clear.

A doorway with a raised step emptied right in front of her, and she quickly snared the spot. It gave her a good view, as well as interesting neighbors, a man and woman dressed in matching turquoise wigs, who seemed more interested in making out than watching a parade.

Took all kinds. And they sure had all kinds here.

Anticipation washed up from her tired feet to the top of her head as she primed herself to experience her first Mardi Gras parade. Travel books had given her a vague idea of what to expect, but the novelty, the unexpected freedom thrilled her.

She could have shared this with Evan, if he hadn't been so obsessed about that note. She wanted to put it out of her mind, but since he'd interrogated her, she found it hard to forget. A trashcan sat ten feet from her; she could simply toss it in and the matter would end.

Or would it?

If this wasn't just a PR stunt, and she'd really been targeted, it might not. Would whoever it was—perhaps Copper Delacroix?—persist?

She couldn't decide.

She didn't want to decide.

She'd wished for adventure, right? Perhaps this was fate's answer. Was it so wrong to desire mystery, something unpredictable in a life normally planned out to the hour?

Her purse carefully closed and strapped across her body instead of hanging from one shoulder, she felt secure. Several people eyed the stoop, so she took up as much of the space as she could to discourage them. Casual conversations with others in the crowd, *where are you from, is this your first parade, make sure you get a Zulu coconut tomorrow*...filled the time until the music turned the corner onto Canal, and the Krewe of Hermes arrived.

A buzz of excitement moved up the street, heralded by the brass and drum of a marching band. A sea of waving arms rippled through the crowd, closer and closer to where she stood, and voices called out, "Throw me something, mister!"

The first float came into view, a vision of tropical color. Black men balancing long metal poles topped with flaming coffee cans walked before the float, moving in a jerky, rhythmic dance, bending gracefully to pick up silver money tossed by the crowd. These were "*flambeaux*," traditionally carriers of lights by which spectators could see the parade after dark. Even though modern street lights provided enough illumination, the reminder of the old tradition put the event in context and allowed her to imagine what it might have been like many years before.

Twenty to thirty people rode on the decorated float base, about the size of a semi-truck bed. The masked riders, costumed in white satin, sequins and feathers, held brightly-colored prizes, displaying them to the almost deafening roar of the crowd.

More daring crowd members approached the float with a personal plea, receiving LED-lit strings of beads and even artificial red roses directly from the gloved hands. Beads flew at the crowd, whirling spots of color, snatched in mid-air. In their enthusiasm, some Krewe members threw necklaces too high for the masses, and the trinkets lodged themselves in trees along the street, suddenly revealing an explanation for those she'd seen from the streetcar along St. Charles Street that morning.

The noise level grew, people jostled her in their excitement, and she became aware of the sheer size of the crowd around her, everyone a total stranger in a city she didn't know. Despite her own enthusiasm and determination to be independent, she'd brought herself to a place she was very much alone in the midst of thousands.

Had she made a mistake?

"Hey!" A voice called from the float, a disguised figure from the upper level pointed at her. When their eyes met, the man's arm arced upward, and a long string of green beads flew toward Brianna. The man watched until she caught them and waved back her surprised thanks.

He looked ahead, then, as the float moved onward. A huge marching band of African-American children strutted along behind the float, lustily playing the theme from a movie of the past season.

Brianna examined the string of beads, each one half an inch across, made of clear glass, as those in the past had been, the string easily thirty inches long. The street lights reflected off the beads with a pure glow. "Incredible," she whispered.

"The man know a good thing when he see it, Mama," said a man in the crowd in front of her. He winked broadly.

She blushed, her anxiety moving a notch down at this simple friendly comment. "Thanks."

The man took one of the many strands of beads from around his own neck, this one of red faceted shiny plastic beads, each reflecting light like a disco ball, and handed it to her. "*Laissez les bon temps rouler!*" he shouted, echoed by several others in the crowd.

Her heart skipped a beat at his exclamation, but a moment later, the translation clicked into her mind— Let the good times roll!—and the man moved on through the crowd.

"He sure do, Mama," came a more familiar voice at her elbow.

She turned to find Evan grinning at her. Surprised and relieved to see him, she hugged him tight. "I thought you had plans!"

He seemed surprised at her sudden expression of affection, but his arms slid around her. "The bars are open late. No reason to head right down, when there's so much to see here."

His tone and the way he looked at her implied that it was her he'd come back to see. She could have pressed him, but she was willing to accept the fact she didn't have to be alone. Nice to have someone covering her back.

"Glad you came," she said, letting her delight in the evening include him.

Another float moved into her line of sight. Armed with her friend and her strings of beads, suddenly she no longer felt like just a spectator, but a participant. She shoved Evan into her spot on the step.

"Hold this place for me, okay? Hey, mister!" she called, stepping forward into the light. "Throw me something, mister!"

In what seemed like no time, the parade passed, float after float, band after band, and the people who'd watched with her moved on to their next activity of the evening.

Brianna owned two dozen necklaces in a rainbow of hues, one with the medallion of the Krewe, and several metal commemorative coins called doubloons. She'd connected with masked strangers on the floats whose faces were hidden, only their eyes smiling back at her pleasure. She'd even found herself flirting with the riders, not to the extent of some women, unzipping their tops to their navel, but revealing herself through a smile or a wink.

*We need to have some dignity, right?*

Evan, on the other hand, fully enjoyed the performance of the other women, scarcely missing an opportunity to catch an eyeful. Every time he managed to get a string of beads, he'd be sure to pass it off to whichever neighbor happened to be most exposed at the moment.

"Now who's a pig?" she asked as the crowd broke up.

"Hey, I'm just promoting an exchange of hospitality, my friend." He winked at one young lady with significant cleavage, stepping aside as she passed. "When in Rome, right?"

"Right," she said, still energized by the vivid panorama of color and flashing lights, the heart-pounding music, the passion and enthusiasm of the Krewe and the crowd, echoing even as the parade moved on. She ran her fingers through her new jewels, reveling as they tapped each other.

"You look very…festive," Evan said.

"Thanks." She grinned. "I had a good time."

Night had set in, and the shadows around the tall downtown buildings were long. People walked by in twos and threes, talking loudly, their voices tinged with an unfamiliar Southern drawl, or even the slang affected by the local blacks.

She had a sudden flash of disorienting anxiety. It wasn't her city, or the comfortable environs of Forbes Avenue or the Cultural District, where people walked about the streets after their plays or other events let out in relative safety.

Her first instinct, to return to the calm safety of the B&B, fluttered before her like the wings of a hungry hummingbird. Should she or shouldn't she? She'd taken most of the precautions, left her credit cards safely back in the room, had worn dressy but comfortable clothes. Her purse was safe. Now that Evan was here, she was reluctant to let him go. Why not try it his way?

"So you've played the white knight," she half-teased. "I suppose the least I can do is accompany you on your debauched rounds."

"I thought you'd never ask." He actually offered his arm, and they walked west on Canal. Within a few blocks and a much bigger crowd, she realized she'd come to Bourbon Street.

*Here I am, Party Central.*

They turned off Canal onto Bourbon. Music poured from the bars and restaurants; predominantly canned pop music from jukeboxes, but occasionally live brass instruments rang clear in the mellow night air. The sidewalk in the wake of this living mechanism that was the multitude was littered with trash and empty "*geaux*" cups (plastic, not glass) and discarded beads. Wouldn't do to trip with so many people around—they'd likely just mash her into the sidewalk and she'd become a permanent fixture, a casualty of the good times having rolled right over her.

Evan's arm guiding her, they followed the general drift of the mob, which overflowed from every open doorway into the street, punctuating their loud chatter with guffaws and obscenities. Some rowdy drinkers shoved against her, but Evan interceded to protect her from several of the more grabby types, and she found herself grateful.

*See, this is why I skip the bar scene. So much better to have a chilled glass of wine in my own apartment, without exposing myself to all the moronic pick-up lines and slobbering idiots who wait Out There.*

Evan didn't seem partial to any of the places they passed, so many of which seemed the same. But finally, at a doorway where soft lights glowed, the lament of a saxophone reached out and wrapped itself around Brianna. She stopped in her tracks, riveted. Peering through the doorway into the room decorated in red velvet, she gauged the interest of the patrons, who seemed to be hushed, listening. "This one," she said.

"You sure?" He leaned closer. "Doesn't look like

they've got many naked people in there."

She gave him the stink-eye. "Surely that's not your only criteria."

He chuckled. "Of course not. Come on, let's go in." His hand placed itself square in the middle of her back and gently edged her inside the door. The mournful musical notes continued, arranged in a blues number that radiated with emotion.

Some of the crowd were dressed up, some dressed down. The saxophone performer swayed and bent as the music moved him in a small cleared space at the far end of the polished wooden bar, slender frame clad in black. His short-sleeved shirt was unbuttoned to the waist. In the muted spotlight, he vaguely resembled the mysterious Copper, drawing magic from the twisted metal in his hands, his eyes closed in ecstasy.

"What do you want?" Evan asked, sidling close to the bar.

"Um…whiskey sour."

She stayed close, watching the musician, feeling the music he played deep inside. The jazz strains pulled and tore at her heartstrings as her foot tapped along with the tune.

A soft voice came from behind her. "What do you seek, p'tit?"

The odd phrasing caught her attention, and she turned to look over her shoulder. Copper Delacroix smiled down at her, as if it were perfectly natural the two of them would end up together in this pleasure-seeking crowd of several thousand.

Caught off-guard, she said, "Oh—hello."

He moved closer, ostensibly pushed by the crowd. His tan linen suit seemed fresh, a light blue print shirt underneath open to mid-chest, revealing curly hair. He wore a small gold earring in his left ear. As he brushed against her, his spicy cologne triumphed over their unwashed and alcohol-drenched neighbors. He studied her with curiosity in his eyes.

"We're here for the music," she said, gesturing to Evan, still waiting for the bartender to fill his requests.

"Magical, isn't it?" Copper smiled, his gaze never leaving hers.

"Certainly."

She tucked her arm over her purse, holding it even closer. The words he'd used echoed those of the note she'd received. Bizarre that he'd turned up in the only bar she'd visited, at the exact same time. Was there something to Evan's paranoia? Perhaps she was truly being stalked.

Evan turned around, holding two cups high to maneuver back to Brianna's side. His eyes narrowed as he saw her talking with Copper. "Friend of yours, Brianna?"

She fidgeted, taking her drink from him. "Someone I met at the airport last night."

His gaze was hard and unfriendly. "Uh-huh. Busy place, that airport."

Copper laughed softly. "I feel I am interrupting. Please, enjoy your evening."

He delivered a gracious nod that encompassed them both and wended his way around the end of the bar to a small table set near the small performance space that opened up as he approached. He raised a hand, and a waitress came immediately to serve him.

"What was going on with you two last night, anyway?" Evan asked, leading her through the crowd to snag a couple of seats along the back wall.

"Last night? What do you mean?"

"I saw you on my way out of the airport. Something in the body language was off. Did he scare you? Or threaten in any way?"

She slipped into her seat, scooting it until she had a good view of the performer. "Not at all. My luggage got lost, and he waited with me till it came. He didn't bother me."

*Even though he was at the airport, then at the streetcar stop, and now here...*

Seemed like an amazing coincidence. Perhaps too amazing.

The jazz player took a break and joined Copper, now seated where she had a clear line on them both. Their dark, velvety eyes were as similar as their builds. Perhaps they were family, of some sort, brothers or cousins. Copper said his mother lived in the city— possible he had a whole extended family.

What did Copper want? Was he making a play for her? He hadn't said anything in the least provocative or flirtatious. Could this be what he meant she was seeking? An exotic, delicious interlude with a self-possessed and handsome native of the Big Easy? That was certainly adventurous.

But that wasn't what she wanted at all.

He might be a fine tour guide. But she had no need to create an exotic fling just for the sake of doing so. Hanging out with another lawyer was daring enough. Especially with the tension over the amount of danger they should ascribe to this mysterious note hanging between them.

Copper caught her eye and raised his glass in a

silent toast. A little embarrassed, she looked away, her cheeks hot under his fixed regard. Evan didn't miss either gesture. He followed her gaze across the crowded room.

"So you have a chance encounter at the airport, and another at a bar the next night. In a city of three-hundred and fifty-thousand? Huh."

"And the streetcar."

The words popped out before she even thought. Horrified, she sensed that bulldog paranoia sink its teeth deep into them.

"Streetcar? The one this morning? How close did he sit?"

She bit her lip, then made the confession. "Right next to me. But my purse sat on my lap."

"He could still have put that in."

Feeling like a witness trapped on the stand, she acknowledged Copper was an obvious candidate.

"Do I have to find a judge to instruct you to answer?" Evan asked. He eyed her, reading her face, and gradually relaxed, taking a long drink of his beer. "I don't think so."

She stole a look at Copper, now speaking with some young men preparing to take the stage. Did his sneaking around have anything to do with his mumbled outburst about the King of Rex?

She'd heard the torment in his voice. Whatever he felt about this man, it wasn't the kind of thing to share with a stranger. Another mystery… one she wasn't ready to share with Evan just yet.

She had to puzzle out the note first. Then she'd see.

"Evan, it's still circumstantial."

He nodded slowly, his eye on Copper, who only

smiled politely. Brianna wasn't sure what Evan was thinking, but he seemed less intent. Maybe having a suspect in mind was settling to him, rather than having to choose from all the crazies in the world. Whatever it was, she hoped it continued for the rest of the evening. Hopeful the crisis had passed, she sipped her drink and loosened up her tight shoulders, settling in to listen to the music.

## Chapter Eleven

*Something about this guy…*

As soon as Evan saw them speaking at the bar, that sixth sense that something wasn't right tingled hard enough to jolt him. The feeling spread through him, slippery and dark like a rainbow-hued oil slick. Brianna looked surprised, but not scared. Like the night before, her body language told him this wasn't expected.

And after the day he'd had, he wanted no more surprises.

But the guy—what did she say his name was? Hi ho silver? Copper?—seemed pleased to keep his distance. That was just fine with Evan.

Now he needed something to get his mind off the problem, if he was going to spend a pleasant evening—or what remained of it—with Brianna.

"So, I filled your ear this morning with all kinds of garbage about my trek into the legal life," he said. "Your turn. Tell me why you wanted this thankless job."

Brianna smiled. "Job security. Why else?"

That was not what he expected.

"Really? I thought you'd be one of those 'I always wanted to help people' types."

Even as the words came out, he heard them through her ears and knew she'd be insulted.

But she amazed him again by just laughing. "You

thought so, did you? Well, you're so wrong."

She drained her glass and set it on the table, leaning closer so they could hear each other talk. Since the musicians had taken a break, the voices around them got louder.

"I don't ever want to be out of work. Like my father. When the mills shut down, he just surrendered and died. I never forgot how bad that felt." She teared up, then looked away, blinking hard.

It was the first time he'd seen a chink in the independent woman's armor. It actually shook him a little. "Brianna, I'm sorry. I…I didn't know."

She shrugged, her emotions coming under control. "No sense in apologizing for the truth. Sure, I'd like to say I was in this to help people. That's one of the greatest parts of this profession. Like Judge Miller said, we're privileged to do something a very few people share. We can represent people who need help before a tribunal. It should be honorable. Sometimes it is. But I do it for the money. That's something I can believe in."

Definitely not what he expected. Fit with Frank's opinion, though. Brianna was a tough opponent, through and through, because she'd already gotten what she wanted before the trial even started.

But it made her no less fascinating.

"Another drink?" he asked.

She raised an eyebrow. "Even after my indelicate confession?"

"Because of it." He laughed. "If anyone needs another drink, it's you."

Distracted for a moment by a couple passing in cleverly-painted beige bodysuits and large diapers, pacifiers hung on strands of green beads around their necks, he hesitated before he stood up. "Now that's something you don't see every day," he mumbled.

"I sure hope not." She stretched a little. "I'll hold the table till you get back."

Evan agreed and elbowed his way through the crowd, nearly taking out a small woman wrapped in crinkly blue foil. "Sorry," he said, cringing as he made sure she wasn't hurt—much. But she wandered on, giggling, so he guessed she was sufficiently alcohol-anesthetized she hadn't noticed.

*Yeah, that was gonna be me. No worries, no thoughts, just a weekend in another world. Before I met her.*

He glanced back at Brianna, who took a mirror from her purse, checking her reflection, then ran a hand through her hair, fluffing it a bit. He started to smile at her girlish vanity, but the smile faded when she took out that note to peruse it.

Why couldn't she leave that damn thing alone?

He growled and made himself concentrate on the line at the bar, buying two more drinks. When he got back to the table, he was stunned to find Copper Delacroix sitting there.

What was it with this guy? Could New Orleans on the weekend before Mardi Gras really be that random, or was something darker going on here?

And why was he the only one who seemed to care?

He paused at the edge of the table. "Hope I'm not interrupting," he said, wryly mocking Copper's earlier comment.

"Not at all." Copper didn't move from the chair Evan had inhabited just a few minutes before.

Brianna's gaze darted up at Evan, then away.

"Maybe we can find another chair—"

"No, that one's just fine," Evan said, setting the cups on the table. "If I could have it back."

Copper eyed him a long moment, and Evan felt he was being measured. The revelers at the table next to theirs got up and left their chairs. Copper smoothly took one, and set it across from Brianna, sitting on it and leaving Evan his.

Trying not to openly growl, Evan pushed past Copper to retake his seat. To Brianna, he said, "I thought we'd made a decision about this."

She fidgeted. "It's a public place."

Copper looked at Brianna, then at Evan. "I trust you're not jealous. You have no reason for such feelings."

"Who said anything about jealousy?" Evan demanded. "I'm just thinking it's pretty damned rude for you to insert yourself in our vacation."

Copper's eyebrow crept upward. "Together? You're vacationing together?" His expression fluctuated a moment. He targeted Brianna with his intent gaze. "You said—"

Brianna stiffened. "I don't owe you any personal information."

Evan bit back his impulse to tell the guy to get the hell out of his presence, but this Copper clearly had clout and connections. No sense stirring up trouble, especially on Copper's home turf. "Thanks for keeping her company while I was at the bar, but we won't keep you."

Copper's expression resolved into a complacent smile.

"I shall leave you to your evening. Our fair city has

many underlayers, exciting avenues that can lead to once-in-a-lifetime experiences. But you have to look for them, and embrace them once they reveal themselves."

Copper's friend/relative was replaced on the small stage by a young white woman with curly dark hair who sang blues to melt the heart, clutching the microphone with both hands as if it were her lifeline. Once she began to sing, the buzz of conversation faded, and Copper stood up.

"Perhaps we'll meet on St. Charles tomorrow. The morning parade passes by the streetcar stop." He winked at Brianna. "May your visit be all you desire."

Once he'd gone, someone snagged his chair. Evan and Brianna were left alone, staring uncomfortably at each other.

"I didn't ask him to sit down, in case you were interested," Brianna finally said.

Evan thought about her brooding about that note, and just bit his tongue. Anything he'd say now would seem petty, and maybe chase her off again. The guy had left; that was the important part.

"I didn't think so. He seems the kind to just move in on someone without being asked."

She seemed relieved to let the subject drop, and turned her attention to the singer. Evan watched Brianna instead, admiring the smooth line of her cheek and the faint auburn highlights in her dark hair. Once again, the sight of her in the courtroom came to him, a vision of her skewering Frank's witness on cross-examination, a triumphant light in her brown eyes. She was really something when she got cranking.

*I wonder if she has the same degree of passion in bed...*

Whoa.

He'd let that train of thought run away with him. Better to focus on not stepping on her toes first, before he got to tickle them. Or anything else.

But he definitely wanted to win that chance. A slow smile came to him. He loved competitive women. Loved capturing their hearts even more.

He sighed and drank from his cup. Six dollars for a beer was pretty prohibitive, but what else did he expect during one of the biggest drinking festivals in the country? Wasn't much more than refreshments at Heinz Field for a Steelers game, after all.

When the next number started, he leaned close to speak to Brianna, but an argument broke out directly behind him. One young man, who looked like a refugee from some Ivy League school, was tackled by another, and dropped his half-full cup onto Evan's table, spilling the contents. Evan was on his feet in a second, and Brianna soon after.

"Hey, watch it!"

Evan tried to separate the two, and a third college-age guy joined the melee, yelling obscenities in their general direction. Someone's fist clipped Evan's jaw just under his left ear, and he stumbled back against the wall.

The three kept shoving, shouting and swinging, till the club's bouncer broke it up.

Brianna scooted behind the table to help Evan to his feet, ducking as one of the wild swings came her way. "Are you all right?"

Evan worked his sore jaw, thinking he'd had a lot worse. But he wouldn't admit it in front of someone he wanted to impress.

"Sure. I'm good."

The college kid weaved, half leaning on his buddy as the bouncer shoved them toward the door. "Sorry, man. I think my friend's had too much to drink."

"Think maybe you have, too. Go home and sleep it off," Evan said.

He imagined there would be far too many drunks out on the street that night to expect a real effort at enforcement. Even as practiced as New Orleans cops must be at dealing with these mad party nights, there were only so many of them, and so much they could do. With luck and hope, the damage to physical property and human bodies was kept to a minimum.

Brianna eyed her empty cup, its contents dumped in the fight. "Maybe it's a sign. I think I'll call it a night."

*Already?*

Evan checked his watch and cloaked his disappointment. It was only eleven. Early for a party boy to head home, but it wouldn't hurt him. Less hangover than that morning, anyway. Which would be a good thing.

"Let me drive you home. It's late and there are a lot of rowdy people on the street."

She hesitated. "You sure you're okay to drive?"

"Comparatively speaking?" He chuckled. "Yeah, I think I only got to drink about a beer and a half. Wearing more than that. Shouldn't be an issue."

"If you say so. I'm just warning you, I'm not licensed to practice here. I might even be subpoenaed as a witness. So you'd best be a good driver."

Her smile showed Evan she'd forgiven him for any earlier slights, and they were back on the positive side.

Determined to keep things that way, he helped Brianna tuck the chairs in so they could get past. He checked to make sure she had her purse, and then out of habit patted his own pockets to remind himself where he'd put his keys. When he hit his back pocket, he had to do it twice to be sure, but his wallet was not where he'd left it.

"What the...?" He checked his other pockets, lightning stabs of panic running through him.

"What's the matter?" Brianna asked.

"My wallet's gone."

Evan's stunned expression and raised voice attracted the attention of those around them, and the peanut gallery chimed in. *What's happ'nin, man? Wallet gone? Welcome to N'awlins.* The last drawled, with an added snicker.

"I had it when I bought the last round." He checked again, his shirt and pants both, but it was definitely MIA. He shot a look at the door, realizing belatedly that he'd been scammed by the college kids. "Damn it."

Brianna looked under the table. "Sure you didn't drop it when you were trying to break up that fight?"

"That wasn't a fight, my dear. That was a well-rehearsed pickpocket routine."

He scowled, thinking he of all people should have been smarter than that.

"Seriously?" she sighed. "Let's get out of here then."

Evan led the way to the door, turning back to make sure Brianna followed him. When he did, he caught sight of Copper. When he saw Evan watching, his hand waved in the air. Not a "goodbye" sort of wave, but a "hocus-pocus" kind of movement.

*For real? Oogly-boogly magic? Hex curses? Casting an evil eye? What was that?*

What the hell kind of evening was this turning out to be?

Outside, they weaved their way through tourists on the street, heading back to the lot by Jackson Square where he'd left his car. Frustrated and angry at his own carelessness, Evan marched along, hands in his empty pockets.

"All the books warn about pickpockets. It's an art form during Mardi Gras," Brianna said, rubbing salt in his wound, though he was sure she meant it sympathetically. "You didn't lose your credit cards, did you?"

He shook his head. "Left all those back at the house. I'm not a total idiot, you know."

"That's good to hear."

He chuckled despite his aggravation. "You really have a bad opinion of everyone affiliated with GD&S, don't you?"

"Yes." She hesitated, then tried to cover a smile. "Well, I did."

"You mean I'm growing on you?"

"Like mold? Maybe."

She laughed softly. The street lights overhead shone around her, giving her the appearance of a halo. He had an impulse to kiss her—a strong one.

Not sure how that would be received, he angled a little nearer, close enough their elbows touched. She didn't pull away. *So, maybe…*

His eyes scanning first to make sure no muggers lurked in the lot, he stepped closer when he opened the door for her. She was practically inside the curve of his arm. He decided to go for it. Half-expecting a fist in the crotch, he leaned in quickly and did the deed.

Her lips were soft, her perfume faint, and her body warm against his as she gently kissed him, too. Sensing success, he held back, because once he'd kissed her he knew he wanted more. Much more.

After several seconds that were too short indeed, she pulled away, regarding him with a knowing look. "Now look what you've done," she said, her voice just above a whisper.

"What's that?" he replied, nearly as breathless as she.

"You've created a serious conflict of interest."

Her eyes twinkled with amusement, and she ducked under his arm to slide into the passenger seat.

*What the…?*

"Oh, hell," he muttered. "Once a lawyer, always a lawyer." He shut her door and came around to get in the car, glad the pickpockets hadn't taken his keys, too.

Still smiling like a cat who'd eaten the canary, Brianna leaned back in the seat.

"Hungry?" he asked, pulling out onto the downtown street. "I'm sure we could find a muffaletta someplace."

Brianna shook her head. "No, thanks," she said. "I think I'm ready for a good night's sleep. Long day tomorrow." She patted her beads. "Two more parades, at least."

"How are you going to get all those home?"

"Home?" She blinked. "Well, I'd thought—I mean, I can take them on the plane, right? They're not contraband?"

"No, Bri, but they weigh a ton." He took a left,

trying to avoid the crowded boulevards by heading east of Magazine Street, the long way around, but it would get them there.

She stared at him a moment. "No one's called me 'Bri' but my mother."

"Oh. If you'd rather I didn't, then—"

"No, I think I like it."

She leaned back, relaxed, and softly hummed along with the popular tune that played on the radio.

"Good." He drove with an eye out for patrolmen, just in case. *No, really, officer, I've only had two beers* tended to be the usual excuse, though in his case, it was true this time.

He couldn't think of another conversation starter, just pleased with his triumph so far. It didn't take too long to return to the Worleys' house, even detouring to avoid the partiers wandering the streets. They pulled up just after midnight.

The lights were still on, but the door was locked. Evan knocked, noticing Brianna covering her yawn. She looked cute, even doing that. He tried not to think about asking her to share his room, guessing it was much too soon.

Terri answered the door in a thick pink bathrobe, an expression of relief on her face. "Finally. I was worried when—oh, Brianna, you're with him." She smiled as she stepped aside to let them in. "Together. How nice."

Feeling like a teenager caught out after curfew, Evan trooped inside under his hostess's delighted eye.

"I'm glad you're back. I realized I hadn't left you a key, so I waited up."

"Thanks. I should have thought of that." Evan

included Brianna in his apology, and she nodded.

"Not to worry. I know you ran out of here on a mission this morning." She beamed at Brianna.

Evan tried not to roll his eyes.

"I had to finish up in here anyway." Terri led them into the kitchen, where she finished scouring the counter with some cleanser and a sponge. "Are you hungry? We have some cold cuts and some king cake left." She gestured to the tiny kitchen table.

The king cake looked very tasty, and Brianna took a small wedge, licking the purple sugar and icing off her fingers. "That hits the spot," she said.

Evan thought better of it. "King cake and beer doesn't sound like a tasty combination. Thanks anyway."

"Since we're all in, I'll just turn off the lights out back," Terri said. "See you for breakfast." She tried to smother her grin, and slipped out to the living room, shutting down all but one light.

"Good night," Brianna said.

Evan's eyes met Brianna's as they shared an expectant silence. Her lips parted, and he thought perhaps she'd approach him for another clinch, but instead she stepped back, creating a definitive space between them.

"Thanks for spending the day with me," she said. "I had a good time."

"Me, too." Reluctant to let her go, he kept talking. "I—do you have plans for tomorrow?"

"Plans, yes." She gave a little sheepish laugh. "I tend to do that. Plan everything. Less chance for surprises that way."

*Not particularly encouraging.*

"But some surprises are good ones, right? I mean….you, and me, and…" He gave his best puppy-dog eyes look and a smile he knew was charming.

Her soft laugh buoyed him up. "Today was a surprise of the best kind." She came to him for a quick peck on the cheek, then headed for the stairs. "Sleep well. Let's see what tomorrow brings, okay?"

"Okay."

He flipped off the light, then followed her to the stairs, just catching a glimpse of her attractive back side as she reached the top. "G'night," he said, still hoping, but she went in her own door and closed it with a firm click.

*That's all right. I've still got four more days.*

He popped in his room for a towel, then made a quick stop in the bathroom for a hot shower, his thoughts about Brianna making him slowly shut off the hot water till the chilly drops cooled him off—in every way.

She'd revealed a couple of different sides to her character that he found fascinating. He couldn't wait to learn more about her.

Her pal Copper, on the other hand, was someone he could care less if he never saw again. Brianna might not think it strange that he showed up every place she did, but Evan wasn't buying it as coincidence for one minute.

And what the hell was that little gesture Copper had made as he was leaving the bar? *Hocus pocus.* That was exactly what it had seemed like. The kind of gesture one would use to put a magic spell on someone.

That must be the alcohol talking. He wasn't that crazy. Or maybe he just hadn't had enough.

He raided his suitcase for his little bottle, and took a long drink, to help him start keying down. First the day with Brianna, then the incident with the note, then the fiasco of his wallet being stolen…

He still couldn't believe he'd fallen for that one.

*Getting soft in your old age, Farrell.*

He doubted anyone would bother to turn in an empty wallet, but he'd call the police in the morning just in case. His cards had all been left safely here, and he'd bought dinner and two rounds of drinks, so his cash couldn't have been more than thirty bucks or so.

*So those turkeys are out of luck, unless they need Starbucks points or a tow from Triple-A.*

Snickering at the stupidity of it all, he climbed into bed, wiggling around until he found a sweet spot and let himself sink into it. He set his mind on colorful dreams that involved himself and one attractive litigator of his acquaintance, but in no way, shape or form, meeting in the courtroom.

Preferably something much more intimate.

With those sweet thoughts, he soon drifted off.

Chapter Twelve

It was a glorious morning.

Brianna woke when the first tendrils of sunlight sneaked between the slats of the mini-blind. She felt good, and relaxed, for the first time in—well, as long as she could remember.

The day before had been a collage of new and unexpected experiences. Delicious food, the joy and soul of the music, even the broad expanse of the Mississippi, all belonged to her now.

The riddle-like note added spice that thrilled her. She'd been a puzzle freak since she was a kid, and didn't intend to stop now because Evan thought it could be "dangerous." She took it as a game to heighten the excitement of her trip.

Even if Copper Delacroix had something to do with it.

He'd certainly seemed to latch on to her since she'd arrived in New Orleans, to the point where she'd term it creepy. Sure, it could be coincidence.

*Maybe.*

If it didn't stop, she'd take measures. Even at carnival time, she was sure stalking still constituted a crime.

Setting Copper aside, she popped into the shower. While the hot water beat down on her skin, she found Evan Farrell sneaking into the corners of her mind. The ghostlike memory of the feel of his lips on hers, the taste of his mouth, the possessive way his arm had slipped around her had kept her from falling asleep once she'd climbed in bed. Even though they'd known each other for less than two days, she really liked him.

She scrubbed floral-scented shampoo into her hair, considering the complications a liaison with Evan might cause. She'd only half joked about the conflict of interest.

It was crazy to think she could make a relationship work with a lawyer from Givens, Dellenbach and Spicer. They'd be sure to be opposing counsel on another case. How could she convince a client or the firm's partners that she'd do an honest job if she was entwined with a lawyer from the other side?

But despite those reservations, Evan could be the one she'd choose.

Drying her hair with a towel, she headed across the hall to get dressed, still engaged in vacation thinking. Throwing on a gauzy peach tunic and white slacks, she added gold earrings and a pair of gold necklaces from her collection the night before. A glimpse of herself in the mirror made her stop and stare. This wasn't her usual look at all.

Not that she wasn't well-maintained—she spent her time on exercise videos and plucked out every incipient gray hair—but her wardrobe was normally well-seated in the business of work. Looking sincere for a jury. Impressing her bosses with serious suits and low heels. Not caring by the time she left the office, exhausted, at seven p.m. or later, what the hell she looked like.

She liked the new Brianna. A lot.

Conceding one decision to sensibility, she left her strappy white sandals in the room and wore sturdy sneakers instead. A little shiny lip gloss and a quick ruffle of a brush through her hair, and she felt ready to conquer the world.

A little disappointed Evan wasn't at the breakfast table, Brianna sampled Terri's *pain perdu,* a fancy New Orleans name for French toast, made with real French bread, which turned out to be tender and delicious. She was prepared for the coffee-with-a-punch this morning, and drank two cups, feeling more energized than ever.

Her shoulders were loose, the sun was shining, and it was all she could do to stay in her seat until she'd finished eating.

"Did y'all have a good time in the Quarter?" Terri asked, a curious eyebrow raised. The Wisconsin couple, resplendent in matching lemon yellow T-shirts, swiveled as one toward Brianna, with a pointedly-interested stare, the kind that went with a roadside accident that you couldn't look away from.

She felt a blush creep up her cheeks.

"Yes, I did," she said, her mouth drying up in a heartbeat. Clearing her throat, she added, "We caught the parade downtown and then found a jazz club with wonderful music."

"Oh," Terri said, with a delighted *yenta* smile. "You were out late. You and Mr. Farrell."

She had no inclination to discuss her potential love life with any of the guests, so she turned the conversation on Evan. Next time he'd get up early enough to defend himself.

"Actually, we had a little bit of trouble. Evan's wallet was stolen."

The Wisconsin Mrs.'s eyes grew wide. "Stolen? Sweet mercy!"

"It's to be expected," came a booming Southern drawl from the kitchen as the male half of the cowboy couple strolled in. "Pickpockets can tell a tourist a mile away. Not that there ain't plenty of them in town this week."

Terri agreed. "It's unfortunate, but true. Did he lose much? Did he call the police? Not that they'll have much luck, I'm afraid."

Brianna shook her head. "He'd left most everything here. He just lost his walking-around money."

"At least you're both all right," Terri said. "A wallet can be replaced."

"Right." She finished her coffee, feeling a need to escape before the conversation turned back to herself. "When is the parade this morning?"

"There's a small parade at ten, and another at eleven-thirty—the Krewe of Iris, which is the women's krewe," Terri said. "Both will be up at St. Charles. They always have pretty floats. You've got time to read the paper, if you'd like."

"Wonderful. Thanks for a delicious breakfast." Brianna gathered up the *Times-Picayune* from the couch. From its wrinkled look, she guessed several people had already perused it thoroughly. She took its remains to the front porch, sitting in a deck chair to soak up some rays before the parade.

The world news was pretty standard: war somewhere, financial boom in one economy and crisis in another. The local section caught Brianna's interest, with bright pictures of the parade she'd seen the evening before, and personal stories of the wealthy debutantes who'd been selected as the queens of today's parades.

Inside, on a page removed from the glitz of Mardi Gras, were other stories, of drug busts and other poverty-driven crimes in the black areas of town. Another situation not improved in the least by the detritus of the hurricane.

The city was full of such contrasts.

Crossing over Canal Street the day before, she'd left modern skyscraper territory for the French Quarter's aging but history-steeped personalities. Architectural styles were eclectic, even within neighborhoods. Great wealth and great indigence lived practically side by side.

Lifting her face to the sun, she closed her eyes. The city illuminated contrasts in her, too. Her law practice tended to define her. She fought battles for impersonal clients to earn money she needed to protect herself from the financial disaster that had destroyed her father.

But until her conversation the day before with Evan, she hadn't really wondered if work was enough. Something in the way he talked about the legal profession and what it "ought" to be resonated with her. There was more to life than work.

*Only for those who could afford to indulge such a whim.*

No, she told that little nagging voice inside. You should be able to do work you enjoy, work that made you feel you'd done something good for others, not just punched an uncaring clock.

And why shouldn't one cultivate a personal life that made her or him happy?

It had to be obvious when even the other-worldly Copper pointed out she put up walls to keep people away.

*So I'll work on that.*

Those walls seemed to be weakening where Evan was concerned. The touch of his lips on hers came to mind again, even here in the sun. The thoughts that followed threatened to take her way off track for her day, so she concentrated on the paper again.

One headline featured a broad reference to the King of Rex. She couldn't forget the cold hatred in Copper's voice on that subject, some not-so-veiled threats there. Could he be serious? And what if he was? Not like she could go to the authorities with some vague "hey, this guy knows who Rex is and doesn't like him."

If Copper really meant the man harm, he'd likely give himself away. Maybe she could use her interrogative skills to snare an admission from him. Her suspicions that he planted the riddle in her purse gave her an opening to pursue him, to determine his motives and intentions.

He'd said he'd see her this morning at the parade...how *very* convenient.

Terri and the others came out, ready to trek to the parade route. Brianna quickly folded the paper and left it inside, joining them as they carried a cooler, some grocery bags and folding chairs down the street to St. Charles.

Once they reached the neutral ground, Terri angled her way through to the front, greeting friends who'd saved her a spot. A round of quick introductions passed by Brianna entirely as smiles flashed and hands were shaken.

She admired the spectacle, scanning the excited crowd. Children perched in protective box seats atop eight-foot ladders leaned forward, waving, to see if the parade was coming. Souvenir vendors rolled rickety carts full of cheap and gaudy plastic inflatables along the route. Passersby wore ostentatious costumes and strings of beads in an array of startling color.

A buzz of excitement and anticipation grew under the shadows of the live oaks, as long-time friends and neighbors greeted each other, and even the eldest acted like small children at their first circus. Which was how Brianna felt as well.

As she acclimated to the noise level she sensed a presence behind her. She knew without looking it was Copper.

He looked her over, then crossed his arms, nodding with approval. "A changed woman from this time yesterday, I see."

What exactly did that mean?

"I have my own beads today." She showed him the pretty golden loops, intentionally changing the subject.

He grinned. "I expect you will have many more by this evening, my lady."

"I hope so." What would she do with them all? She had no idea. She needed only a few as souvenirs. She could hang a few on her lampshades. Perhaps she could gift the more jewelry-like ones to her clerical staff. No point in worrying about it. Beads were for catching, and having, living in the moment. Consequences could be worked out later.

Copper surveyed the crowd. "Where is your friend?"

"Terri's over—" She searched out her hostess, spotting the bright fuchsia T-shirt. "There."

"No, I mean the gentleman with you last night. He had a bit of trouble, didn't he? Is he all right?"

*Copper didn't miss much.* Evan's "trouble" had taken place after Copper had left their table. "Evan? He's fine, I think. No real harm done, except to his pride."

Copper nodded. "In such a man, that sort of injury can be severe."

She chuckled, knowing many men to whom that sentiment might apply. She was more interested in his observation that she had "changed." She felt less like a caterpillar and more like a butterfly. But the metamorphosis was not by any means complete.

"Here they come!" cried out a small girl in front.

Determined not to miss a moment of the excitement, Brianna stepped between the well-braced ladders and leaned forward to catch a glimpse of the floats coming up the street. People began calling to those on the floats, arms raised to catch some bit of finery. The game was about to start again. She opened her hand and smiled.

"Throw me something, mister!"

Chapter Thirteen

Evan heard the bustle outside his room as the hard-core "tourists" got ready to abandon the house to collect more beads. A stolen peek through half-open eyes showed him it wasn't yet eight-thirty.

*It's my day off. No, thanks.*

The rumble of their passing reminded him of the old-style movie elephant stampede. By contrast, the silence after their exit gave him an excellent opportunity to fall back to sleep.

As he stretched awake again about eleven, his mind clicked into action, ticking off things he had to do. Report the theft of his wallet, on the long shot that someone might have turned it in. *Ha. Fat chance of that.*

But stranger things happened.

First things first.

He tumbled over the side of the bed, feet thudding on the floor, body protesting his departure from the spot where he'd slept on the very comfortable mattress. His jeans lay on the floor where he'd tossed them. He slid them on, mindful of the possible presence of other late sleepers.

As he washed his face and took care of his other needs in the bathroom, he remembered that Copper fellow saying he'd meet Brianna on St. Charles this morning. That lit a fire under him. He recalled the way

Brianna's face looked when speaking with the slender, tawny-skinned man. He hadn't liked it.

How had she not realized Copper was right out of Whackyville? She was a smart woman. She didn't seem like the kind to take crazy risks for no reason. What did this guy have on her?

That made Evan even more determined. He was prepared to follow her into whatever she planned to get herself into. Even if it was dangerous. Especially if it was dangerous. Under those circumstances, she'd be a lot better off with him at her side.

So, it looked like Evan would be taking in a parade or two, just to make sure that this "spooky" guy didn't get his hooks in Evan's would-be chick. He just had to approach this in the spirit of Mardi Gras in New Orleans. The purpose of being here was to relax and have fun.

If they could work through this to a point where they could do that, perhaps they could find themselves enjoying each other's company on a more permanent basis.

He scanned the stack of cards in the top drawer of the small dresser, grateful for his instinct to leave them behind the night before. His two major credit cards were there, along with his bank access card, which he stuck in his front pants pocket. The convenience store at the end of the street would surely have a machine, so at least he could have some spending money. Those were the three he used most often. What else had he lost?

A couple of gas company cards, some photos—he winced, thinking of the picture of his sister's graduation, the only one he had of her—Bar Association card and half a dozen rewards cards.

Maybe a dozen. He had way too many. Business cards, with his office address and phone. That was regrettable. What else?

The stamp card from his favorite sub sandwich shop. He'd almost had a full card, too. That would have direct impact on his waistline. *Damn. Wonder how you explain that on an insurance claim form...*

He glanced at his reflection. His jeans and plain blue shirt didn't seem festive enough, so he clipped on a pair of rainbow-striped suspenders. Nothing said 'ready to party" like fancy suspenders, right?

Hoping there was still coffee left at the ripe hour of eleven-thirty, he ran his fingers through his hair, cultivating a Stephen Baldwin loose-cannon look, and left his room, heading downstairs. The house was empty, but the coffeepot was hot in the kitchen. Evan poured himself half a cup and gulped it quickly. The back door scraped open, and Hank Worley shambled in, shovel in hand, a stunning vision of sweaty host.

"Good morning," Evan said, wondering what the big man had been up to. *Burying the body of a partier who didn't survive?*

"Hey," Hank said. Dirt smeared in a ragged line above his brow. He reached for a tall ice-filled glass of tea on the counter and downed half of the cool liquid in a few swallows.

"Everyone's down at St. Charles," he said. "Except me. Terri wanted me to put in an azalea, so it would look nice for the picnic Mardi Gras Day."

The poor guy looked so winded, Evan felt compelled to offer assistance. "Need some help?"

Hank cut him off with a wave. "You'd best hurry. Iris parade'll be comin' past soon."

Evan nodded, relieved. Yard work wasn't exactly his idea of vacation. "See you later."

He trudged out the front door and down the short driveway to the uneven sidewalk, cracked and tipsy from the live oak roots spreading under the concrete. Others walked alongside him past the homes painted in assorted pastels, up toward St. Charles, where a crowd gathered along the streetcar line.

A skinny black man called to Evan from his front step, where he struggled with a red and white cooler. "Hey, man! Help me cart this box, and I'll give you a brew!"

"Sounds like a deal." Grinning, Evan grabbed one handle and walked with the man, followed down the street by a group of skipping, yelling children. He thought there were four, but they moved too fast for him to keep an exact count.

"Just set it down there, in the neutral ground," the man said with a bright smile. "Sandy, keep an eye on your bubba, there!" he admonished the oldest girl as the children immediately wandered off in opposite directions.

True to his word, the man opened the chest and handed Evan a beer from the collection packed in crushed ice. "Thanks, brother."

"No problem." Evan nodded to him, then set off to find Brianna and the others.

The early parade units, the horseback royalty handing out theme doubloons, passed as he joined the party. The throng was a fraction of the crowd downtown the night before; the ranks perhaps five people thick, instead of ten. Nearly everyone wore some sort of beads, some thickly draped.

The front row along the avenue was lined with eight-foot stepladders topped with wooden boxes holding preschoolers huddled two and three to a seat. Watchful parents stood behind their children on the ladders, anchoring them to the ground lest they get too wiggly.

In the area which the man had referred to as the "neutral ground," whole families had set up for the day, with folding chairs and coolers. Picnics ranged from homemade peanut butter and jellies to the elegant group sipping white wine and munching from a vegetable and dip tray. Children weaved in and out of the gathered lawn chairs, some clapping their hands in time with the approaching band.

Evan squirmed gently through to the front row, trying to get a better view of the crowd so he could find Brianna. Oblivious to the passing float, he moved along the street's edge as those before him raised their arms, trying to garner the attention of the masked riders. He craned his neck, looking for a familiar face.

Suddenly he was smacked on the top of the head by a toss from the float. He ducked to avoid the grasping hands reaching for whatever had hit him, but the bauble slid into his front pocket. As he bent over slightly, another arm hit him in the back of the head.

"Hey, watch it!"

When he tried to stand straight again, another handful of beads flew before his face, but he leaned back as someone snatched the gold chain in midair.

"Evan!"

A hand reached out to grab Evan's arm and pull him into the crowd, temporarily safe from the more zealous bead collectors. Brianna checked him over.

"What are you doing? You're going to lose an eye out there."

"I'm fine," he grumbled. She looked fine, too. More than fine, dressed in a loose blouse the color of ripe peaches that just lit her up. She sparkled with bead necklaces already.

"What did you catch?" she asked with a smile. "At the rate the sharks were after that throw, it must have been something wonderful." Her gaze flicked to his shirt pocket.

"I don't even know." His hand patted his chest for the enlarged pocket, then reached inside to discover a deep violet string of tiny abacus-type beads, narrow and strung closely together.

"Ooooo," Brianna gasped. "Those are beautiful."

"They're yours. They haven't been very lucky for me so far." He rubbed the back of his head where they'd landed.

"Thanks." She slipped them around her neck, her face glowing. "Look what else I got," she said, running her fingers through the beads that hung across her chest to display them.

What did she see in a bunch of plastic junk probably made in China? "Uh-huh." Evan popped the top of his beer can. "All alone? Or are Terri and the others handy?"

"Copper was here, actually." Her gaze flicked away.

"Great. Funny how he's always on your heels, hmm?" He scanned the crowd, and sure enough, spotted Copper talking with several black women nearby.

Brianna bit her lip and turned her attention to the street as another spectacularly-colored float, rising some fifteen feet high, crawled by them, decorated in giant papier-mâché kangaroos and crocodiles for an Australian theme. The masked women of the Krewe of Iris stood on double decks, tossing beads, toys and plastic cups to those who caught their eye.

Distracted from the riders by the shadow of Copper's presence, Evan subtly moved to stand between them.

Brianna relaxed and called to the riders like any other tourist, but Copper came to stand behind Brianna, a little smirk riding on his lips. His cool good looks seemed to attract the eyes of the ladies on the floats. When he smiled and held up his hand, it was like wizardry. They tossed him golden chains, and tri-color beads four feet long. One woman even leaned down to hand him a long-stemmed red silk rose. He nodded, as if the gifts were his due, then passed his treasures on to those with him, including a delighted Brianna, when they moved on.

Evan seethed silently, then downed his beer to free up his hands as a marching band that passed, majorettes and cheerleaders kicking high and performing baton tricks, crown jewels among the instrument-carrying youths.

Did Copper think he could win Brianna's heart with his little presents?

Two could play that game.

Iris was an all-female Krewe. Evan knew how to handle them just fine.

The next float, bedecked with orange, yellow and red flowers and the Mexican flag, passed slowly as the band marched on. Evan put on his best bad-boy grin and stepped closer, so those on the float could easily see him.

"Hola, senoritas!" he called. "What do you have for me?"

Several women looked in his direction, smiling under the loose half-masks they wore. Two scrambled to be the first to cast a string of beads in his direction. Evan caught one in each hand and acknowledged them with a wink. He looped the green and the gold beads around his own neck hastily, as another threw him a baseball cap with the Krewe insignia. He grabbed it and waved his gratitude, placing the cap on his head.

From the corner of his eye, he saw Copper step aside to allow Brianna to catch a Krewe bead strand, shiny red plastic with a medallion bearing the likeness of a goddess, which she added to her thick collection of many colors.

Growling, Evan stepped closer to Brianna, determined to impress her. At the back of the float, he spied a tall brunette in lilac, whose dark eyes smiled into his. She pointed at Evan, then leaned forward to toss a lengthy string of 3/4" pearl-like beads into his outstretched hand.

From the gasps around him, Evan guessed he had caught a real prize. He blew a kiss of gratitude to the masked woman, running the beads through his hands, marveling at their weight. After the float had moved on, he turned to Brianna, holding them out.

"I think these would suit you better than me."

Copper's stare burned into him, and he gave it right back.

*Yeah, I did that. What are you gonna do about it, Copper man?*

"They're incredible." She reached out with a finger

to touch them, wonder written on her face. "I couldn't take them, though. They're yours."

Evan grinned. "But they don't really match my ensemble. Here. Let's conduct this formally. I'll give you this for one of yours as consideration. That makes it a valid contract."

She laughed softly. "Always business with you." She sorted through to find a shorter red string that matched a stripe in Evan's suspenders. "This?"

"Sure." Evan reached out to place the pearls around her neck solemnly, and took the red ones as she handed them to him. "Very beautiful," he said.

She blushed, then stammered, "T-Terri's over t-there, with the people from Wisconsin," pointing up the street toward downtown.

Following the direction of her finger, Evan saw his hostess with both the northern tourists and the cowboys, too, far enough away they couldn't really speak, so he waved. The Cheeseheads still appeared dazed from the excitement, but they'd accumulated a nice little batch of beads of their own. "More plastic crap," he muttered.

"It's Mardi Gras," Copper said softly, suddenly near Evan's ear. "It is impossible to avoid the delights of the season."

Evan twitched, startled by Copper's proximity and his words, and pulled away. Was the man a mindreader, too?

Copper smiled as if he'd heard Evan speak aloud. "Especially in the company of such a lovely woman."

"Right." Evan turned away. The man just rubbed him wrong. And not only because of the way he'd latched on to Brianna. Something else… disturbing.

Copper wouldn't let it drop. He nodded in

Brianna's direction as she parceled out some beads to a young black girl next to her. "She is lovely," he said. His tone was that of someone handing around a plate of appetizers, clearly encouraging Evan to help himself.

"She sure is."

Copper acknowledged his comment with another nod, then stepped back.

The next float passed, but Evan didn't bother to raise his hand for more beads. Instead, he puzzled through Copper's implication. He'd thought Copper a potential rival. But his words weren't proprietary. They seemed, rather, to be encouraging Evan's interest in Brianna.

But that's not how it goes. How can he not be interested in her? She's a real prize—beauty, brains and successful life, too.

There had to be some other motive.

Maybe Copper was trying to up the stakes.

That had to be it.

Did he think Evan wasn't in it to win it? Shows what he knows, huh? Copper thought he had to add wood to the fire of love, to make their contest more real and the stakes higher. Brianna wasn't enough of a prize—he wanted to really challenge Evan, man to man.

The thought sparked his competitive spirit. He could beat this guy at his own game, beat him easy.

Evan smiled and looked back at Brianna, seemingly oblivious to the contest and immersed again in her quest for plastic finery. Well, he was a guy, and he'd rise to the occasion.

*You're on, Copper. You're on.*

Chapter Fourteen

From the moment Evan joined her at the parade, the atmosphere changed, more than the sparring between Copper and Evan. She could easily ignore that. What drew her like a super magnet was the way Evan played the float riders to impress her.

After he'd received the pearls, which her neighbors in the crowd assured her were spectacular, he'd unbuttoned his shirt a couple more notches to reveal a chest with a comfortable amount of curly brown hair.

But, in her opinion, not the shirt, but the smile captured the hearts of the ladies. There was something of mischief about it, the face of the little boy who'd just picked all his mom's prize roses to present them lovingly to her.

She wasn't immune to it herself.

He scored a chain of shiny red hearts and brought it to her, his grin triumphant.

"Thanks, but you don't have to prostitute yourself on my account, you know," she said.

He huffed in mock insult. "Prostitute? What are you talking about? Believe me, I wouldn't sell myself for any woman."

"Really?" Brianna asked.

"Really."

Copper observed him coolly. "I believe something in you would sacrifice itself for a woman. The *right* woman."

Evan scoffed. His eyes narrowed. "Yeah? What makes you such a great expert, pal?"

"Copper knows many things about men and women…and love."

The last float rolled toward downtown, amid entreating cries for the dregs of the beads. The crowd began to disband, and Terri and her following came to join them.

"I think you've got the hang of it, girl." She winked at Brianna. "Look at your loot!"

"I may have been a little greedy—my neck's starting to ache." She took several heavier loops from her neck and tucked them in a plastic grocery bag Terri handed her.

Terri's gaze flicked from Evan to Copper and back again. "Mr. Farrell, I see you've had your share."

Evan smiled and strutted a little. "With so many beautiful women competing to throw me things, it's hard to remain humble."

"I'm sure it is." Terri grinned at him. She eyed Brianna's other companion. "Who's this, Brianna?"

"We met at the airport the night I lost my luggage. This is Copper Delacroix."

Terri's eyes widened. Her lips closed together with a near-snap. "Really!" was all she said.

Copper's eyes sparkled. "My mother is Felicity Delacroix."

"We should be going," Terri said, her tone imperative. "Lunch will be ready at the house—"

Copper interrupted Terri. "Brianna, do you have plans for this afternoon?"

Uncomfortable at the snub to her hostess, Brianna

tried to recall the notes she'd made. Saturday, Saturday... "I think a visit to the voodoo display at the art Museum."

A flash of alarm streaked across Terri's face.

Copper smiled widely. "You are interested in the religion of voodoo? I'm sure you will find it fascinating."

Evan scowled and stepped closer. "Voodoo? That's just something from old movies, isn't it? It's not real."

Copper's dark eyes turned on Evan, hard to read. "Oh, yes, Mr. Farrell, voodoo is alive and well in New Orleans. At the Voodoo Museum, a practitioner will meet with you to tell your future, or discover your secret admirer—"

"Or put a hex on someone who has wronged you?" Terri said.

"A hex!" gasped Mrs. Nielssen, standing behind Terri.

The big Texan spit out a guffaw. "Now really, ma'am, you don't need to worry about that."

Something ominous stretched between Terri and Copper. Copper stood his ground for a few moments, then bowed to Brianna.

"I will leave you with your friends. Enjoy the day in our fair city."

He smoothly turned away to stroll down St. Charles, leaving Brianna intrigued. What was so wrong with voodoo? Surely some people believed in its power, but she relegated it to the level of carrying a rabbit's foot for good luck.

*Wasn't good luck for the rabbit, though, was it?* Her father's usual question jabbed her.

*Not now.*

Once Copper was out of earshot, Terri demanded, "Where did you meet him, again?"

"At the airport. He was a perfect gentleman. I've run into him several times since I arrived."

"Yeah, like that's not suspicious," Evan muttered.

"I'm not hunting him, Evan."

"Right, he magically appears where you do. On the street, on the streetcar, at a bar… everywhere." He frowned. "Back in Pittsburgh we'd call that stalking."

Brianna eyed Terri. "What's the matter with Copper? Who is Felicity Delacroix?"

Terri gestured in the direction Copper had gone. He walked alone, even in a crowd, as though people made space to let him pass. Her voice trembled a little as she spoke. "Mama Delacroix is a notorious voodoo queen."

McCurdy, the Texan who had pooh-poohed the mention of "hexing," said, "Now, come on, ma'am. You can't really take that seriously."

Brianna was struck by the chill in Terri's tone.

"Mr. McCurdy, a supervisor in my office was the victim of a voodoo curse. He took ill with a debilitating ailment which was never diagnosed. Then a week later, he died."

Mrs. Nielssen gasped. "Sweet Jesus!"

Terri went on, "The rumor went around that he'd sexually harassed one of the secretaries. She said something about seeing Mama, shortly before it all happened."

She shuddered. "So, yes, I believe voodoo curses are alive and well. And that man is in the thick of the magic. You stay away from him!"

She waved a finger in Brianna's direction.

"Now let's go back to the house."

Terri didn't wait for agreement. She walked away toward the B&B. The others followed along, Evan and McCurdy bringing the chairs and cooler.

Despite what she'd heard, Brianna found it hard to believe Copper meant her harm. He'd been charming, enigmatic, and mysterious. *But voodoo? Really?*

Terri went straight upstairs to lie down, leaving Brianna no chance to apologize. Hank followed her, mystified. The others took a break from the rising heat, refreshing themselves with chilled drinks before scattering for their chosen afternoon occupations.

When the dust settled, Brianna and Evan found themselves alone in the kitchen.

"Now we'd better have a little talk," Evan said. "Time for a powwow." His brow was furrowed, and Brianna decided it was no time to argue with him, police officer's paranoia or not.

"Bring it on," she said.

## Chapter Fifteen

They took iced tea onto the back patio, then stood at the far end of the deck, observing the garden.

"Is that what you're going to claim next?" he asked. "That old Copper has cast a magic voodoo spell on you and that's why you keep ending up together?"

Brianna tore her gaze away from the coral hibiscus and tropical magenta bougainvillea, staring at Evan in disbelief. "Get serious."

"You know he planted that note." Evan paced on the deck. "What are you going to do about it?"

"Nothing. Yet."

She debated sharing about Copper and the King of Rex, but Evan growled like he thought she was an idiot. *Nothing like making him think I'm completely nuts...*

"Do you believe in voodoo?" He glanced back toward the house, as if someone might overhear them.

"Of course not." She set her glass down, afraid she'd spill it, all the while controlling an urge to haul off and smack him. *Was he really going there? For heaven's sake.*

"I'd intended to see that exhibit long before I came here or met him. It's part of the city's heritage. If I was in Kansas, I'd see the World's Largest Ball of Twine. If I were in San Francisco, I'd see the Golden Gate and maybe Alcatraz. It's just— " She waved her hand. "It's what one does here."

"Well, what one does *not* do is screw around with someone who thinks he's some kind of voodoo priest. Especially someone as shady as Copper Delacroix."

Before she could protest, he added, "I think I'd believe Terri, since you've been here exactly two days and she lives here year-round."

He might have been right, but she'd have clawed herself before she admitted it at this point.

When she didn't reply, he frowned. "Do you believe?" he asked again.

"Evan, I'm not sure why it—"

He stepped closer and dropped his voice. "Listen, something happened last night." He chewed his lip, more unsure than she'd ever seen him. His cocky attitude from the first night in the Worley's living room was nowhere to be found.

"Something what?"

She tried to imagine what could have happened between Evan and Copper. Even in the bar, she couldn't recall a moment when they'd been alone together.

"When we left the bar. Your ooga-booga pal made this…little hand gesture." He almost squirmed with discomfiture.

"What kind of gesture?"

"I don't know. It was almost like a…I don't know. A…zap."

*What the hell?* "A zap?"

"Yeah. Like this." He took his hand and half-waved it at Brianna, his fingers first spreading, then coming together with a little poke.

"Not just a wave? Like, 'see you around'?"

She couldn't take her eyes from his face. He was so

serious. Whatever he'd seen had shaken him. "You really think it was something sinister? A spell? Hexes?"

Though she spoke lightly, her mind wrestled with the mental picture she'd received at the costume store, when she pulled that note out of her purse: Copper, his face painted and his clothing that of some sort of warrior priest. Was that what a voodoo practitioner looked like? Was it a warning?

"Hell, Brianna. I don't know. But when you assemble pieces of evidence, you start to build a real case."

He took a drink of his tea, staring off into the neighbor's yard, where a couple of small children chased a puppy around, as if things like voodoo didn't even exist. "So I'll ask again. Do you believe?"

She cleared her throat. "No, I wouldn't say so. But I'm not a particularly religious person. I tend to function more from a place of tangible proof and hard evidence."

Evan shrugged and turned his sapphire gaze back to hers.

"Faith is a funny thing. Most of the time it doesn't involve logic and rational thought—believers move onto a higher plane. Catholics believe bread and wine is transformed into body and blood, as part of their religious ritual. Christians believe the soul leaves the body after death and takes up existence in another place. Those who believe in reincarnation think the soul moves on to another life. These theories aren't about proof. It's what you believe—or don't."

He came closer. Uneasiness emanated from him like magnetic rays, unseen but toxic. The longer he talked, the more chills ran up her back, even in the bright sunshine.

He went on, "If someone is convinced a hex will kill them, most likely it will, whether the sender has power or not. It's mind over matter. Whatever you consider true is the grounding on which you base your life. You have to believe in something."

The longer he stood so close to her, memories of the night before tugged at her mind. Almost without volition, she took a step toward him, needing his presence and support. The next minute she was in his arms.

He didn't seem surprised or alarmed. He just held her close.

Her head on his chest, she listened for a long moment, realizing his heartbeat had sped up. Something told her it was time to trust him. "Evan, there's something else."

He stiffened, but didn't release her. "I'm listening."

"Copper said something very odd on the streetcar the other day. We were looking at the paper and got to talking about the Rex Krewe and the King of Rex."

"The what?"

"It's a Mardi Gras tradition. Rex rules Carnival. The honor usually goes to one of the city's movers and shakers, who belongs to many civic organizations. He's a philanthropic star. It's considered a real mark of respect to be chosen, but it's always a huge mystery. He's revealed on Lundi Gras. Monday night."

"Yeah? What's that got to do with Copper?"

She sighed, not sure how to approach the subject. Evan had a tendency to flip out about things he thought were dangerous.

And maybe that wasn't such a bad thing.

"He started muttering that he knew Rex's identity. Then he said those who wronged Copper will suffer."

Evan pulled away gently and looked her in the eye. "So he made a threat against this King of Rex guy?"

"Not exactly. He didn't say for sure who it was—"

"Well, someone must know. The committee, or whoever. Someone should warn him."

"What would we say? That's a pretty vague threat, if it even is one. He could have just been blowing off steam about a bad business deal."

Evan cleared his throat. "Maybe, maybe. So what should we do?"

"Maybe the place to start is get some education. We can skip the display at the art museum and go to the real Voodoo Museum." She remembered a mention in her guidebooks. "I've got the address upstairs."

"You're sure you want to pursue this?"

With him looking down into her eyes, she almost faltered. *We could be doing other things that have nothing to do with crazy kinds of people like this.*

But her stubborn nature wouldn't let go. "I think we should. Just until we have a little more. Something that might really interest the police. Or else we find this is all a fantasy of smoke and mirrors and we walk away."

He frowned and shrugged. "All right, all right. If you say so. But I'm going with you every step of the way, so you don't get yourself in trouble. Hear me?"

Secretly pleased he wanted to accompany her, she didn't want him to get too cocky, either. "Well, if you have to."

Now he outright scowled. "Yes, damn it, I have to." He drained his glass and set it on the picnic table.

"Go get your book and bring that note, too. Maybe someone there can make sense of it."

Brianna went quietly upstairs, trying not to disturb Terri. She went into her room and took off all her beads, setting aside the treasures she'd collected that morning, back before everything had become so serious.

She tucked the guidebook into her purse, the note already inside. Her fingers tingled, remembering the buzz when she first touched up the triangle-folded paper. *Magical indeed.* She hurried back downstairs. Evan waited by the front door, car keys in hand. Brianna flipped through the pages of her guide book as Evan drove, searching for their destination.

"Here it is, the Voodoo Museum on Dumaine Street between Royal and Bourbon." Reading on, she said, "Psychics may conduct private readings, tarot cards, palm readings and such."

"Hmmmph." Evan shifted up and kept driving, heading down to Magazine Street, where afternoon antique and art buyers strolled from shop to shop. He took a left on Magazine for the Quarter as Brianna read aloud.

"'Voodoo originally came with the slaves from Africa, but they had to modify their practices under their Catholic masters to be allowed to continue to practice their ancient religions. They noticed that the Catholics used to pray to saints to intercede with their God, so Voodoo practitioners substituted intermediaries known as the Loa, that interact with worshippers and even possess them in secret ceremonies.'"

Stumbling over the unfamiliar jargon, Brianna went on, "'About fifteen percent of the population still practices Voodoo.'"

"Really?" He eyed her while waiting for a light to change. "Then this Copper fellow could be in it up to his neck."

She clutched the book as if it might save her. "I suppose so. But even if he is, that doesn't mean he's some evil priest. It says voodoo is more about predicting the future and revealing hidden truths in yourself than in casting spells and raising the dead."

She blinked and read that paragraph again. *Say what? Raising the dead? Now that's something I don't want to hear about at all!*

Evan chuckled suddenly, startling her from her reading.

"What's so funny?"

"You. Me. Us. Talking about raising people from the dead and searching graveyards for prizes. We're just a couple of lawyers on vacation. What are we doing? This is crazy."

"Crazy. Probably." She leaned back in the seat. She wouldn't feel right walking away, if someone's life was truly at stake. What if Copper killed this man and she'd been able to stop him? That would be hard for her conscience to live with.

Besides, Evan had promised he'd stay with her the whole time. She wanted more time with him, that she was sure of.

So this mission had taken on a couple of layers beyond just puzzling out the mystery.

"I don't know, Evan. I mean, we could drink ourselves into oblivion every night like the rest of the Mardi Gras partiers. But we've been invited into a side of New Orleans others don't see. You know, that adventure thing we were talking about yesterday."

He glanced sideways at her. "You trying to convince me, or yourself?"

Her reply stuck in her throat.

They pulled up in a parking lot near the French Quarter and walked down in search of the Museum. Happy, excited voices echoed off the brick and stucco buildings on either side of the narrow streets. Some cars endeavored to force their way through the crowd spilling off the sidewalks into the streets, but they were few and far between. Most people were smarter than that. This was definitely a pedestrian area for the week.

Evan lagged behind, and she looked over her shoulder every so often to make sure he was still coming. The talk of magic and voodoo had her second-guessing. She was still fired up by the sense of adventure, but clearly he wasn't convinced. Maybe what they learned at the museum would make the difference.

She almost missed it.

Expecting a large building set aside from the rest, like the Carnegie museums in downtown Pittsburgh, she walked right by the door. Evan whistled sharply and she stopped.

"I think this is it," he said. He pointed to the darkly-carved wooden sign that hung over the door.

"Oh." She studied the sign, as well as the entrance, its windows covered with red curtains. An electric jolt of anxiety zipped down her back. She stiffened her shoulders in response.

*I can do this.*

"Ready?" He pulled open the door. "After you."

It was put up or shut up time.

She nodded and stepped inside, half expecting to be possessed as soon as she crossed the threshold. The ambience was spooky, to be sure, grotesque statues, bones and skulls displayed in the lobby. She paid their entrance fee to a wizened old man, hardly more than a skeleton himself, and they were invited to the inner sanctum.

The hallway to the large back room was hung with photographs and paintings, news stories of the workings of voodoo. Much of the history seemed attached to a woman named Marie Laveau, a famous priestess. The name belonged to both a mother and daughter, but the daughter made voodoo her own source of strength. Several paintings of Marie stared down upon the museum visitors; she looked powerful, but not malicious.

Unlike a number of the other artifacts that would no doubt haunt Brianna for days.

Wanting to educate herself, she forced herself to peer into the jars on the shadowed shelves, the twisted dead things in them misshapen and ugly. She read the explanations of the *gris-gris,* either an amulet of protection, or a magic incantation that would bring a thing to pass. She studied the altars, bright as flower gardens with their gifts of beads, fruits, and other valuables seeking approval of the voodoo gods.

Coming face to face with a seven-foot-high carved wood black depiction of a "zombi", she tried her best not to shiver, though her gut told her to break and run.

Evan, on the other hand, seemed to wax more enthusiastic around every corner. "This is incredible!" he gasped. "Zombies. Who knew? I love zombies. Look at all this neat skeleton stuff. What's this? Snakes. I *love* this snake." He pointed to the sinuous carved form of a black snake that hung, diagonal, on the wall. "I want one for my house."

Brianna eyed him as if he were one of the eerie oddities. "Are you out of your mind?"

"I think so," he agreed, excitement dancing in his eyes. "I think I have totally taken leave of my senses. Why not? Makes more sense than dealing with this situation like an adult."

A flush of irritation crept up her cheeks, and she was glad for the spooky red lights of the museum that would hide it from Evan. She'd learned what she thought she needed to know, anyway. Time to move forward.

"Come on, let's find out how to consult with the spirit woman."

She made her way through the wide-eyed tourists to the lobby to find the elderly man who'd collected their fee. He wasn't there.

She stepped aside, trying not to turn her back to anything creepy, not easy in this place. Evan continued to read and examine the various plaques along the walls, finding each one more fascinating than the one before.

At least he was interested now. That was a good thing.

The more she'd seen today, the more she was glad to have a companion on this "adventure." Ceremonies drenched in blood, sacrifice of animals, ghosts of ancestors, and other bizarre occurrences were a far distance from her white-bread suburban childhood existence. The artifacts alone were enough to convince her this religion was one of mystical proportions she might not be equipped to deal with.

She crossed her arms, almost hugging herself for comfort. *If that old man doesn't reappear here in just a minute, I'm going to bail. Before something gets me.*

And just that quickly, the clerk stepped from behind a black curtain that led to some nether region of the facility. He took a seat on his rickety stool and began collecting money from several others waiting in line to see the museum. When they'd all passed, he turned his dark, interested gaze on Brianna and Evan.

"Haven't seen enough?" he rumbled.

*I've seen plenty.*

Brianna cut off her first response and forced a smile instead. "We were told we could arrange a meeting? With a spiritual advisor?"

He broke into a grin, his teeth so white against his dark skin and the shadows of the room. "You want information about wedding?" he asked.

"No!" both lawyers said as one, their vehemence causing him to blink and rock in his seat.

"No need to eat old Albert's head, now. Consult for both, that is sixty dollars."

"Sixty—wow."

Nothing about this trip was going to be inexpensive, that was for sure. She gave the man her credit card, since Evan seemed oblivious. He vanished into the back a moment, then came with a receipt for her to sign. When she'd finished, and she had her card safely back in her purse, he pointed to a second curtain, this one red and textured, off to the left. "You go through to the courtyard in back. Someone will help you there."

"Thank you."

When Evan remained enthralled by the things in jars, she grabbed his sleeve to drag him along.

"I was coming," he muttered.

"Good."

She took a deep breath. The next few minutes would set her on a new path, one way or the other. Perhaps the woman was a fake, and clearly string them along, in which case Brianna could discount this whole episode as crap and go back to her vacation. Or if she took the note seriously and had something to offer as advice, the adventure would continue.

Heart racing with anticipation, Brianna headed down the short hallway to embrace her fate.

Chapter Sixteen

The back door led to a sunlit courtyard, a different atmosphere than the dark, dusty collection inside. A weight lifted off Evan as they came out into the light.

"Did you see that collection of bones?" he asked. "Previous generations right there, ready to ask for their wisdom and experience in your daily life. It's like the Chinese or Native American traditions of invoking the presence of the ancestors. Really fascinating stuff." He smiled broadly. "And that snake!"

He'd found the experience much more interesting than he'd expected, including the depictions of gods in various forms, especially the thick python, said to participate in all rituals performed by those with the Museum.

"Yes, I saw them," she said.

"That's it? 'I saw them'? I thought you were the one all hell-bent to jump into the world of voodoo."

She didn't even respond, but he just grinned. Who would have suspected she was one of those girly girls? Doesn't like spiders and snakes… Ha! She was just too proud to say so.

"What next?"

"The readings are done through here. I guess we just wait and see."

As if summoned, a turbaned black woman in a long dark dress passed through from the museum. "You desire a reading?" she asked, holding out her hand for the receipt. "Our priestess, Madame Masika, will help you. Come this way."

She led the way into a darkened waiting room hung with black and red draperies, lit with multicolored candles that gave off a musky scent that approached cloying, as far as Evan was concerned. Gesturing for them to sit, she slipped through a hand-woven curtain in the back.

Evan perched on the edge of a mat-covered soft chair, studying their surroundings. The oil paintings on three of the walls depicted ceremonies or rituals, groups of dark-skinned men and women dancing in impossible postures, sacrificing animals, burning fires on altars and other bizarre acts.

His early Methodist training rebelled, as did his sense of logic. How could these people possibly believe slitting a chicken's throat would bring them what they wished?

Any crazier than he and Brianna tossing quarters into a public fountain and making a wish? Or those afore-mentioned transmogrifications of body to bread, blood to wine? When's the last time he stepped on a crack, hmm? Just in case?

This was definitely a to-each-his-own sort of event. Now that they were here, he just needed to fasten his seatbelt and see where the ride took them.

"Feel like a real country mouse," he whispered.

Eyes wide, Brianna nodded.

The woman re-appeared through the curtained door. "The priestess will see you now."

Evan got to his feet, pausing at the door, not sure if chivalry dictated he should let Brianna precede him, or if his street-trained cop sense would put him between her and any potential danger. How bad could it be? Probably some Whoopi-Goldberg type faker with a glass ball...

Brianna hesitated, so he took the initiative and stepped through first into a much better-lit room with only dried natural things hanging on the walls, fruits and grains, and was that—?

*Cool! A dead animal on the wall!*

Brianna gasped behind him and looked away. *Girly girl.* He snickered, but not loud enough that she could hear.

The atmosphere slowly closed in on him. As they moved forward to the two hard wooden chairs that awaited them, his smile faded. The very air seemed to thicken with a smoky flavor, probably incense of some sort.

His breath caught as he came under the scrutiny of the dark eyes of the aged black woman seated at the table before them. She wore bright red and gold, a resplendent shawl with lines of multi-colored embroidery around her shoulders. Her turban sat tall and proud, though she herself was a tiny woman.

She didn't feel small, though.

If he closed his eyes, he could sense her presence, a warm glow like an embrous fire, that rose eight feet in the air.

But the setting detracted from her personal power. The diminutive table was spread with a red cloth, worn shiny in places, and in the center was an honest-to-God crystal ball. Just like in the movies. How corny could you get?

The turbaned priestess watched them, bird-like, her

head tilting off-center as she sized them up, wrinkled hands resting lightly on the cloth as they stood before her.

Brianna moved closer to Evan, their arms nearly touching. The hair on his arms stood from the electric anxiety that passed between them. Personally, he would have felt less unsteady if the woman had been holding a pistol. Voodoo, or whatever mystical practice she dealt in, was totally removed from his body of experience.

Brianna made the first move, taking one of the chairs across from the old woman. Evan followed her example.

"Good," the woman said, smiling crookedly, exposing a gold tooth. The smile didn't penetrate her eyes, he noticed. Her voice had a Caribbean lilt. "You have questions for Madame Masika, or do you want me to tell you what I see?"

Brianna glanced at Evan, looking for moral support.

*Hell, this was her game, let her play it. Drag the note out, get whatever heeby-jeeby words this woman has to offer and let's go. I could be sitting on a barstool listening to jazz right now. Or hanging out with those cool zombies instead.*

He just shrugged.

She cleared her throat a couple of times before she spoke. "Please, tell us what you see."

Evan frowned, as Brianna dodged the direct route. Who knew where that would lead? This woman could come up with anything.

The priestess looked from one to the other. "Alike, but different. You don't know each other well."

*Like that was hard to discern from our body*

*language and style of dress. I could do this job. But I'd look like an idiot in a turban.*

"Both searching for something you believe you cannot find."

More pop psychology? Who did she think she was, Dr. Phil in a babushka?

Evan's focus trailed away from her, drawn to the stuffed corpse of the animal, trying to determine what kind of animal it might be. Non-descript reddish-brown fur, larger than a cat, but not really fox-like, he couldn't really tell. He thought back to dead things he'd found as a kid, running with his friends in the woods behind his rural Morgantown home. They had the same pinched look and the same empty eyes.

The recollection made him shiver.

"You take money to perpetuate disagreements between others, instead of healing their wounds." The priestess's eyes were accusatory.

Brianna's face drained of color, and she gave Evan a quick glance.

Startled by the statement, it wasn't hard to see how the old woman might discover that. He snorted with derision. "Did you get that when you ran the credit card? Checked Google for a name? I'm sure there's a computer back here someplace."

The priestess studied him a long moment, examining him like an insect on a pin, before it was stuck into a collection. "You do not believe."

"In this? Damn straight I don't." He eyed her right back. He believed in plenty of things, like the power of doing good deeds and the kind of love his parents had known. But fortune telling? No way.

This dried-up little raisin didn't scare him.

She just shook her head, and turned back to Brianna. "You, though, have an open mind. And a question." She reached across the table, her hand palm up, gesturing for Brianna to take her hand. "Tell me what troubles you, *bébé.*"

Brianna placed her hand in the old woman's. "A mystery, Madame. Someone left me a message, and it troubles me."

"A message?"

"Yes. With references to voodoo practices or places." Brianna took a deep breath and squared her shoulders. "We think someone may be in danger, and we wanted help in deciphering this message."

The priestess never moved, her fingers still clenched around Brianna's. "A message from whom?"

Brianna eyed her purse. "We aren't sure."

"Should that not be your first question?"

Enough playing games.

Evan interjected, "We think the note's from Copper Delacroix."

The woman's eyes widened, and her interest fanned an obvious spark. "Is that so?" She appeared to consider them with considerably more significance, then released her grip on Brianna's hand, gesturing with her fingers. "Give it to me."

Brianna did so, wordlessly.

Madame Masika closed her eyes, holding the paper over the crystal ball, rubbing its edges between her fingers. Rocking a little in her seat, she brought it near her face, eyes still closed, then placed it flat on the table before her, moving her fingers across it like a person reading Braille. At last, her hands came to a standstill and she sat like a statue, labored breathing evident in the trembling of her chest as it rose and fell.

*What the hell? Isn't she even going to look at it? I mean, I know it's all about the show, but—*

The priestess' eyes opened abruptly, giving them both a jolt.

Evan mentally kicked himself for letting her dramatic presentation get to him. *Sucker's born every minute, pal. Guess she got you.*

The tiny woman sat a little taller, patted the paper on the table. "The son of Mama Delacroix—his hand I feel in this magic."

A moment of regret zipped through him, and he realized perhaps he believed more than he admitted to himself. He'd hoped to be convinced by what she said, and this was just a rehash of what he'd already told her. Perhaps he should have let her try it cold.

*Let's hope she's not going to just tell us what we want to hear.*

"Now, the message." The old woman examined the paper before her. "That which you seek is within your grasp," she read. She eyed Brianna. "You? What is it you seek?"

Brianna shrugged, her cheeks taking on color. "I want to know what to do." She gave a furtive glance toward Evan.

The woman continued to observe her, then looked back at the note. "To secure your answers, you must travel a path of danger, where sand becomes water, and the greatest peril is to be alone."

"Where sand becomes water?" Evan repeated. "Now that's a little mysterious, isn't it—"

The old woman glared at him, and he felt himself stop talking, not of his own will, but by hers apparently.

He struggled to object, but nothing came out. What the hell?

Brianna appeared not to notice his unnatural silence, focused on the old woman and the divination process.

Frustrated, he fidgeted in his chair, drawing another glare from the priestess. Geez, what else could she do to him? Turn him into a newt? Realizing she had shut him up for real, he thought better of pushing the issue. This was out of his league. A thrill of fear shot through him, but he shoved it deep within. He couldn't let the women see it.

Madame Masika tapped the table before Brianna. "Sand becomes water. Many places there are in the Bayou Barataria where one may stand on what seems like solid ground, only to find it shifting beneath one's feet as it sucks them into the earth."

"Quicksand," Brianna said, nodding. "The most obvious interpretation. But what are you saying? We have to go to the swamp?" Her voice trailed off with lack of enthusiasm.

"You must not go alone," the woman warned. "The words are very specific. The danger will grow if you are alone." Her eyes flicked over to Evan, then away, as if she had assessed him and found him lacking.

Oh, really? Now this old witch was going to decide what his capabilities were?

Swamp, huh? When there sowed many bright activities with loud music and beer flowing expensive water, why would he choose to slosh around in a swamp looking for quicksand? His mental picture swelled to contain the bugs, the oppressive heat, the moss hanging down over the muddy water, and the snap of alligator jaws...

Not at all what he'd planned.

But as he sat, trapped in silence, Copper's words haunted him. *I believe there is something in you that would sacrifice itself for a woman.*

Brianna was now hanging on the old woman's every word. She was going to play out this charade to the end, wasn't she? He hoped she remembered they were discovering the facts about the threat to Rex, not going on a full-scale crazy hike.

"Who is my enemy?" Brianna asked, clutching the edge of the table. "Is it Copper?"

Madame Masika leaned forward, speaking in a low, intense voice. "Enemies are all around us. Some are in the human world, some in the natural world, and others come from the realm of spirit." She shook her head. "You can gain an enemy even without taking action."

Discouraged, Brianna slouched back into her chair.

Evan wished he had words to buck up her spirits, convince her there was still time to throw the damned paper away and spend the next three days enjoying herself. But the eye of the priestess pinned him to his chair.

"That is no longer possible, monsieur."

"What?" Startled, Brianna turned and stared at him.

His eyes widened. He hadn't spoken aloud, and Brianna knew it, too. Had the old witch *heard* him? Inside his head?

"This journey has been chosen for her. She must follow the path before her feet."

Still spooked, Brianna returned her focus to the note. "So you're saying I must investigate this before I leave, is that right?"

The woman nodded, her face set in stone.

Brianna glanced at Evan, surely knowing what he was thinking; he'd said it often enough. "What happens if I ignore this message?"

Madame Masika folded her hands over the note as if trying to suck up any other meaning she could gather from it. "Then you risk the wrath of Damballah. This is something you should not challenge. Damballah will protect you if you carry out the task he has charged you with, but if you fail him…" She shrugged.

This was a crock of crap.

He really thought so.

But here he sat, frozen and speechless on a chair in a room with dead animals on the wall and what appeared to be a real, honest to God voodoo priestess three feet from him. How could he believe otherwise?

Digesting the old woman's words, Brianna seemed to be thinking along the same track. The look on her face convinced him. He'd seen enough of her spirit, in and out of the courtroom, to know how seriously she took challenges.

Once she'd made up her mind, he'd never be able to persuade her otherwise.

*All the women visiting New Orleans during Mardi Gras—what, some 50,000 of them?—and I hook up with the one who's got a voodoo curse to deal with? When does that start being fun?*

Evan felt a growl of frustration in his throat. Heard it, too. *So this Madame isn't all powerful.* He relaxed, let go of his resistance, hoping her control would fade away. His mind raced.

If Brianna was determined to pursue this wild

goose chase, then she shouldn't go alone, as the priestess had reminded her. He knew his capabilities. He could protect her from most things. Who else was there? Hank? Copper?

The thought that Brianna might ask Copper for help in escaping this situation he had himself created was the final straw that committed Evan to the quest. *Over my dead body*, he thought, and hoped he didn't mean it.

The old woman continued. "I see your enemy's possession will fall into your hands without any act on your part. Your task is to recognize it for what it is and take steps to keep it safe."

Brianna gasped. "You mean you don't know what it is?"

The turbaned head shook, the expression on her face one of sadness. "That is not revealed."

Brianna cocked her head. "We discovered that the Cities of the Dead are the cemeteries. I don't suppose you could tell us which one?"

"Again, that is not revealed. But St. Louis I is a place with strong magic. It is where Marie Laveau is buried."

"Marie?" Evan was surprised to hear himself say. Grateful the old witch had released him, he continued, determined not to offend again. "The Marie Laveau from the Museum?"

"The same. Marie Laveau was the greatest voodoo priestess in the history of New Orleans. Both mother and daughter are both buried there." She inspected the paper again. "Search out the flower, and present the gods with what you bring from the swamp."

"Whatever that is," Brianna said softly.

"A final sacrifice will be demanded of you, child. But if you meet your fate with courage, you shall be rewarded with the knowledge you seek, and receive direction as to what steps to take with that knowledge."

Evan wondered what "wish" Brianna might have that was so crucial that she'd be willing to go to these lengths. *Must be a good one.*

The priestess rose to her feet. Evan realized they were being dismissed.

"Thank you, Madame," Brianna said, taking the note back.

The old priestess inclined her head, then went to a carved wooden box on a shelf behind her. She reached inside, then handed Brianna a small green cloth bag. "It will help protect you."

Brianna sniffed at the bag, holding it gingerly. "*Gris-gris*?" she asked.

"Yes. An enchanted collection of herbs and other defenses. Keep it close to you always."

Evan eyed the old woman. "So you believe that Copper Delacroix owns these magical powers? That he's dangerous? Could he kill someone if he felt they'd wronged him?"

She studied him a moment, her arms crossed. Something in her eyes spoke of much more than she was willing to reveal.

"The son of Mama Delacroix has his own reasons for what he does. It is not my task to explain them." Her glance flicked to Brianna. "But I warn you to be careful. What seems pleasant on the outside can be dark and twisted under the surface."

She stiffened, her lips snapping shut as if she'd said too much, then she turned away from them and hobbled out the back.

Somehow, that didn't set his mind at ease.

But at least they were done. He put on a happier face for Brianna.

"Had enough fun yet?"

## Chapter Seventeen

Brianna followed Evan out, holding the *gris-gris* bag as if it contained a live snake. After what they'd just experienced, she wouldn't be surprised.

She'd tucked the note safely back into her purse. She stopped to buy a couple of reference books in the shop, since research was her standard preparation. When they returned to the sunlight outside, she answered his question.

"Fun?" she snapped.

"Sorry," Evan said. "I'm just trying to lighten the mood a little."

His dog-whipped tone made her sorry immediately. "I-I know. It's not your fault."

She must have expected that this fortune teller woman would pooh-pooh her imagination, and rain on her adventure parade. The note could have been some sort of hoax, some practical joke she could toss aside. Something to share with those back home as those "crazy Mardi Gras moments."

But this had gone way beyond whimsical exploration of a New Orleans cultural oddity.

When the priestess divined that Copper was involved just by a touch of the paper, and when she'd interpreted this seemingly-random series of events, and when she'd warned Brianna to complete this path or…what had she said? Risk the wrath of Damballah?

Those things sank a foundation of that spiritual world into reality.

A cold sweat came over her, and she shivered in the warm afternoon sun.

Evan must have noticed, because he took her in his arms, holding her close. "Come on, now, don't worry. We'll figure this out," he murmured, his lips close to her ear. "Remember she said you can't do this alone. Guess that means you're stuck with me."

His arms around her felt like a shield, like a flak jacket, protecting her, and gratitude washed over her. Her lips so close to his, she was drawn to kiss him, the delicate touch something magical, a promise and a guarantee that everything would be all right. She actually believed he could keep her safe.

She didn't know how long they remained lost in that wonderful feeling, but eventually the world around them started to intrude.

"Get a room, man," someone muttered as they shoved past on the busy sidewalk. His companion laughed, and Evan shook himself loose. He held her at arm's length, studying her.

"You look like hell. You want to get a drink?" he said.

She looked at her watch. They'd been at the Museum nearly three hours. It hadn't seemed that long—where had the time gone? Alcohol didn't feel like the right answer. She felt dazed and drained. "I don't think so. I'd rather go back to the Worleys' to lay down for a few minutes."

"Sure, if that's what you'd like." He took her hand, and they started for the car. The crowds moved around them, going about their business as though the world hadn't just shifted.

As if someone Brianna thought was a friend hadn't set her up, with this note and a curse that she couldn't escape.

She'd trusted Copper Delacroix, wanting to discount what others said about him. But if the old priestess was correct, Copper had created this path to lead her to quicksand and a swamp and how many other sites of potential death and destruction?

She held tight to Evan's fingers, because they felt real, an anchor to the world of the sane.

"What—what did you conclude about what she said, Evan? The Madame?"

Something cautious flashed in his eyes, but she wasn't up to dissecting it at the moment. "Oh, that? Lot of mumbo jumbo. Didn't you think so? Standard crystal ball fakery."

"I didn't, actually."

When he didn't come back with some smart aleck answer, she glanced over at him, spotting worried lines of tension around his mouth and across his forehead. So he wasn't as blasé about this as he wanted her to think.

*Why does that worry me even more?*

When they got in the car, she fastened her seatbelt . Brooding, she watched out the open window as they headed into the Garden District. When they stopped for a traffic light, Brianna noticed a group of elementary-aged black girls jumping rope and singing on the sidewalk. The words were hard to catch, but Brianna found herself compelled to listen. Some of the words were in English, but some she just couldn't recognize, some sort of patois.

One of the girls turning the rope suddenly turned

and stared at Brianna, her eyes intense, never missing a beat as she sang.

*See my king all dressed in red,*
*i-ko, i-ko an-ay*
*betcha five dollars he kill you dead...*

Brianna shuddered from the malice in the smile that accompanied the child's words. Once her gaze connected with the child's, that venom clearly having its effect, the girl turned back to her game, her face malleably morphing to that of an innocent child, as if that horrible scowl and the implied threat had never occurred.

Was she searching out impending doom at every turn now? Even little kids on the street? Ridiculous.

She looked over to see if Evan had noticed, but he accelerated as the light changed, oblivious to her distress.

*Maybe I'm just seeing things. That's it.*
*Just seeing things.*
*I hope.*

Looking over her shoulder, she watched till the girls were out of sight. But they didn't leave her mind for a long, long time.

\*\*\*\*

Back at the house, Hank greeted them from his seat in front of the television, absorbed in a basketball game. Evan immediately latched on to the score, and the two men were off and running on the subject of the upcoming tournaments. It was fine with Brianna. She took the stairs, thinking a hot shower might wash away the doom-filled cloud she felt hanging over her.

Mid-afternoon, while the other guests were away, turned out to be the best time to use the shared bathroom. She stripped off her clothes, then climbed under the steaming flow.

Loving the lilac-scented guest soap that Terri had laid out, Brianna scoured the long-dead dust of the museum from every inch of her, trying not to imagine the dry caress of snakeskin against hers.

No matter how hard she scrubbed, that conversation with Madame Masika replayed in her head like a stuck record. Her skin crawled with the memories of that dark, ghastly museum. She didn't care if she ever heard about zombies again. Ever.

What was she going to do now?

First thing was to eat a little crow, annoyed with herself more than him to admit Evan had been right about Copper Delacroix all along. *Yeah, he'll just love that.*

Was he right about the rest of it, too? Could she ignore what Madame Masika—and that damned note—said? Or was she now "cursed" and compelled to carry out its terms?

No.

She didn't think so.

Well, maybe not.

*I'm just not sure.*

She gave up on the scrubbing and let the water run over her face. She wasn't usually wishy-washy on life choices. Her answers might not always be correct, but she tended to jump fast and hard on her first instinct.

Like her initial impression of Evan Farrell. If they'd met back in Pittsburgh, she wouldn't have given that insolent jerk another thought.

But here, out of their element, she found she cared about him. He'd stuck with her and promised to keep on. If she asked, she'd bet her life that he'd really follow her right into the monster's lair, as he'd said.

But she couldn't ask him to do that.

The note warned her not to go alone. What other choice did she have? She should make Copper accompany her, since it was his big plan.

Maybe that *was* his big plan.

Maybe he'd thought she'd be so desperate that she'd go off alone with him.

Then what would happen?

A cold shiver ran through her. No, that wasn't the right choice. If he'd go to such lengths to follow her, to set her up, he couldn't be trusted. Who could she choose?

Finally cleansed, she got out of the shower and got dressed in an airy pink sundress she'd bought new at the end of the previous summer, but had never gotten the chance to wear before winter dumped on the Steel City. Small daisy earrings forced a cheerful outlook, her white sandals, a bit of lip gloss. There. She felt better, and paused to assess herself in the full-length mirror. The reflected room contained a detail that hadn't been there before.

A small piece of blue paper lay neatly folded on her pillow.

Maybe Evan had invited her to have more tea on the veranda. Better than having him join her in the shower—wasn't it? A smile coming to her, she walked over to retrieve it. When she picked up the paper, a familiar electric shock stung her fingers again. She dropped it onto the bed, suddenly terrified.

Copper.

What now? He'd done enough to ruin her vacation.

How the hell had he gotten in here?

Knowing Terri's aversion, there was no way she would have let him in the front door or taken a message to pass on.

*It had to be magic.*

That chilly shiver ran through her again, and she really considered tossing it in the trash. Then an almost movie-like vision passed before her eyes where this note would come hunt her down, trailing along behind her through the streets until she acknowledged its existence, and then—

All right, all right. She'd read it.

*Not like it'll kill me.*

Maybe it held a clue, or some absolution. An apology for her anxiety. Maybe it ended the game. Biting her lip against the prickle of recognition that ran through her fingers a second time, she picked up the note and carefully unfolded it. The letters were formed in the same hand as the other note. Definitely from Copper.

*Come to the west end of the Bayou Barataria this evening to take your place in the grand drama about to unfold. You will gain the power to change your world.*

*Your greatest wish will be granted when you have fulfilled your obligation. The quest awaits; do not disappoint the gods.*

That and a set of GPS coordinates, was all it said. The words filled her with a cold dread. What "grand drama" was he talking about? All she could think of was Madame Masika saying she must obey in order to free herself of this voodoo. Nearly four p.m., and the note commanded her to go to the swamp that evening. The same one Madame Masika had mentioned.

*That means we'll be there after dark. In the swamp. Where we've never been. With mosquitoes, alligators and worse.*

Evan was going to love this.

She took one more look at herself in her pretty, girlish attire and sighed. Hardly suited for tromping through the mud. She took it all off and changed into her plainest T-shirt, jeans and socks and sneakers, ready to lay this set of distractions to rest once and for all.

Holding the note in her hand, she headed downstairs to share the "good news" with Evan.

## Chapter Eighteen

Nagged by the events of the day, Evan lost interest in the basketball game pretty quickly. After talking with Hank long enough to be polite, he excused himself, taking his cell phone and the phone book out onto the back porch. It was difficult for him to believe the police department wouldn't have anything to do with matters like this. Particularly when everyone seemed to shy away from the subject of the Delacroix family.

He dialed the police department non-emergency number, then identified himself as law enforcement and asked for the duty sergeant. While he waited, he put on his best game face, knowing it would boost his confidence, then dug his old precinct info out of his memory.

"Lambeau," growled the sergeant.

"Sgt. Lambeau, my name is Evan Farrell. I'm a police sergeant from Pittsburgh, Pennsylvania, badge number 8047, here on vacation. My companion's run into some trouble, and I think we need police intervention."

Lambeau's tone warmed, but not much. He sounded tired. "What can I do for you, sergeant?"

*Good question. Maybe just arrest this bastard so we can get on with our lives?*

Evan cleared his throat. "Someone planted a note in her purse." He explained the circumstances, then asked, "Now, I hope there's no cause for alarm. Note from a stranger and all. I guess we're just curious how much credence the local police puts in these kind of things."

A long silence on the other end of the line, before Lambeau answered.

"You're calling me about a love note someone stashed in your girlfriend's purse? We busted ninety-six people for indecent exposure yesterday alone. I got no one available to process those people already, and we've got a whole stack of warrants ready to be served for felonies. You want me to send someone out because of a piece of paper?" He snorted, derision clear in the delivery. Evan could almost hear him shrug. "How do you do things up north, man?"

Evan refused to give up.

"What's the name Copper Delacroix do for you? He's apparently the author of the note, and he's stalking her around town, unwelcome and uninvited."

That name certainly seemed to carry its own magic. Lambeau's interest perked up.

"I'll send someone to check it out, but I'm not sure it will be today." He took the address and promised to keep track of the request. "Meantime, you end up with a body, call us back."

"Come on, friend. What's the chances of something real happening to her? Just because people keep mentioning Delacroix and voodoo?"

Another silence. The sergeant's voice sounded a little choked when he responded.

"We get dead people all the time their family says died from voodoo. It happens."

*Damn. That is not what I wanted to hear.*

"And if he's got a grudge against someone?"

"Then I wouldn't want to be that someone."

Evan wrestled with the issue of whether to share what Brianna had told him, then acknowledged they really didn't have enough. "Okay, how about a stolen wallet?" Evan said quickly, before he could get cut off.

"I'll put you through to lost and found." The line clicked shut and was answered a few minutes later by some young woman, a clerk who seemed at least interested. *Must not have been around long enough to become jaded.*

To his surprise, his wallet was there. "Someone turned this in this morning, sir," she chirped.

"I suppose it's empty."

"No, sir, there's all kinds of cards and money in it. Gentleman said it was found in the French Quarter, outside Antoine's."

"Fine, thanks. I'll come pick it up."

Evan stared at his phone after he hung up. What kind of madness was this?

Someone found his wallet, a gentleman, she'd said. A wallet laying in the street, money intact, just turned in to the police department lost and found? Now that was almost as big a mystery as Brianna's note.

But at least he'd confirmed that the police took voodoo seriously. Which meant he and Brianna should, too.

Brianna came through the sliding door onto the back porch dressed to go ATVing rather than to a nice dinner and a parade. Her face was pale, her eyes anxious and frightened.

"What now?" he asked.

"Another note." She held it out to him.

"This guy's worse than the Phantom of the Opera." Evan grabbed it and read its few lines. "This evening, huh? He thinks we're dumb enough to ride into the swamp in the middle of the night?"

"Well, it says me. You don't have to go." Her voice trembled, then her hands clenched into fists. She glanced away at the neighbor's yard, as if she couldn't bear to look him in the eye. She seemed so defeated, it caused him physical pain thinking how unfair this was to her.

*When I get my hands on this guy...*

She seemed more vulnerable than he'd ever seen a woman before. He crossed the few feet between them, driven to make her feel better. He swept her into his arms and hugged her close, inhaling her faint aroma of lilacs.

"Of course I wouldn't send you alone, Brianna."

She reached her arms around him, holding on tight. "I'm so grateful you'd stand by me on this. It's so insane. But I can't just walk away. You heard her. You *heard* her."

"I know, I know."

He continued to hold her, because she felt good in his arms, and he felt good protecting her. Without thinking, he kissed the top of her head. "Your white knight is here, my lady. Just point me at those windmills."

She gently pulled away, smoothing her shirt, her eyes wet with incipient tears. "I'm sorry—"

"No, Brianna. You have nothing to be sorry about. This isn't your fault. We'll get the one who's responsible. I promise you."

He moved closer, tipped her chin up and looked

deep in her eyes. "I'm in, now. I'm not leaving your side till we do this thing."

Then things happened fast. Her sad eyes entreated him to cheer her up. She was beautiful, and so close…

Impulse drove him to kiss her again. Her lips were sweet and soft as she yielded to him, and she slipped back into his arms. He tasted her and it was wonderful. Her body pressed against his, seeking comfort.

*More comfort than I have time to give her right now, if we've got to go to the bayou.*

*Damn Copper Delacroix!*

His misgivings must have seeped into his lips, because she drew back.

"What's the matter?" Belatedly, she noticed the cell phone in his hand. "Did you call the police? About your wallet? We should have stopped at the station while we were downtown."

"I, ah…yeah, I called them about the wallet." He didn't see any point in sharing the rest of his conversation; she looked rattled enough.

"Someone turned it in, with everything still intact. We can pick it up whenever. Maybe this city isn't as dangerous as its reputation."

"All right. That sounds like a good idea, before it gets misplaced in all the mayhem." She took a deep breath and let it out slowly. "Then what?"

"Then, I guess we're heading to the swamp."

\*\*\*\*

The evening yielded a spectacular hour-long sunset along the westbound road Evan took to the bayou. He'd stopped at a store on the way to pick up a backpack and supplies including candles, matches, flashlights and snacks, in case they got lost.

Brianna had second thoughts all the way there. *This is nuts*, she kept telling herself. But the old woman's warning about the wrath of Damballah struck through to her heart.

*Damballah manifested as one ugly and vicious snake. I don't want anything to do with it. Nothing. I'd be happy to not even look at it again. Ever.*

She used the time in transit to skim her books, researching this expedition as heavily as a brief for court. Copper had specifically invited her, so he must believe her participation would be mandatory in the ritual. It felt very intentional, not like a wild-goose chase.

But would anything they saw this night help her save herself?

Interesting how Evan had chosen "Phantom of the Opera" as a comparative example. It had always been a favorite of Brianna's, the story of a young woman manipulated by a powerful man with apparent magical abilities. She hadn't realized until this moment how that story resonated with her own, a woman challenged to put her own life on the line to save others.

That was her intention.

Her participation in this charade was only designed to lead Copper on, until he revealed what his words about the King of Rex had meant, and whether he truly intended the man harm. When she had enough information to make a formal report, they might save this man's life.

*But we'd best not lose our own in the process.*

It hadn't been easy to locate a boat to go into the swamp after dark, but Evan found VISA really could get him anywhere he wanted to be.

One tour service was unwilling to take them out, but would rent them a boat and give them a map of the area, as long as they signed a waiver saying the tour company wasn't responsible for anything that happened.

"Now, if ye'd wait till morning," the old man said, walking to the dock with them as twilight approached, "I could take ye out, show ye where some of the big Indian fights took place, and so on." He scratched his leg through his worn brown pants, and waved his other hand to chase away mosquitoes who were only too evident. And hungry.

Brianna couldn't take her eyes off the dull surface of the black water under the overhanging trees and moss. What hid in there that could hurt them? Pictures came to her mind, movie monsters she'd seen over the years, moonshine-soaked hillbillies out to slice up unsuspecting or too-stupid-to-live tourists. She should have spoken up, told Evan they had to abandon the idea. But by then, she was running on sheer adrenaline and fear.

The tour owner sidled up to Evan, speaking in a tone meant to be man-to-man. "The swamp ain't a place to take ladies after dark, ye know. Strange goings-on in there. Much too dangerous. Room in town's much cheaper and more romantic, if ye get me drift."

Now that was one hell of an understatement.

*Not like I want to be here, either.*

Evan nodded wearily. "If there was anywhere else we could be tonight, you'd better believe I'd be there," he said. "Something we just have to do."

The old man shook his head and pocketed his credit card receipt. Brianna could just hear him thinking they were irresponsible tourists out for a cheap thrill. "Oars are in the boat. They'd better be returned, or it'll cost ye."

"We'll get them." Evan left the old man muttering about "damnYankees not having a lick of common sense" and came to join her.

The swamp wasn't inviting. This didn't look good.

The same eerie feeling had run through her when Evan picked up his wallet at the police station before they'd left the city. Almost everything had still been in it. Almost. The only this he reported missing was his sandwich club card, the kind he'd licked stamps and stuck them on. Something was odd about that.

But of everything that could have been stolen, that seemed like the least economic loss. Evan was upbeat about it; Brianna let it slip from her mind.

Better to concentrate on not dying in the swamp.

Reluctant, she hung back as they approached the dock where the ten-foot boat awaited them. Reality set in. The thought that they were about to set off into a dangerous, unfamiliar environment in a thin metal boat just as dark arrived made her nauseous.

*You don't have to do this.*

But she did.

She didn't know if it was Madame Masika's urging, or Copper's notes, or, hell, if it was voodoo. Every quarter-mile closer they'd come to this place, a compelling draw in the pit of her stomach, like a string or rope, pulled her closer. Something obligated her to see this through. She'd been told this was the way to solve the problem, and like all lawyers, she bore a problem-solver. That was really the basic definition of her job: people came to her with a problem and she would use the law in the best way she could to fix it.

But what law dealt with the mysterious world of voodoo and the backwaters of Louisiana?

Evan hesitated near the head of the dock, looking like the brave hero of any movie she'd ever seen. *Well, maybe not the gladiator movies.* His shoulders were square, his jaw set, his eyes bright; he was out to save her.

That, in itself, gave her a small smile and the courage to go on.

"Ready?" He held out his hand.

She nodded wordlessly and took it.

Evan flicked on one of the flashlights they'd brought, but all it revealed was the ooze of mud. Brianna felt it suck on her sneakers the closer they got to the water, so she walked a little faster, both of them hurrying onto the splintered wood of the dock.

*So, the sand becomes water almost before our journey begins.*

He climbed into the boat nearest the end of the dock. It rocked violently before he caught his balance, then he extended a hand to Brianna and helped her in.

She sat in the front quickly, remembering that being low in a small boat was the safest way to travel. The boat was sturdier than she'd thought, with room for five or six people and it came with both oars and a small motor.

She turned on her phone and activated the GPS app, finding they had several miles to go before they arrived at the coordinates they'd been given. While a powered ride would be noisy against the natural sounds of the swamp, surely it would be better to arrive before the middle of the night.

Evan fired up the motor, and they started off into the black water.

The trip was uneventful. Apparently the touring companies kept these waterways fairly clear by constant use, so they ran into no issues with tangled rotors or belligerent wildlife. When they'd come within what she hoped was shouting distance of the place, they agreed to cut the engine and switch to paddles. Evan insisted that he be the one to steer them, "because I'm the man," which annoyed her, but left her free to keep watch.

The moon started to rise, so they weren't left in complete darkness. Brianna turned off her flashlight to save the battery, absorbed in the symphony of the swamp.

Frogs and crickets peeped in harmonic rhythm, an occasional splash of water indicating the presence of some of the swamp's larger residents. The noise from distant airboats on the water became more apparent as her ears adjusted to the natural sounds. Pinpoints of firefly light blinked on and off along the water's surface and the branches overhead.

Along with the gentle sound of the oars entering the water, pushing them forward, the voyage could have been soothing and wonderful if they'd really been here as tourists, instead of tensely anticipating whatever Copper had planned for them.

"There's a current here," Evan said softly. He quit rowing. The boat continued to move forward. They went on like that, the crickets waxing and waning as they passed.

Then they heard the drums.

## Chapter Nineteen

The sound was soft at first but gradually got louder till it eclipsed Brianna's heartbeat. The crickets and frogs who'd serenaded them so far fell curiously still, the sounds of the drums echoed off the trees and the dark surface of the water.

Suddenly the drums cut off and a haunting sound came from ahead of them, its tone almost that of a horn, but not one of brass. Three long notes, almost a summons. The sound ran chills down her back. She'd heard the sound before, but it took her a moment to identify it—someone blowing on a conch shell.

*A lot more disturbing in person.*

Ahead of them, the darkness took on a faint light, then the dim glow resolved itself into a clearing. A dozen or more people gathered there, their faces lit by reflected firelight. More filled the clearing, but the shadows were too deep for Brianna to identify what else awaited them there.

Still carried on the current, the boat scraped the bottom then stopped. In the eerie silence that followed the drums, Brianna's heart leaped in alarm at the grating noise. She held her breath.

Several long moments of silence felt like they stretched for hours before the drums started again, louder, playing in a hypnotizing cadence.

Brianna and Evan took advantage of the noise to

climb out of the boat near shore, the splash and suck of their feet in the mud lost in the pounding rhythms. They pulled the boat out of the water and set it next to a thick tree hung with Spanish moss, waving away dangling spiders as they climbed out from under the mossy curtain.

Guided by the flickering of firelight on the dark tree trunks, they approached the group. Brianna moved slowly, testing each placement of her foot cautiously, trying to find a solid path.

No one seemed to have noticed their arrival, activity by the kettled fires continuing undisturbed. What was she supposed to do now?

*This is what we are meant to see. But I can't just walk up there. Not yet.*

Heart in her throat, she hunkered down behind a fallen tree trunk to get a clear view of what was happening. Now that they'd come near, perhaps twenty feet away, she recognized the construct as a table with an altar, similar to the ones pictured in her books.

The fire illuminated the multi-tiered altar and some of those who gathered around it. Painted with tribal markings in black and white, the three drummers' faces stood out like bare skulls against the reflected flames. The people in the back row were silhouettes only, dark outlines swaying to the rhythm of the drums.

On the altar, Brianna identified a Damballah cross on the top level, surrounded by a number of unlit candles, and some small statues. On the next level sat a bottle of liquor. A large bowl and some cups on a tray were laid out before it, and what looked like a loaf of bread next to a large machete, blade gleaming in the firelight. Bright, tropical flowers decorated all the levels.

Finally, on the ground to the left of the table was a large box with a screen on the front, that appeared to be a carrying case for an animal, something alive.

*A snake.*

It was one thing to see these items laid out in a cold array at a museum; quite another when an actual voodoo ritual was taking place before her eyes. Avoiding the thrill of fright blazing through her, she focused on the table, searching for clues to why they'd been summoned.

As the drums continued their spellbinding beat, a dark figure eased into the light before the altar, a tall, slender person dressed in black. Moving gracefully to the rhythm, the priest approached, bearing a tall black candle, which he used to light the other candles.

Eyes closed, chanting words Brianna could not understand, the priest turned slowly around to face the others. Those seated before him on rough wooden benches rocked from side to side.

She gasped when she recognized Copper, dressed as she'd seen him in her mind's eye when she'd touched that first note, a red turban on his head and, on his face, jagged red paint slashes like bloody lightning.

Instinctively, she pulled back, hoping they couldn't be seen in the shadows.

He turned to the altar and lit two long sticks of incense, which soon filled the clearing with an exotic smoky scent. Walking in lock-step with the beat of the drum, he reached for a cup and one of the bottles. He poured red liquid into the cup, then held it up.

The drums stopped.

He spoke loudly in English, gesturing with the cup

to the four corners of the clearing.

"By the power of St. Anthony of Padua, Legba Atibon, guardian of the crossroads, Legba, guardian of the bush, Legba, guardian of the house, *Ago, ago si, Ago la!*"

After the words passed, the drummers played again, even louder. Copper took a drink of the liquid, pouring some also into the fire where it hissed into smoke. He handed the closest drummer the bottle, and he drank from it, then passed it to the man on his left. He drank as well, and did the same. Whatever was in the bottle seemed to inspire them. Their drums reverberated with sound until Brianna could hardly breathe.

Copper leaned down before the altar, shaking something onto the ground. Brianna couldn't see what he was doing, so she inched up until she stood behind the thick tree trunk next to her. He held some sort of painted tin, and from it, he dropped a white substance on the dirt in a distinct design.

"What's that?" Evan whispered.

"That would be the *veve*," Brianna whispered back. "It's the sign for a particular deity or spirit. First, there should be the drummer's *veve*, then there will be others, depending on which spirit they are calling forward."

Her heart pounded so hard, she couldn't believe Copper didn't hear it.

Copper drew a second figure on the ground. The drums' rhythm changed. Several people in flowing robes rose from the first row and began a seductive, erotic dance. The dancers thrust their hips forward and sideways in a frenzied manner, moving around the fire kettles oblivious to each other until the drums stopped again. They froze.

"*Gator Guede, le bon ton roulette, ye, ye, ye.*"

He raised the cup to the sky, then took a long drink before dumping some in the fire, causing it to flare up. He poured the remaining contents of the bottle into the large bowl, then added a red liquid Brianna hoped was wine, swirling the bowl in a large gesture before his chest.

The drums beat a new rhythm, so compelling Brianna could hardly keep still. The lead dancer took the bowl from Copper and passed it among the participants.

When all had drunk, the dancers returned to the area before the fire and danced again, the drummers changing rhythm to something more primal. The silhouettes moved between Brianna, Evan and the fire, rotating their shoulders and bouncing up and down. They left a respectful space between themselves and Copper, who continued to create more designs on the ground, evenly spaced and spreading out toward the edges of the clearing.

He began to chant again, this time echoed by a chorus from those seated on the ground. Brianna felt herself drawn into the give-and-take, her head and thoughts growing fuzzy.

"Do you know what they're saying?" Evan asked.

Brianna pulled herself back with difficulty. She shook her head, a little dazed.

Here, hold my hand," she whispered. "I feel so strange. If I look like I'm getting—" She stopped, unsure how to explain what she was experiencing.

She didn't believe in this stuff. Not at all.

*Then why do I feel like there's spiders crawling*

*around inside me?*

"It's hypnotizing, isn't it?" he said, holding her hand tight.

Grateful he understood, she kept a firm grip on his hand and let it anchor her to reality.

The remaining bottle was passed around, and the singing rose to a more intense level. Copper moved among the gathered, holding his hand above each one's head as he passed, as though blessing them.

In his other hand was a small wooden boat, which he held over his own head. As he passed each person, he or she would raise a hand toward the boat. A small puff of smoke floated upward to land in it.

"Those would be the requests of those petitioning the spirits," she said.

"Spirits, right." Evan's voice resonated with disbelief.

Once Copper had traversed the entire group, he paused before the altar, while the dancers continued to react to the beat of the drums. He held up the boat and said, "Now we shall send our spirit prayers to heaven."

He started to set the boat down into one of the fires, but froze in mid-gesture. The drums and dancers slowed, then stopped, watching Copper for their next cue.

Chin held high, Copper looked from one side of the clearing to another.

"There are those present who have not sent their wishes to the spirits. Come forward!" he commanded.

Brianna suddenly felt herself compelled to move toward the fires. Her ragged breaths dragged against the urge to move, but she couldn't stop. A rush of panic drenched her.

"Evan?"

"You wanted to know what would happen," he reminded her with less I-told-you-so than she expected. "I promise I won't let anything happen to you. Let's see why we're here."

Her legs dragged unwilling feet toward the clearing. Evan walked beside her. Copper waited for her, even in the horrifying makeup looking regal. Her eyes met Copper's glittering dark ones for a long, silent exchange.

Something happened then, nothing she could describe. Copper seemed to be inside her head, pleading with her, rewarding her, all at once. All she had to do was release herself to him.

*No, I can't do that.*

Panicked thoughts bounced around inside her mind, but she couldn't speak.

Evan tried several times to come between her and Copper, but it looked like he crashed into an invisible wall. He couldn't get any closer.

Copper spoke to the drummers. The rhythms began again. The dancers moved in place, dark eyes watching the newcomers.

Once the drums began, she lost control. Something in the rhythm simply sucked her willpower away. Copper reached out and put two fingers under her chin, turned her face to look at him. Brianna felt an eerie calm settle over her, and her fear was gone.

In a voice that sounded round and full, like it would fill an ocean, Copper asked, "Do you bring a petition for Damballah?"

*Not at all.*

She thought the words, but they didn't come out.

She didn't believe in Damballah, or want to ask him for anything at all.

*You can have your snake-gods—just leave me alone!*

The words remained trapped in her mind.

Copper gestured to one of the dancers, and the robed woman handed him the cup which had earlier been passed. He gave it to Brianna, indicating she should drink.

Evan shook his head. She knew she shouldn't taste a drop. But Copper's eyes held an odd light of intense excitement and determination.

"Drink!" he commanded. He raised his hand slowly. Her traitorous hand brought the cup to her mouth. Inside, she was screaming. But she had no physical will to oppose him. She took a deep swallow, the drink burning her throat.

A few seconds later, she was light-headed and wavered on her feet.

*What was in that cup? Some kind of super alcohol—or supernatural substance? Don't be ridiculous. This can't happen.*

*This can't happen...*

The incense filled her senses. The drums began to pound in her head and Copper continued to stare into her eyes. Her self-conscious desires began to slip away as her body joined in the dance. Time seemed suspended as she moved with the others in an ancient circle that seemed as old as the world.

Chapter Twenty

Evan entered the clearing but found himself held in place ten feet from the altar. He could do nothing as Brianna dream-walked through the worshipers. At one point, her movements changed from jerky to smooth, as if she'd quit fighting whatever held her. Standing before the priest, the look on her face was almost angelic.

Copper looked down at her without expression, without movement. Almost frozen.

*Frozen...like me!*

Through his anger, Evan struggled against the unseen forces immobilizing him. His quick mind and body had kept him alive as a cop. He was used to having these faculties readily at hand. This was untenable. He continued to struggle, but couldn't break the compulsion holding him.

One of the dancers handed Brianna a cup.

*Don't drink that!*

She hesitated, almost as if she had heard him, but drank anyway. She shuddered, and her knees bent, nearly gave way. But the drummers picked up the beat, and Brianna began to move with the brightly-robed dancers. A faraway expression graced her face.

She'd been drugged, he was sure of it.

Copper turned toward him, and he stiffened with as much rebellion as he could muster.

*What does he want from me? I'm not going to give him the satisfaction of turning into some zombie.*

The voodoo priest just smiled.

Brianna's hypnotic state approached ecstasy as she danced and twirled with the others. What did Copper want her for? Did they intend to use her as a sacrifice? On the table, the firelight glinted malevolently off the blade of the machete.

Evan swallowed, hard.

Copper approached Brianna, holding his hand over her head, as he'd done with the others. She stopped moving. Her hand lifted toward the small wooden boat Copper still held, releasing a puff of white smoke that went into the boat with the others.

She stood still, breathing deeply, swaying as the drums continued.

Copper released her with a gesture, and the dance possessed her again.

The priest beckoned Evan forward. He found his legs suddenly free to move, but only in the direction of the last place he wanted to go.

At least it was closer to Brianna.

Resisting with every bit of his will, he shuffled to stand before Copper.

What he needed was the firepower he'd carried back on the streets in Pittsburgh. *I'd give this guy a straight ticket into Heaven. Or maybe Hell. You bet I would.*

"Do you have a petition for Damballah?" Copper asked.

*Yeah, I'd like to tell him to take a flying...*

Evan caught a glimpse behind Copper of Brianna sensuously swinging her hips. She was practically an animal, her whole being infused with a wild passion Evan had never seen in her. His desire for her grew. He wanted her like nothing he'd ever wanted before. The raw feeling threatened to overpower him. He wanted to take her into his bed and make her his, make her do things to him, make her happy.

"Yes, yes, Damballah is powerful and strong. He can grant the wish you seek." Copper's grin split his face.

Wait a minute. What was happening here?

Evan hadn't entertained such passionate thoughts about Brianna. But once he'd thought them, they seemed to take charge of his heart, his loins, every part of him. The drums pounded inside his head, through his blood. Finally they stole his train of thought altogether.

He was called back to focus when Copper moved closer, holding the wooden boat high, his hand over Evan's head. When Copper lowered his hand, Evan felt a release, as if some problem that consumed him had been solved.

Copper directed a nearby dancer to pour liquor into a cup. Evan knew he shouldn't drink, but when the woman brought it to him, he was powerless to resist.

He tasted the red wine, expecting to get all spacy like Brianna, but found the only effect was a rush of warmth. Wine always affected him that way. As the seconds ticked by, he decided it wasn't what they'd given Brianna. Or else his mind was stronger than hers, and she'd let herself get sucked in to this whole "adventure," as she insisted on referring to it.

The realization gave him hope. If he wasn't impaired, perhaps he'd have the chance to stop them if they intended to hurt her. What other reason would they have to alter her conscious state? He couldn't even imagine why they'd dragged her all the way out here otherwise.

He had to do something.

So much of this depended on what he let himself believe. The same applied to Brianna. *Come on, Brianna. Fight it.*

Copper led him to a bench in the front row and sat him down. Evan's gaze followed Brianna. Every time he spotted her, a wave of desire and will to possess her washed over him.

*She will be mine.*

Copper placed the boat in the fire, and it vanished in a burst of white flame.

"Damballah has received your petitions!" he proclaimed. "We shall now glorify him!"

He bent before the altar and reached into a screened box. A flourish of drums preceded a moment of reverent silence as Copper drew out a huge gold-flecked python. He held the undulating snake up in the firelight. The monster had to be at least ten feet long.

A dancer moved forward to take it from the priest. It curled around her as Copper oiled his hands from a jar on the altar, then massaged the snake.

"Great God Damballah, we hail your presence among us," he intoned. "Those who have gathered pray your blessings upon us and the granting of our deepest desires."

The dancers slowly weaved forward in a line, backs undulating in rhythm, giving the appearance of a snake themselves. In sharp contrast, Brianna now stood still, eyes closed.

Evan wanted to call out to her, but found his voice

missing. Again.

What was it with these ooga-booga guys anyway? The next one that shut him up would have his attitude seriously adjusted.

Copper moved toward Brianna, a silver dagger in his hand. *Where had that come from?*

The dancer with the snake followed close behind him.

Evan tried to jump up but found himself stuck to the bench.

Copper took Brianna's hand, turning it palm up. A slice of the dagger slit her finger. She didn't even react.

Red blood collected on her finger, and Copper held it over the snake's head until it dripped onto its nose. The snake's tongue flicked out, tasting the blood. Copper pulled gently on Brianna's arm until it was extended. The snake inched up Brianna's stiff arm, poking its ugly face around the back of her neck, slithering down her other arm until it graced her like an evening stole. She shifted to bear its weight, standing with her arms out as if crucified.

His own skin crawled, as the snake moved around Brianna's bewitched body. She'd shared with him how much she'd hated all the snake depictions at the museum. How could she calmly let this happen? Evan didn't understand.

The dancers chanted, drawing into a circle around Copper and Brianna. Copper squeezed her bleeding finger, holding a small black cup to catch the blood.

"Your blood for his blood," Copper whispered with the intensity of hate. "Your blood for his blood."

The priest's voice deepened, now deadly serious. Here was the crux of Copper's mission. That nameless "him" was in real trouble. *The King of Rex?* His earlier distraction with her body had disappeared. All he wanted now was to rescue her. But his body failed to respond.

Suddenly Copper straightened, thrusting his arms upward. The drums stopped like a heartbeat's end.

"*Damballah Wedo!*" he sang, turning slightly to the right, then, "*Damballah Lele!*" turning to the left. "*Ago si, ago la,*" he went on, slowly, moving back to the center as the drums picked up softly. "*Damballah o, Damballah ye,*" he sang, echoed by those reflected in the fire. "*Le grand serpan, allon roulay.*"

He went on singing in a foreign language with a French intonation. The snake slithered off Brianna and returned to the arms of the dancer. Brianna stood like a statue, oblivious. The dancers seemed to complete some kind of chant sequence, the volume of the drums dialing up as they finished, then they followed the snake dancer to the side. Copper's eye fell on Evan.

"Come forward," he said.

*Tell you what, pal. I'm not playing along. Not at all.*

Determined now to remain seated on the bench, Evan growled as his body wrenched to its feet, jerked like a puppet on strings, and lurched toward the altar.

Whose blood would be spilled next? His?

His resistance was almost painful, as he battled his own nerves and muscles for control. The drums rose in tempo and volume, so loud conscious thought was almost impossible.

Brianna joined him in front of Copper. Her blank stare gave no indication she recognized him. They faced each other, an arm's length apart, as the dancers swirled around the clearing, behind and before the altar, circling the drummers.

Copper lit a new stick of incense, heavily clouding the air with smoke and cloying perfume, waving it around the two of them until the rest of the scene took on an unreal haze. Unsure what was reality and what wasn't, Evan's thoughts became a nightmarish miasma.

Neither moved as Copper took a wicker basket from beside the table and chanted strange words over the contents, small cloth bags like the one Madame Masika had given Brianna. He passed the basket to one of the dancers, who distributed gris-gris to all.

Stepping forward, Copper held one hand over each of their heads, delivering an incantation of some sort. Recognition sharply entered Brianna's eyes as she wakened from whatever trance she'd been in. She didn't seem frightened. Instead her expression radiated a peaceful acceptance and serenity.

Must be the drug, Evan thought, but her pupils seemed normal-size, and she was almost smiling. Her dark eyes seemed to communicate warm thoughts.

She loved him.

That he could see from her eyes. They were meant to be together. They'd always been together, only separated by circumstances that Damballah had not rectified. Following in his way, they would be rewarded with the goodness of their love.

*No, wait. That's not right.*

His mind reeled in a whirlpool, trying to grab on to anything that made sense. For a moment, he recalled that malicious muttering as Copper had collected Brianna's blood. That—…now *that* was real. He was out for someone's blood.

179

But when Evan looked into Brianna's eyes again, that evil faded and he was filled with the loving feelings they shared.

He didn't know which of them moved first, but suddenly they were in each other's' arms, their skins hot and feverish, blazing with feeling everywhere they touched.

Her lips were like fire, but he couldn't stop kissing her, holding her, his hands sliding up and down her arms, pulling her hips close, feeling every inch of her against him. She responded to him, her fingers exploring his body, her tongue doing the same to his mouth.

Ignited, their fervor caught fire, and he lost track of everything around him. His world was only Brianna, and hers him.

They acted on that fire, letting their hidden wants rule them, releasing their inhibitions while the chanting continued, the drumbeats driving them to consummate their desires. The scene felt like a waking dream, the smoke and the potion hiding the real world from them, leaving only this wonderful fantasy…

Until it was gone.

## Chapter Twenty-One

It was half-light when Evan opened his eyes.

He lay in a soft pile of trampled mud, the stale scent of burnt incense in the air. A rustling in the leaves by his head made him twist slightly to discover what it was. A large rat checked him out, eye to eye, its nose sniffing in Evan's direction.

"Oh, hell no." He quickly stretched out his arm to bat it away.

The rodent scampered off and Evan pushed himself upright.

The sun cracked its way over the horizon. He surveyed the area around him, the center of a clearing, surrounded by a bunch of old moss-covered trees in a swamp.

Real hazy on the details of where he was and how he'd gotten—

*Brianna.*

He lurched to his feet, unsteady as if he'd been asleep for days. He'd lost his shirt, and insects had gone to town on his bare skin, the itching driving him mad. All he could remember for sure was that he'd been there with Brianna.

Where was she?

"Brianna?"

He paced the length of the clearing, his blood pressure rising. Parts of his memory's puzzle clicked into place, but not enough to provide him answers.

Copper had conducted a ceremony here. Yes. Right there on the small hill. But the dancers, drummer, the altar, everything had disappeared. The smell of incense was all that remained to prove there had ever been a ritual performed on this spot.

"Brianna!"

His skin crawled as he wondered whether Copper had taken her, when Evan hadn't been able to protect her, under the influence of whatever the hell had happened.

Before despair took him, a faint moan came from behind some trees. He found Brianna lying on the ground, her forehead marred by dried blood. He checked her over as she began to wake up. She didn't seem to be injured. Her clothing was torn and mud-stained, although she had most everything on but her shoes.

"Evan?" she asked, her mouth moving awkwardly, like it was full of cotton. "What...where...?" She glanced around, a little frantic.

"Where's Copper?" she asked. "And the dancers? Drummers? Where did they go? Were they even here? Or did I...I swear there were dancers here. A dozen or more! Weren't there?"

Practically hyperventilating, she looked up at him in utter confusion, tears rolling down her cheeks. He knelt down beside her and took her in his arms.

This was one emotion he completely understood right now, because he was as confused as she.

"Yes, love, they were," he reassured her.

"Okay, then I'm not going crazy."

"Not unless we both are."

She held on tight for a long moment. The contact stirred memories of the night before, when she'd been in his arms, too, dancing to the beat of that music, rubbing up against him in a very sexy way…

"Where's my shoes?" she asked, tearing him away from those recollections just in time.

"I'm not sure."

She pulled back from him a little, looking at his bare skin. "And what happened to your shirt?"

He'd seen the scene in that brief flashback. She'd torn it off him like a wild Amazon. *Somehow I don't think that's what she wants to hear right now.*

"Yeah, that's a mystery, too. The morning mosquitoes are ready for brunch, though, and I think we should start heading out of here."

She let him pull her to her feet, then wandered across the clearing, as if she'd find the dancers hiding behind a tree. The evidence of their being here was all around them: burnt matches, the remainder of an incense stick, footprints in the mud. He tried to remember what had gone on, parts of it flashing into his mind. The fire. The drums.

The snake.

*I'm not telling her that part, either, just yet.*

"Are you all right?"

She looked herself up and down. "I—I think so. My finger hurts." She peered down at it, seeming confused by the healing wound there. "And my head."

"You must have bumped your head when you hit the ground. It looks okay now. You don't remember what happened?"

She shook her head.

He pointed to her finger. "That was courtesy of

your good friend Copper."

Her eyes became saucers. "What?"

The bugs were really starting to get to him now, itchy bumps covered his body. He did his best to brush them off. "Look, we can do the full recap later. Let's go."

Her mouth hanging open in bewilderment, she nodded. "Okay. But…" She surveyed the empty glade, her finger, his clothing covered in mud, her confusion a clear ache in her soul.

She reached out and he took her hand, finally something solid in the fog that rolled over from the night before. As soon as their hands connected, he was flooded with a sensation of comfort and love. It felt strange to him, but the change in her expression told him that she felt the same.

Maybe this was how it was supposed to be.

The dawn fully engaged now, they walked back to the boat, which he was pleased to find where they'd left it. Imagine if Copper and his merry men had trashed the boat, too. That could have been a disaster.

They carried the boat the few feet to the bank, then he pulled the boat just into the water, so it would clear the bottom once they got in. Knee-deep in the dark water, he held the boat steady while she climbed in, shadows deep from the trees overhead.

Something splashed in the water behind him just as he was about to climb into the boat, and he missed his step. He fell headlong into the bayou.

Brianna laughed weakly. "Come on, I don't want to ride with you all—"

Something swished past his legs underwater. Something big.

"Shhh," he said, jerking himself upright and heading for shore. "There's something in the water."

"What?" She leaned forward, scrambling in her pack for a flashlight, which she waved from side to side around the boat, scanning the water for danger. "What is it?"

"Throw the rope over here, and I'll pull you in." He caught movement out of the corner of his eye as Brianna turned to look behind her.

"What was that? An alligator?"

As if she'd summoned it, the animal's ridged back snaked past the boat, rocking it by the force of its passing. The damned thing was huge.

She shrieked and grabbed on to the sides of the boat.

He had to get her out of the water, now. "Come on, Brianna, throw the rope. You're safer on shore."

To his dismay, she only fumbled with the rope, instead staring at the water where trouble now waited. The creature made several more passes, surfacing just enough for him to see it was a monster, maybe twelve feet long and thick as a submarine.

It bumped the boat, jarring it violently.

"Brianna, now!"

She clung to the sides of the boat, ignoring him, her eyes focused on the beast.

He debated the usefulness of jumping in and physically manhandling her onto dry land, but that 'gator seemed a big deterrent. "The rope, Brianna?"

Finally, she seemed to grasp his words. Still not taking her regard off the reptile, she tossed the rope toward the shore. It fell short.

He lunged into the shallow water and grabbed it.

With one strong yank, he pulled the boat half onto shore while the alligator swam away, perhaps startled by the movement.

"Give me your hand, Bri. I'll get you out of there."

She sat frozen, arms crossed tight.

"For crying out loud." He surveyed the immediate vicinity in the growing light, seeing not even a trace of the water rippling. "I think it's gone," he said, relieved. "Come on, let me help you over here."

"Are you sure?"

*Hell, no, I'm not sure.*

Wait, who was going to wear the pants in this relationship? When the trusty knight gave orders, the princess jumped. No time for this nonsense.

"Of course I am. Hurry now."

She shivered and took a deep breath, still studying the water. When nothing happened, she stood up, a little shaky, and held out her hand.

He seized it and dragged her ashore just as he caught movement in his peripheral vision. Across the inlet, the alligator's huge tail smacked the water in challenge, and it charged straight for the boat.

"Look out!" Brianna yelled.

She snatched up the wooden oar Evan had dropped on the ground and headed for the water before Evan could stop her. The alligator launched itself into the now-abandoned boat, its mouth open, hissing horribly, and inches-long teeth snapped at her.

Brianna swung the oar toward the open mouth of the creature. The impact of its jaws clamping down on the paddle nearly wrenched it loose from her hands. She wrestled for control of the oar, then the alligator jerked on the it, pulling her into the shallow water.

*Lunatic woman. What's she thinking? I've got to do something before she gets eaten.*

A distraction, that's what was needed.

*Here goes...*

He launched himself into the swamp downstream from the monster. "Hey!" he shouted. "Hey, over here!" He smacked the water, trying to get the alligator's attention.

"Evan, what are you doing?" Brianna gasped, yanking the oar back as the beast released it.

*I'm being a friggin idiot, apparently.*

"Come on, you big jerk, come and get me!"

He continued to splash, only then recalling there might be more alligators in the water. Sure he felt nips at his legs and ankles, he tried to be logical. *Surely with an old daddy this big, no one else dares come in his territory, right? We should be fine.*

*Should be.*

"When he gets out of the boat, you get in and head the other way, all right? We need to get the hell out of here."

"Me? Row the boat?"

"Just do it."

He waited until the gator slid back over the edge of the boat into the dark water, its claws scraping down the wood, an awful sound, as it shoved off.

*That's my cue.*

He half walked, half-swam for solid ground. Tree roots gave him purchase to drag himself out of the water, and he kicked some fallen logs into the water to keep the monster's interest. When the old gator came to investigate, he ran along the bank, finding Brianna just where he'd left her.

Brianna, trembling, clutched the sides of the rocking boat, and gave a little screech as he seized the grounded end of the boat and shoved it into the water before duck-and-rolling himself into the boat with her. He grabbed the oars and started rowing the other direction for all he was worth.

"Oh, my Lord," she whispered, a hand over her heart. "I thought you'd taken Copper's words about sacrifice to heart. When I heard all that splashing—"

"No, just threw some old logs in. I was trying to make something else sound more interesting than you."

Breathing hard, he kept rowing, returning the way they'd come in. The swamp looked so different in the daytime. Kind of Uncle Remus-y, almost. Sure, Br'er Rabbit and Br'er Frog might appear at any moment now.

*Long as it wasn't an alligator.*

Relieved, he breathed deeply, letting the out-breaths time his oar strokes. "So much for Mamma Whats-Her-Name's promise that if you came out here you'd be rewarded. You'd think Copper would have at least given you that, since he dragged us out here."

"Yeah." She sounded spooked and tired.

He didn't disagree. They'd been up all night and not in the usual Mardi Gras party way. All the mud and sweat and blood…

As he worked the oars, something caught his eye, a flash of white. "What is that?"

"Hold it still. Let me see," she said.

With a worried glance back in the direction they'd come, he acquiesced. "Just for a second. Then we have to make our escape."

He pulled the oar into the boat, and turned it over

to reveal what he'd seen: a brilliant white object protruding from the wood. She leaned closer to check it out, then started laughing.

"You're seeing something funny here? We almost became alligator chow."

"Look what we have," she cried triumphantly.

She pried the two-inch-long tooth from the oar and dropped it into his hand. "The possession of my enemy." Its sliminess chilled him, but this could definitely fit the clue they'd been given.

"Unbelievable," he said. "Just unbelievable."

He gave the tooth back to her.

She closed her hand around it, then tucked it into her pocket.

He notched the oar back into its cradle and piloted the boat into deep enough water to use the motor. No need to be quiet this morning. Better to get home before the vampiric mosquito population drained them altogether.

Yawning, he started the motor and headed back to the dock.

"I need some sleep, a drink, and a shower. Maybe not in that order."

"I'd recommend the shower first," Brianna said absently, her eyes scanning the water's surface.

"You're not exactly Miss Sweet-Smelling yourself, you know."

A squawking came from the trees overhead to the left, announcing the dive-bombing run of a low-flying black crow. It came straight for the boat. Brianna leaned forward and covered her face. He ducked to the right as it passed close enough he could feel the rush of wind off its feathers. It continued to harass them all the way out to the dock.

*If I didn't know better, I'd say the damned thing was watching us, making sure we leave the swamp.*

*If I didn't know better.*

He was being ridiculous. The crow was probably just looking for something to eat. Tourists likely fed every animal in the swamp, just to get a chance to see wildlife close up.

But he had no further need for wildlife encounter. He'd had enough to last a couple of years. Maybe the rest of his life.

He sped up, arriving back at the dock in much less time than it had taken to get out to the clearing the night before. Brianna was dozing by that time. He only woke her to help get the boat tied up.

Then they headed back to the city, their precious and hard-won prize safely tucked away.

Chapter Twenty-Two

Brianna woke bathed in alarm, feeling trapped, smothered…

Then she realized as she came fully awake that she was only tangled in her sheets. She must have been thrashing around for hours. The travel clock next to her bed said 12:10, and the sun was shining out the window.

After noon?

She sat bolt upright. It was Lundi Gras, Mardi Gras Monday, and half the day was gone. What was she thinking? When had she gone to bed?

She couldn't even remember going to bed. Or changing into this nightshirt.

A deep breath helped dissolve the fog clouding her memories. What came to her was Terri's concerned face earlier that morning, sitting at the breakfast table when Brianna and Evan came stumbling in. Close on the heels of that picture came another, fuzzier, of the drums and the spicy incense, and... Copper.

The thought of his name put the rest into focus, and she remembered their mission into the swamp. She jumped out of bed and grabbed her jeans off the floor. Slipping her hand into the pocket, she found the alligator tooth. It popped out, slightly yellowed, into her palm.

*It really happened, then.*

As her recall sharpened, she remembered snatches of the ritual, the rhythm of the drums that became her heartbeat when Copper called her to him. The sharp incense, the moaning chant of the devotees, the utter freedom of the dancing, these first tiptoed into her mind as cold thoughts, then settled into her body with the reminder of how they had possessed her.

A shifty memory of a heavy weight on her arms and shoulders tapped at her recall. She focused, trying to remember what that had been. When the answer came to her mind, she shot straight up with a little scream.

That snake. That horrible, horrible snake.

Impossible.

But she knew it to be true.

Brianna stared at the tooth in her hand. Remembering the jaws of the alligator, she shuddered. As if the snake wasn't enough…

She'd been violated by that man, mesmerized, somehow, her mind taken over by his cruel commands. How had she let that happen?

This tooth, if it was the "prize" they'd been sent to find, had to be taken to the cemetery. Or so dictated the note. Was she still bound to its commands?

And why in heaven's name would she be, after all this?

She tossed the tooth onto the dresser, wiping her hands on her muddy jeans. "That's it. I'm done. Evan was right. This is a matter for the police."

A glance as she passed the mirror caught the scab on her forehead. Another souvenir from their evening enchanted by voodoo.

It didn't look bad, though. Someone had cleaned it.

*Probably Evan. He'd been so kind to her in the swamp. He'd tried to save her from the alligator. He'd...*

A very different picture came into her mind of Evan. This one brought a flush of heat up through her body. Every nerve ending tingled with remembered touches.

She knew instantly, just as she had with the snake, that this, too, was real. She and Evan had been stirred by those voodoo drums into a sexual encounter.

As disbelief struggled with memory, her desire for him resurfaced.

She had wanted to become intimate with him, perhaps later than sooner, so she hadn't been made to do anything against her will. The kisses she'd shared with Evan before last night had promised this sort of passion.

Only her personal inhibitions had stopped her from acting on them on her own.

Copper's ceremony must have just been a catalyst of sorts.

A soft knock came at her door.

She sat down on the edge of the bed, pulling a sheet around to cover her bare legs. "Come in."

Evan opened the door, peeking his head around it before he came in. "I wasn't sure if you'd be awake yet."

He took in her posture and the clutched bed sheet and closed the door behind him. His face held weary lines of fatigue, but the sight of him flooded her with a rush of emotion.

Her mind flashed back to the moment the two of them stood opposite each other in the candlelight and drumbeats. She'd felt such comfort in Evan's presence, such love as she'd not felt since her parents had died.

His presence now re-evoked those feelings, almost joyous and all-consuming. As long as he was here, she would be loved and all would be well.

At the same time, something burned within that wanted to drag him into bed with her, letting that fire play itself out the rest of the day until their passion was spent.

But that couldn't be right. She tried to push that idea aside. "D-Didn't you sleep?" she got out at last.

He crossed to sit on the edge of the bed next to her. "A little. You know Terri was concerned when we didn't come back last night. She wanted to hear what we'd been up to."

"You didn't tell her?"

The thought of explaining their night brought a quick swirl of nausea to her stomach. Not that they were accountable to anyone, because they were adults of free will.

*Oh, really?*

But it still sounded crazy.

His eyes twinkled. "Hardly. No one I know would believe what we saw...and did."

"What did you say then?" Suddenly conscious of the faint scent of his aftershave, the rumpled softness of his hair, she concentrated on rubbing her fingers over the bumpy chenille of the bedspread, to distract her from his proximity.

He cleared his throat.

"I, um, told her we went out parking west of the city and ran out of gas. Then we got lost looking for a gas station and landed in the bayou."

Brianna covered her face with her hands. "Parking? Oh, geez. You really said that?" She peeked out between her fingers.

He nodded.

"And they believed you?"

He shrugged. "Dunno. But it sounded as good as anything. I mean, we show up, just in time for breakfast, covered in mud, obviously having been out all night. Sounded reasonable to me. At least my mom would have bought it."

She tried to remember their arrival and gradually the picture came together. The look on Terri's face as they stumbled in, exhausted, wet and somewhat dazed was nothing so much as a teenager's mother concerned for her child who she thought was dead in a ditch.

"Thank God!" Terri had said, jumping up from her place at the table. "We were just about to call the police!"

She came around to look more closely. "Where have you been?"

Mrs. Nielssen stared as if her eyes would pop, while the tall Texan just smirked. Weaving on her feet, Brianna was glad when Evan's arm came around her, bracing her upright.

"We've had quite an adventure," he said. "But I think Brianna needs to get to bed first. I'll be back down in a few minutes to tell you all about it. You've got coffee?" he asked hopefully, looking over at the table.

Terri assured him there was plenty for them both, but Brianna headed on to the stairs, Evan close on her heels. Outside her door, she pulled her dignity together and said, "I can manage."

"I'm sure you can. But let me help anyway."

He walked her to the bathroom, where he washed her face and other exposed areas with a warm, soapy washcloth, then took her across the hall, letting her get changed, then tucking her in with a warm kiss good night.

*Or good morning, really. Guess it was all where your reference point was.*

Those pieces of the morning falling into place, Brianna nodded. "All right, I remember now."

The other thing she remembered was a dream, a frightening dream, where Copper was urging her to do something she did not want to do. Right after that, she'd woken up feeling trapped.

"Did Terri really say the police had been called?"

"She said they were going to report us missing. We came home just in time. You had quite a night. We both did."

The affection in his voice started the pilot light of passion inside her again, and she slid close to him. He slipped his arm around her.

"How's your finger?"

Puzzled, she looked at her hands. "Why? What happened?"

He took her right hand and turned it from side to side.

"There," he said at last. He pointed to a fading dark red mark half an inch long. "That's got to be it. I saw Copper cut you, when he had the snake. He dripped blood from your hand onto the snake. I didn't know if he wanted the snake to bite you or what."

"The snake bit me?"

"No! No, it didn't. I just didn't know. The whole

scene was pretty trippy, and your buddy had control of everything. He whammied both of us somehow, dragging us up to be part of that ritual. Half of it wasn't even in English. I don't know what it was about. And I really don't know how he did it."

*Copper cut me?* she thought, stomach twisting with dismay. *Why don't I remember that?*

"The...um... more personal items the practitioner has in his possession, the more easily the victim will be controlled. For example, a blouse or shirt would work, but actual cast-off parts of the person, like fingernail clippings, skin, hair..."

Her voice drifted off when she suddenly remembered during her very first encounter with Copper, that he'd gotten her hair caught on his ring. What had he done after that? Had he kept those strands of hair for his voodoo dreams?

And what did he have on Evan?

"What is it?" Evan asked.

She explained what had happened. "He could have hair of mine to use in his rituals."

Evan frowned. His hand went up, almost automatically, as if to make sure it was still there. "He didn't get any of my hair. So what then? How did he make me his puppet?"

"What did you say was stolen from your wallet?"

"A sandwich rewards card. It's kind of old, the kind that they gave you stamps to lick and put on it. Why?"

"That was it? No money, nothing else?"

"That was it."

*Licked them. A personal body fluid.*

With a wrenching of her stomach, she suddenly

knew that Copper's people had taken the card, and for what purpose. To cast a solid spell, it was necessary to have something of one's body. This would allow them access to Evan's spirit.

He eyed her curiously. "What are you thinking?"

"If Copper needs something personal, something—biological—if you will, to make that connection and gain control, that card would give him just what he needed." She explained her thought process, bolstered by what she'd read in her books.

"Oh." He hesitated, looking like he'd taken a sharp kick to the gut. "So, what then? Do you think that's enough for the police?"

"I'm not positive that's anything but circumstantial evidence, Evan. Maybe someone was just hungry and wanted a free sandwich."

His expression and tone were both sarcastic. "In Pittsburgh. Really? Makes for a long drive for a sub."

"Yes, I know it sounds ridiculous. But I honestly don't know what we should do."

A long moment of silence dragged out between them, and he slid his hand down her arm. The motion gave her shivers. She looked into his eyes, seeing the same feeling burning there for her. Before she knew it, her hand had slipped behind his neck, pulling his face to hers. Passion burst from them both in an uncontrollable wave.

He slid up higher on the bed, lifting her up to meet him, hands caressing her as their lips fastened on each other for kiss after kiss. She grabbed the hem of his polo shirt and pulled it up, over his head, tossing it behind him onto the floor, the smell of his skin igniting her desire even further.

With a quick push of her right hand, she rolled him onto his back, then slid on top of him, sitting astride him, feeling the very physical manifestation of his need for her pressing into her feminine parts.

"What about the others?" he said, glancing over her shoulder.

"We'll be quiet." Feeling a rush of power and control blow through her, she smiled, leaning forward very slowly, teasing him, her hands pressing his shoulders onto the bed, her breasts just out of his reach.

"Honey, the way you make me feel, I don't know if I can be." He watched her for a moment, his breath catching in his throat as she moved her hips very gently back and forth, rocking them in the way most calculated to stimulate him. "Oh, no you don't."

He reached up to grab her shoulders, and before she could flex her legs to strengthen her position, he flipped their positions, trading so that he was on top. He was stronger than she was, and longer, and when she would have continued to tease him, he pinned her with his ankles and elbows, lying directly along her body. Then he lowered his head, kissing her till her lips felt bruised, but she didn't care. She wanted more.

"Don't stop, love," she murmured. "Don't stop."

"I don't intend to, not at all." He reached down and unbuttoned his jeans, wiggling out of his clothes in a way that only built up her anticipation. Her lingerie vanished in a single rip, and he was inside her.

Their mutual climax came much too soon for Brianna, though it was wonderful in every way. Evan was just the partner she'd been looking for, and he pleased her very much. Afterward, though, when she lay nestled in the curve of his body, she began to wonder when she'd started believing that.

His thoughts must have taken the same track, because he asked, "Did that seem… odd… to you?"

She sighed, content. "That seemed amazing to me. Something I'd waited much too long for."

"Maybe that's it," he said.

"Maybe that's what?"

He gently turned her face to his. "A couple of days ago we didn't even know each other. Then we didn't like each other. But all of a sudden, we're in bed together, having the best sex of our lives. That doesn't seem odd?"

She just heard the part she wanted to. "That was the best?"

"Brianna, I'm serious."

His sharp tone jarred her, and her yearnings began to subside. "What are you saying?"

"I'm not sure. I just hope like hell this is real, and not something else old crazy Copper put together. You know, proving his point that I need to sacrifice something for a woman."

She searched his eyes, finding true feeling there, leaving her reassured.

"Evan, I was attracted to you already. Well, when you weren't being an ass. I don't know that I would have acted on it so soon."

She leaned close and kissed up the side of his cheek, ending with a kiss on the forehead. "But I'm not upset in the least. If all this tension and mystery has given us a boost in the right direction, then I'm glad for it."

He cupped her cheek and smiled at her. "Tell me, right now, how you feel about me."

She hesitated, formulating a response, wanting to make sure the words were right. Then she wasn't sure she could find the words at all.

Her feelings were so confused.

She thought she loved him. Her body certainly had.

But did it make sense that she could be in love with Evan Farrell three days after they'd met?

She never would have believed it.

"Evan, I don't know. I mean, I do have feelings for you." A rush of heat flamed her cheeks. "Obviously. But, I'm not sure how to describe them."

She thought he'd be hurt, but he only nodded.

"That's what I expected. We're not thinking clearly, either one of us." To her relief, he leaned in and kissed her lips softly. "But I'm willing to give it time."

His expression one of reluctance, he pulled away from her and stood up, retrieving his clothing and putting it on. "We should join everyone else. Come down when you're dressed, and I'll see if Terri's got any muffalettas left."

Thinking of the tall seeded buns loaded with olives and meat she'd seen in shops in the French Quarter, her stomach growled. She was famished.

"Good. I'll be right down."

He stepped out and she dressed once again in the pretty dress she'd tried on the afternoon before, and she added makeup and earrings. Nothing would spoil her day today. She'd gone to the swamp and survived. She had the tooth. Now, she'd go to the cemetery and get this curse off her back once and for all.

Remembering what Evan had told her, she rubbed the tip of her finger, wondering how it healed so quickly.

Perhaps Copper's magic extended to the mending of torn flesh as well.

Checking her reflection before she went downstairs, motion outside caught her eye. She inched closer, lifting the shade. A large black crow sat on a branch, distinctly looking in at her. She dropped the shade and took a step backward.

*Don't be an idiot, Bri. It's a bird.*

*Birds don't watch people, except for their own protection.*

But then she remembered the crow that had chased them from the swamp.

*Just a coincidence.*

Then from behind the shade, she heard a sound like a heavy beak tapping on the window. Terrified, she grabbed her purse and left the room, flying down the stairs, where Evan met her.

"Brianna, what's the matter?"

He shoved her behind him, glaring up the stairs to discover what was chasing her.

Hank got up from his spot on the couch. "You all right, hon?" He frowned and looked up the stairs, too, as if he expected the hounds of hell to come baying down.

Her breaths came ragged and hard, her heart pounding, and she concentrated on getting control. "There was a-a bird..."

"A bird?" Hank's face turned speculative. He eyed the upstairs again. "In the house?"

She shook her head, realizing she sounded ridiculous. "No, no. Listen, it's nothing. I'm sorry for causing a fuss."

At least no one else was there. She'd been a

spectacle enough for one day.

Evan pulled her into the kitchen, leaving Hank shaking his head as he returned to his well-worn cushion. He got them both sandwiches and some sweet tea, then led the way onto the porch. "Tell me exactly what you saw," he asked, once they were seated.

Half convinced she was seeing things by then, she replied, "Nothing. I guess I'm just overtired."

"A crow?" he persisted.

She looked up sharply. "How did you know?"

Evan nodded. "I've seen one a couple different times. And again in the swamp last night—this morning. Whenever it was."

"It seemed to be watching me." That even sounded ridiculous to her own ears. "But—never mind. I'm sure it's nothing. Like I said."

She glanced back toward the house, a little self-conscious. With the police on call and the other trouble Brianna's "friendship" with Copper had caused, Hank might be regretting Brianna's presence here. "I'm seeing shadows everywhere."

His laugh lacked the warmth she'd come to expect.

"This certainly has kicked all my old police reflexes into high gear. Doesn't seem to make sense, any of it."

"I know. And I've ruined your vacation. You've done so much to help me, and I'm really grateful."

"I'm not complaining, Brianna, not at all." He reached over and squeezed her hand in reassurance. "I'm just dealing with my changed expectations."

"Yeah."

She wished she could laugh, but that just wasn't in her heart. "None of us are getting what we expected, I suppose. Was Terri angry? Should I look for somewhere else to stay?"

He chuckled. "Tell you the truth, I think she was taking credit for it all. What interested her most was the success of her matchmaking."

Brianna half-smiled, because she liked their hostess and thought she meant well.

But Terri wasn't the only one convinced she and Evan belonged together. Copper consistently said the same thing. She thought he'd done something, in her murky memories of the ritual, to try to cement their feelings for each other. She couldn't figure out, though, what he could gain from that.

She wouldn't worry Evan with those questions. She'd been much too much trouble for him already. She'd be lucky if he ever spoke to her once they'd returned to Pittsburgh.

And she wanted him to speak to her. She wanted that very much.

Chapter Twenty-Three

"So what are we going to do now?" Evan asked.

"If we're sticking to the plan, we're bound for the cemetery." She checked to see if she had her map and her guidebooks in her purse, as well as the all-important "prize." Flipping through the book, she located the page on the cemeteries.

"Look. St. Louis One, where Marie Laveau is buried, is just north of the French Quarter. We could take the streetcar down. It'll save time and looking for a space to put your car."

He hesitated, and she could almost see him wondering whether Copper would materialize if they took public transportation through the Garden District, but he finally agreed.

Leaving Hank to his game, they headed out. She read about the cemeteries as they walked up the block to the streetcar stop. "St. Louis One is only one square block, but they believe thousands of people are buried there."

"Thousands? In one square block?" He shuddered as he walked next to her. "You sure you want to go?"

"We're going," she said firmly. She kept reading. "Homer Plessy? Are you kidding?"

"Who?"

"Plessy. As in Plessy versus Ferguson? The Supreme Court decision that validated segregation?"

Every law student learned this case in the first year; it was one of the foremost cases on American civil rights issues. She remembered hating most of that year.

Evan blinked in surprise. "Really? *The* Plessy? Huh."

He avoided a pile of empty beer cans on the sidewalk, detritus of some Mardi Gras celebration or other. "All the same, it is a cemetery, right? Let's not stay there any longer than we must to get the job done."

She grinned at his equivocation. "What? Mr. I-Love-Zombies is afraid of a cement cemetery?"

He scowled. "Not at all. I'd just like to have one part of this go right, without problems or incidents."

"I'm all for that."

She sighed. "Marie's tomb is fairly close to the gate. We should be able to get in and out without too much trouble."

They arrived at the stop in time to wait for the next streetcar rolling up the line, still a number of blocks away. She studied his face, the dark circles under his eyes. He hadn't slept much. He'd been too busy taking care of her.

*Well, we'll get this wrapped up this afternoon and have one last day in New Orleans completely unclouded by this mess. Tomorrow will be a blast.*

She slipped her hand into his.

He squeezed it. "So Hank was saying this King of Rex will be in the Spanish Plaza tonight."

"Lundi Gras, right. He's supposed to arrive by boat in some fancy ceremony, and he'll get the key to the city."

He eyed her, one eyebrow cocked. "You've really studied up on all this."

"Guess not all of us waste our time reading Grisham on the flights down."

As the streetcar pulled up, he grabbed his chest in mock pain. "You wound me, madam. You wound me."

They boarded and took a seat near an open window, the scent of fresh flowers passing through with the breeze. He leaned back in the seat, putting his arm gently around her shoulders, and she relaxed into it. Their proximity felt good, natural.

They continued along St. Charles to Canal Street, then got off the streetcar to walk the several blocks to the cemetery. So odd, this block of small white buildings just off Basin Street, crowded in on each other like refugees in a food line, the sad, pale stepchildren of the skyscrapers of the city.

They arrived at the gate just as a tour was entering, and they filed in after that chatty group. Brianna found it interesting the light conversation faded as the group moved into the cemetery. The place had an air of solemnity, even in the face of the bright white buildings, practically glowing in the mid-afternoon sun.

She and Evan slipped away from the group, using the map to find Marie Laveau's tomb. The guide suggested it would likely have a number of triple-Xs inscribed on it, left by those wishing for favor from the Voodoo Queen of New Orleans. Once they tracked that down, it was easy to identify. They approached it from the side, making their way between the tombs till they came to the front of the tall, narrow rectangular mausoleum.

The tomb served as the final resting place for everyone in the Glapion family, that of Marie's husband. Brianna studied the space, not much larger than a good-sized sedan set on its side. How many bodies might be in there?

She also found it intriguing that New Orleans, which sat mostly below sea level, used above-ground tombs to bury its dead. In addition to St. Louis the I, there were two more St. Louis cemeteries, a little farther from the center of town. Bodies were placed on top of bodies inside those whitewashed buildings for generations, because there was nowhere to dig.

"Here," Evan said. He drew her attention to a small vase set on the northwest corner of the mausoleum that held a single red hibiscus.

"The red flower," she gasped.

"Where's the tooth? Put it there."

She glanced around, seeing the avaricious eyes of a thin white man watching them from behind the corner of another tomb set diagonally from the one they stood before. She'd read that the homeless often cruised the graveyards, taking the gifts of food and other valuable items that might be left by supplicants. *No need to take longer in this place of death.*

She dug in her purse and pulled out the tooth, which she'd wrapped in a tissue. Crouching down, she left it next to the vase. She couldn't resist reaching out to tap her fingers three times lightly on the tomb, then whispering a traditional-style wish for Marie's blessing.

"Marie Laveau, queen of those in New Orleans, I have done as I've been commanded. Please grant my wish today to be free of this curse."

"Amen," Evan said, over her shoulder.

She stood up, feeling like there was more she should do. But then the tour came toward them, and she felt a bit crowded.

When Evan took her arm and drew her away, she let him. They walked slowly back toward the city, hand in hand. She'd fulfilled the terms of the note.

That should be the end of it.

Evan was uncharacteristically silent as they approached Canal Street. "What's the matter?" she asked him.

He continued silent another minute, then turned to Brianna. "What next?"

"Next? I think that was all we were supposed to do—"

"No." He pulled her to an abrupt stop. "I mean, what's next for us? Has this sudden attraction just been part of this process? If we finish—if this was all there was—does this mean we're done, too?"

She swallowed hard, not expecting this turn of conversation. "I haven't really thought beyond getting past this."

Her thoughts hesitated on the top of a sheer icy slope tilted toward certain turmoil. Evan Farrell had been a constant part of her life for the last several tumultuous days. Their intensity made it difficult for her to remember what life had been like without him.

"These last four days, I've been voodooed and cursed and up and down. Frankly, my head's spinning," he said. "But one thing I know for sure. I don't want to get on an airplane Wednesday to fly home without knowing where we stand."

"You'll see me around," she said weakly.

"That's not what I mean. We've…"

He looked in her eyes, and that bond between them evidenced itself beyond any chance of misunderstanding. "You know what we are to each other. This experience has changed our lives, and more than just these few days. What you said, about the conflict of interest, it's true in so many ways."

Brianna bit her lip, considering what he'd said. It was easy to shove serious contemplation aside behind the excuse that these days in New Orleans had been hell on wheels. But he was right. Their lives had changed. As extraordinary as her situation had been, he'd stood by her through it. He'd shown himself to be a steadfast, reliable, strong companion, someone she could believe in.

*Not so far-fetched, is it? You can touch him, hold him. Maybe money isn't the only path to security after all.*

Then he really shocked her.

"You know, I think we're both looking for a more personal touch, something more meaningful from life." He took a deep breath, and as he let it out, the words tumbled from his lips. "Maybe we can take this as a sign. We could open a practice together, our own little firm. Make a partnership and practice the kind of law we want, you know, rescue the oppressed and save the children and right the wrongs, and..."

She wouldn't have been more surprised if he'd actually proposed marriage. Abandon her job? Start over again?

Needing movement, she started walking toward downtown.

"L-Leave Brannigan?" she said at last.

He nodded. "Like I said the other day, I've questioned my usefulness at GDS for some time now. I just haven't had a great alternative till now. We could work together, instead of on opposite sides, and take only the cases we want to do."

Could she survive working as an independent attorney and not having a big firm's steady paycheck? Were they rushing this, or was he right, and this had been a sign given to them?

*Do I have that much faith?*

It was a lot to think about, and this just wasn't the time.

"That would be sweet, wouldn't it? But honestly, I don't know…"

The sounds of passing traffic filled in the need for conversation for several blocks, then Evan let it drop. Instead he leaned close with a teasing expression.

"So what was that wish, exactly? The one back at the tomb?"

Her face colored, her cheeks hot. "I'll tell you if it comes to pass," she demurred. "You know wishes don't come true if you tell."

"Oh, so that's how it is. You risk your life to help a damsel in distress and she won't even tell you why." Amusement twinkled in his eyes.

She wanted to smile along with him, but the shadow of a cloud still hung over her.

The first relief of accomplishing their "mission" had started to fade. Sure, they'd done everything in the note. They'd gone to the swamp, wrestled an alligator, for Heaven's sake, and visited the cemetery. But that implied that Copper had simply done a good deed for a stranger, setting up a little vacation adventure.

No harm, no foul—wasn't that great?

Copper didn't seem like the type to do something for nothing.

What else could be on the table then? What did he

really want from them?

Evan took her elbow as they reached St. Charles, pulling her out of the streams of people passing after the parade of the Krewe of Proteus.

"You're a million miles away, counselor. What's the matter? And don't tell me nothing, because I can sense something's on your mind."

Should she keep her concerns to herself?

*My crazy lawyer brain could be working overtime on this. Sometimes a cigar IS just a cigar.*

"Bri, I'm not kidding here. We've come close to losing our lives on this merry jaunt, and I'm not risking losing you again. Tell me. Now."

Steel blue determination shone in his eyes.

She wouldn't win this argument. With a sigh, she capitulated. "What…what if Copper didn't go to that much trouble just to get us to the swamp the other night?"

"What do you mean?" he demanded. He didn't let go of her arm. If anything, his fingers clamped tighter. She tried to ignore it.

"Terri's right. He has a darker side. I remember his anger, barely controlled, about the man who's been selected as King of Rex. He's hip-deep in something." She shook her head. "I just don't know what."

Evan must have realized he still held her, because he suddenly let go and leaned back against the building.

*Back's to the wall, right?* She thought, but she didn't say it aloud. Actually, it seemed like a good idea, and she stepped up next to him, both of them now facing the sidewalk. She hardly noticed those passing by.

"He's definitely no one's freaking fairy godmother,

popping in to grant wishes of his city's visitors." His growl was tempered with several shades of disappointment.

He shot her a sidelong look.

"What he did for you had to be something you wanted to do. Even against the best advice."

*Yeah, yeah. Whatever.* She tried to ignore his jab, but it hit true.

Maybe she could have rejected this all along, if she'd started at the beginning. But when had that been? On the streetcar? At the airport? Before she'd even gotten on the plane?

She tried to keep her voice from trembling, frightened to think someone else could hold real power over her. Did he have something of hers? Had he kept some blood from the ceremony in the swamp? What could it be?

"So there must be something else. Something I don't want to do."

"Something *we* don't want to do," he amended.

She shook her head. "But I don't believe in voodoo."

Evan snorted. "You couldn't have convinced me of that the other night, while you were boogeying to the drums with Copper in the swamp. You were as far gone as anyone else there."

She felt tears well up. "But did I say anything? Did I wish anything? Did I agree to anything? How can he still make me do things?"

"You didn't say a word. I've got no clue what happened between all of us. Unless…"

"Unless what?" She looked at him, desperate for a small bit of hope.

"Unless because of the hair, and the blood, and the saliva, like you said, he really has some sort of pull."

"You're not buying this, Evan, are you? It's ridiculous. Like you said, we wanted to go to the swamp. That's what mattered. Not because he *wished* us there."

Her foot tapped almost of its own accord, nerves running loose.

*But love had been given to her. The love she'd wished for at the fountain. The wish promised to her by the note. She'd jumped through the hoops and been rewarded.*

*All that remained was that the bill be handed to her: time to pay up.*

"Honestly, Brianna, I don't know. We're both strong-willed people. We're professional, educated and not even from this culture. But we've gone places, done things that we both know weren't our idea, and over our objections."

"I know." Her turn to sigh. "We shouldn't go anywhere, then. Maybe back to the Worley's until we can figure out what he's going to do next."

Evan nodded. "We'll just grab some dinner and go back early. We deserve an easy night after what we've been through."

"Right." The current started to change, and she felt better again. If Evan was right about the power of the mind, maybe they could simply decide to be done with the voodoo priest. They'd just stay out of Copper's way, and everything would turn out just fine.

Chapter Twenty-Four

Evan was even more disturbed than he'd let on about Brianna's concerns. He'd considered himself beyond the reach of Copper Delacroix, believing his interest in Brianna had carried him along this passage of magic.

He'd hoped once they left the cemetery they were finished with this whole voodoo mess and would be free to enjoy the remaining day of Mardi Gras like everyone else—R and R. After all, they both had to return to their other life by the end of the week, advocating for clients before the judges of the Pennsylvania courts. They deserved some fun.

Whatever Copper's motivation, his machinations had given the relationship between Evan and Brianna at least one little shove. After the shock of their initial reaction to each other, and his remorse for projecting Frank Dellenbach's attitude onto the petite brunette, he was grateful they'd gotten past it and spent time together.

The zombies, snakes and the swamp adventure had certainly added an edge of excitement to his trip he hadn't expected, but he was the kind of guy to examine new opportunities and grab the ones that had meaning.

Like when he'd joined Givens, Dellenbach and Spicer in the beginning.

Like when he'd decided to become Brianna's

champion.

He sincerely meant what he said about starting a practice with her. The reputation of her work quality was outstanding, but more, he admired the kind of person she was. He could see them working together. Was it a rash decision? Maybe. But it sat in his gut like a warm batch of cookies. It surely felt right.

But he had to agree with her. Their business with Copper didn't feel "done."

Evan would have preferred to let law enforcement handle the mess. But his experience on the Pittsburgh force didn't carry much weight here. The large-scale issues managed by the NOLA force during this event left them much too short-handed for "maybes" and "ifs." They wouldn't get involved short of actual physical harm, and even considering their opinion of the Delacroix name, they would want proof up front showing Copper was involved.

*And Copper was no idiot. He'd make sure that proof vanished like the smoke of his swampland fires.*

Frustrated, he had to conceded her plan was probably the safest one. *We've certainly had enough of the craziness. Take the night off, shake this from our minds and start fresh tomorrow.* "All right then. Dinner, then back home to watch the parade on the television tonight."

"Good." She smiled through receding tears. They were on the right track again.

They crossed the street for the streetcar, but Brianna didn't stop when Evan paused at the marker. She kept walking up St. Charles Street toward the Garden District.

"Brianna?"

"Evan, help!" Her voice vibrated with panic like a taut violin string. "I can't stop myself!"

He reached for her but she pulled away into the crowd.

Alarmed, he followed her, gently moving his way through the crowd, all of whom seemed to be going the other direction. Eventually he had to push harder to keep up. He grabbed Brianna's hand, but she slipped away from him.

When he caught up again, he planted himself in front of her. "Where are you going?"

Her response was near-hysterical. "How should I know?"

Slipping into crisis mode as taught at the police academy, he first shoved panic aside. He had to retain his ability to make the best decisions. Even when being interrogated by a bench full of appellate judges, his response was always cold and calculated rather than hot and panicked. *This bastard's no different.*

She pushed hard against him, then slipped by his left, her pace picking up. He lost sight of her in a split second. With one of the biggest parades of the week about to pass, the streets were crowded. One person shoving through the mix really wouldn't be a big deal.

Damn. This was like hypnosis. What was it they said about hypnosis? They couldn't make you do anything you didn't want to do. Sure Brianna was on her way to wherever Copper was, he knew that was not where they needed to be.

He placed that negative square in his mind, concentrating on it as he caught sight of her.

Running now, he drew even with her. "Do you trust me? I want to try something."

217

"Just help me," she whimpered.

"All right. Close your eyes."

He jerked her sideways, just in line with a light pole ahead, and held onto her with both arms. *Here goes...*

He closed his eyes just before impact, the connection a jarring clip to his right shoulder that sent spikes of pain all the way down his arm and around to his rib cage. "Ow!" he yelped.

"Oh, Evan! Are you all right?"

A woman in a bright blue headdress laughed as they bounced off the pole. "Had too much to drink, there, friend? Here you go." She handed him a flyer for a hangover recovery clinic.

The impact had loosened his grip on Brianna, and she was gone again.

Damn it. Nearly winded, he hurried after her. Whatever that painful crash had done for him, it had not broken the spell.

"Are you all right?" she asked, wincing. "That looked like it hurt."

"Yeah, yeah it did." He growled. "Your buddy Copper has a hell of an ass-kicking coming to him. You know that."

"I know. I'm so sorry." She glanced ahead and then back to him. "There, Evan—a police officer! Get his attention!" Brianna cried.

*Perfect.* Copper caught *in flagrante delicto*, voodooing some innocent lawyers from out of town. "Officer?" he called. "Hey, officer!"

Her compelled path took them closer to the two uniformed officers, who were yelling at some hapless man in a green T-shirt and jeans. They ignored Evan as they castigated the young man for urinating on the sidewalk.

"How'd you like it if we come up to DC and piss on the Washington Monument, huh? What kinda jerk are you anyway?"

*Really? That's what you have to do to get police attention around here?*

Evan actually considered fumbling with his belt buckle and taking a whiz right there if it would help them. But likely all it would do was get him arrested, and then Brianna would be on her own. He couldn't let that happen.

Before he could really decide, her quick pace had taken them right past the officers, on to Poydras Street, but she didn't stop there.

Despite all his attempts to halt her progress, they continued five more blocks to Julia Street, where they finally turned off. Down two more blocks, then they finally halted before an old warehouse, its paint peeling. Many of its windows were broken out, giving the feeling of a gap-toothed mouth.

*This didn't look good.*

People, costumed and otherwise, all happy and loud, passed by them heading up to the parade route. Evan tried to reach out to one of them, but found they looked through him. He honestly couldn't get their attention, even when he reached out to them.

So now they were back to the control issue? His fight to control his fear wavered, and for the first time he thought perhaps he would lose that one. This was the craziest thing he'd ever seen. All because of a little bit of spit?

They were drawn to the back door of the decrepit

building. No number or other identifying marks graced the gray metal. The door was opened by a tall black woman, wearing a red turban, otherwise dressed all in black. She bid them enter, and they followed her through a short hallway to the main room of the warehouse, dimly lit from windows on the second level. Dust hung in the thick air, the smell reminiscent of the incense from the swamp.

"Ah, you have come."

The words released them from the compulsion. Brianna stumbled a little, and Evan reached out to catch her.

He kept her in his arms, shocked at the sight of Copper, regal in a tan linen suit, a pale colored scarf around his neck instead of a tie. sitting atop a tall throne, looking down on those gathered before him. Not just he and Brianna, but perhaps a dozen people of varying ages and races performed tasks around the room, obviously under Copper's direction. *What the hell?*

*Wait. Not a throne.*

As he studied the scene more closely, he saw that it wasn't really a throne, just an upholstered chair on top of a platform. *Just a little boy playing King of the Mountain, hmm? Sorry, pal, I don't really feel like playing games today.*

"What do you want, Delacroix?" Evan demanded. He was furious at Copper's condescending attitude and by his own helplessness against the constraint which made him do as Copper wished.

Copper climbed down the stairs at the side of his chair, still in powerful dictator mode, and walked right up to Brianna. She jerked away. He snapped his fingers and she froze in place. Evan reached for her, but Copper raised a hand in his direction, too and he was again powerless to move.

Copper ran his finger across her shoulder and up under her chin, tipping her face up until she looked into his dark eyes. Something happened when they made contact, Evan didn't know what exactly, but Brianna's eyes closed, and her hips swayed ever so slightly, as if she could hear the swamp drums again.

"What I want from you," he said, voice dripping with malevolence, "is strict obedience to the orders I give you. I command you, by Damballah's will, and you know this is so."

"Brianna! Brianna, don't listen to him!" Evan yelled, but she didn't respond with so much as a flutter of her eyelashes. She was under Copper's influence again.

Copper smiled. "You see, my power over her has grown until she can hear only me." He caressed her cheek. Brianna's body shuddered, but gave no other reaction.

*If I could get my hands on that guy's neck...* Evan fumed, trapped into petrified immobility. "What orders?" he said, his voice lined with venom.

Copper moved away at last, strutting before them, sentences bursting from his mouth like machine-gun fire.

"She will go to the Spanish Plaza at Riverwalk to await the arrival of the King of Rex. When the fireworks begin, she will kill him."

## Chapter Twenty-Five

*No way in hell!*

Evan couldn't believe what he'd just heard, but as he opened his mouth to protest, Copper touched his throat and he could say nothing.

"I've heard enough from you, my friend. Don't remind me that I only need you as leverage."

*I wish he'd stop doing that,* Evan growled silently. *He is seriously ticking me off.*

*And leverage for what? Brianna's not going to kill anyone. No way could Copper overpower her good nature that way.*

Copper returned to Brianna, staring down into her eyes. She'd stopped moving when he turned away, but as he came face to face with her again, she started swaying to a rhythm Evan couldn't hear. Similar to the dance at the swamp ritual, it had a personal element now, Copper standing close to Brianna, moving with her, his body touching hers in an almost sexual way. Her eyes still closed, she danced, unseeing, with the dark man.

Copper's hands moved up and down Brianna's bare arms lightly, like the hands of a lover. He touched her face, smoothing her brow, caressing her cheeks and her neck. Her dancing grew more erotic as she was touched, and Copper moved close, whispered into her ear.

She moaned, but whether with pleasure or rejection of what he was saying, Evan couldn't tell. A flash of anger burned through him, bright as burning saltpeter, but he couldn't move a muscle.

Copper called out toward the back of the warehouse. Two women dressed in somber brown robes came to his side and began removing Brianna's clothing.

Evan strained to regain control of his muscles, but couldn't overcome the compulsion which had somehow turned him to stone. What was he going to do, rape Brianna right here? In front of him? His thoughts were murderous.

Copper must have known it, because he looked over at Evan and smiled. "I will not harm her, my friend. She has much to do in my aid this night."

One woman took the clothing away and returned with a full-skirted rose-colored dress and petticoats, obviously an antebellum costume. The women then dressed her in the outfit, Copper maintaining physical contact with his entranced subject by a hand, a touch, changing his point of connection as he needed to accommodate the women dressing her.

Another snap of Copper's fingers brought a flowered headdress with a mask, which was fitted onto her head. With another snap, he released her and she stood still. She was a vision of a Mardi Gras participant, gowned, masked and ready to celebrate an evening of good times. She looked beautiful.

"Now your turn," Copper said to Evan. The women had already vanished into the back, then they came forward with a plantation-look suit, not quite Colonel Sanders white, that would have made Rhett Butler proud. They quickly stripped Evan of his clothing—and his dignity—and dressed him, as they had Brianna. The pair now looked like any other couple about to attend one of the big Krewe balls.

When he was satisfied with their appearance, Copper walked over to his platform and pulled from its shadowed foundation a small white lady's evening bag, which he handed to Brianna. "This you will keep with you all evening," he instructed her.

"All evening," she whispered.

From his pocket, he took a snub-nosed .38-caliber gun. "You will forget this is in your bag, *p'tit*, until the fireworks begin. Then you will move quickly through the crowd to the front, until you can see the King of Rex. He is an evil man and deserves to die."

"Evil man…deserves to die…" she repeated.

*Are you out of your mind?* Evan raged silently. *She's not going to kill anyone!*

"When you are sure he is dead, you will drop the gun and walk away quickly."

What was he saying?

On the plaza, there would be hundreds of witnesses, television cameras, news photos, all of whom would identify Brianna as the murderer. Evan was appalled at the cleverness of the plan. Copper would achieve his result. Brianna would be arrested and charged with premeditated homicide.

She probably wouldn't even have a defense. What would she say? The devil made her do it? He imagined how much weight he'd have given to that excuse in his own law enforcement days. *Not a hell of a lot.*

He strained again against the compulsion that held him still, but couldn't break it.

*How can I help her when I can't even help myself?*

Copper slipped the gun into the evening bag, and stepped back, satisfied. "There."

He returned to Evan and grinned, a dark amusement in his eyes. "Now. Let me hear what you have to say, before you burst a blood vessel." He touched Evan's throat, and the words came spilling out.

"You son-of-a-bitch! You can't do this! You'll rot in jail, if someone doesn't end you first!"

Copper backhanded him across the face. "Do not ever speak of my mother." His eyes seethed with pain. "I do this to prove to her I am worthy."

*Push him on the sore points now. Make him reconsider.* "Must be sad when your own mother doesn't even believe in you."

"She will now."

Copper turned away again, retreating to the pedestal again. He picked up a newspaper that looked like the same edition Evan had read that morning at the Worley home.

The headline speculated on the identity of the King of Rex.

"Edwin DeArment, financier, man about town, philanthropist...The man who is revered in this community for a thousand different acts, and is so rewarded by being named the King of Rex."

Copper spit on the floor. "King of Carnival! The *cochon* doesn't deserve to draw breath!"

The others drew back toward the walls, giving Copper a clear berth as he stalked around the room, kicking things out of his path.

"DeArment closed me out of a financial deal to bring a pharmaceuticals company into New Orleans after the hurricane. That business would have set me for life, since I own the property which was under consideration. He had no reason to disrespect me. None!"

An empty cardboard box went flying.

"He did this for no business reason, but out of disrespect!"

A heavy-looking crate skidded away across the floor.

"He cast aspersions on my character because of my ties to the voodoo community. So it is fitting that Damballah aids me in taking my revenge. If he is frightened of voodoo, let us show him it is for good reason!"

Copper's followers murmured praise to their god and their leader, in blind devotion that sent chills up Evan's spine. He wondered how he fit into Copper's grand scheme. The only rational plan Copper Delacroix could have was to kill Evan as well.

"Don't discount your importance, *mon ami*," Copper said, coming back to him.

"Yeah? Don't discount mine, either, pal. I'm not going to let you set Brianna up for *murder!*"

He hoped his yell would snatch Brianna's attention from the enchanted place where it rested.

But she paid no heed to him, swaying silent and withdrawn in that bright-colored costume. Every eye would be on her when she took that shot.

*And that would be the end of all their hopes and wishes.*

Copper smiled, self-confidence radiating from him. "You don't seem to understand that what you will, or won't, makes no difference to me. I have asked the help of Damballah, and he will not deny me."

Evan scrambled to find some chink in this plan. "You set this up that night in the swamp, didn't you? What was it, some sort of post-hypnotic suggestion?"

All that hocus-pocus, the blood-letting...that span of time between what Evan remembered and when they woke up, alone in the mire. What had Copper done to bind Brianna to him?

"Long before that night, my friend. I began the night she arrived."

Copper examined his fingernails, wiping them clean. "We bound her to us with hair from her body the first night she set foot on New Orleans soil. From that moment, she was bound to follow the demands of the god."

Because Evan was frozen, he couldn't shudder; instead that discomfort rumbled around inside of him, grating against his injured shoulder, and leaving him nauseous.

"What about the swamp?" Evan persisted. "That note you gave her? Did that have any meaning at all?"

Copper laughed. "There is nothing I do without significance, friend. Brianna felt lonely, so I arranged to find a constant companion. Once I interceded with Damballah on her behalf, then she could only trust me more. The plan succeeded, wouldn't you say? You're here."

*Not because I wanted to be.*

The man's ego was enormous. He loved talking about himself and his evil plans, just like a bad-movie villain.

Evan needed to keep him talking. Any minute he was engaged with Evan kept his attention focused off

Brianna. If he held the man's awareness long enough, maybe Brianna would come to her senses.

*Come on, love—wake up!*

"I sure am. Nothing better than a front row seat to watch you crash and burn. That's what they say, right? The bigger they are, the harder they fall?"

Copper's eyes flashed with spite. "I shall not lose this battle. Damballah has promised me."

*Oooh, got him one. Push him again...*

"So you need your momma to think you're a good guy? Is that it? Do you get to inherit the family crystal ball then? Or do you just get a really big snake?"

Copper marched over, breathing hard, his nostrils flared. Fury burned in his eyes. "I told you never to speak of my mother!"

Evan stole a glance at Brianna, who wavered a bit. *Yes! It's working!*

"Why? What makes her so special, other than the fact she's birthed the biggest idiot this side of Lake Pontchartrain? If you think this could work—"

He didn't get to finish his taunt. Copper's anger burst from him in the form of a mean right hook. Unable to avoid it, Evan took the punch right on the jaw and went down, unconscious.

Chapter Twenty-Six

The worst part was reaching for her thoughts—thoughts she so desperately needed—and then having them spin away, sucked into the cotton-wrapped rhythm of the drums in her head.

Ever since Copper had touched her, she'd been lost in a foreign place, where a wood fire sent smoky tendrils into the air, a hint of incense on the wind, and everywhere the beat of those big drums. The longer she remained, even her heartbeat took on that same cadence.

She couldn't find her way back.

*But I must.*

Despite the smells and sounds that engulfed her, she knew Evan was with her, back on solid ground, back in the warehouse with Copper. He had come to save her when Copper's pernicious persuasion had dragged her helplessly along through the crowd.

She wore satin, a dress in a stunning shade of pink she knew was not her own. Vaguely, she remembered the women dressing her in it. Copper had whispered words to her then, using the tone of a lover. He'd given her something. A package. A gift. Something she needed to do. She didn't remember what.

Why couldn't she focus?

She would have stamped her foot in frustration if she could, but she was petrified in place. She kept trying to move, trying to concentrate. Sometimes, for a brief second, she was rewarded with a bit of progress. One such moment, she managed to half-turn, just in time to see Copper strike Evan with his fist, sending him to the floor.

"Evan!" she gasped.

Hearing her voice, Copper whirled, his eyes wild.

"No, no, *p'tit*, you must not think of him now. Copper bids you what to do. You must carry out the will of Damballah."

Pinned by his intent gaze, she couldn't move again. Her tongue, however, still worked. *At least for now.*

"Please. Let him go. It might be too late for me, but he doesn't need to be here." Tears burned in her eyes and flowed down her cheeks unrestrained. She couldn't even wipe them away.

"Oh, but he does." Copper came close, trailed his carefully-manicured fingers down the skin of her arm, sending chills through her.

"Because, you see, he's my last piece of insurance. As long as he follows, I know you will do as you've been told." He leaned close. "Because if you don't, I will kill him. In the most unpleasant way I can think of."

His breath touched her ear, its moist heat an intimacy that repulsed her. But along with it came a mental picture of Evan writhing in pain, covered in a mass of squirming snakes, screaming as they chewed him into bits. The gruesome picture was so clear it sucked the breath from her, leaving her gasping.

"As I have always promised you, *p'tit*, Damballah well rewards those who serve him." His lips brushed her cheek. "But those who fail him die in agony."

Her thoughts finally started coming together, but only in desperate ways. She must do what Copper had commanded if she was to save Evan from that horrible fate. *Now what was it again?*

"Tell me," she said, barely able to conjure up enough voice to be heard. "Tell me again what I have to do."

"That's my good girl." He smiled without warmth. "You will be taken to the Spanish Plaza at sunset to rid the world of an evil man.

"When the fireworks begin, you will approach him and shoot him with the gun in your bag. He must die for you to complete your task, so do not think to bend my commands to your own will. Shoot him, then drop the gun and walk away. Mr. Farrell will be with me. I will release him once DeArment is dead."

She choked, thinking she'd heard him wrong. "No. Copper, I can't kill someone in cold blood."

"You will." He held up his left hand, his third finger encircled by an oddly-textured ring. "Do you know what this is?" He put it close to her face.

She discerned beaded threads of purple, gold and green, as well as dark strands twisted into the ring. She had no idea, so she didn't answer.

"These dark hairs here, *p'tit*? They belong to you. They are of your own hair. Do you remember, our meeting at the airport? I have braided them into this ring to make sure we are bonded. We will be one in action."

She stared in disbelief. Could he really make her shoot someone, against her will, on the crowded street, in front of a broadcast audience of thousands?

*Insanity.*

But he'd brought them to the altar in the swamp. He'd brought her here from Canal Street. Why couldn't he do this as well?

Horror soaked into her bones like a winter chill coming off the Monongahela River back in Pittsburgh.

She couldn't get away with such a heinous, cold-blooded act. She'd go to jail. She'd lose her license to practice law.

She'd lose…Evan.

*Everything.*

Behind Copper, Evan stirred. One eye opened, scouting the territory around him, then he stiffened. Brianna quickly returned her attention to Copper, hoping she kept his interest long enough for Evan to release himself, to think of something to save the day.

*Not much I can do in this state.*

"Why?" she asked. "Why me? I—I don't understand."

Copper shrugged. "No reason in particular, my sweet Brianna. I'd been at the airport for several nights, waiting for just the right person to come along. You were so trusting, so appealing. As soon as I spied you by the luggage carousel, I knew you were the one."

"But surely you have enough minions for the job right here in the city."

"Of course I do." He crossed his arms, tapping his fingers on the sleeve of his jacket, a little impatient, his voice a little louder, acknowledging those who toiled in the room with them. "My own people are quite loyal. I will reward them with many gifts and long life."

"So you could sacrifice an outsider without feeling one ounce of remorse?" The words tasted bitter in her mouth.

His eyes warmed with mirth. "Perceptive as always. But you will admit, you got your wish, didn't you?" He glanced over his shoulder at Evan. "True love. Thanks to me and to Damballah."

He studied her for a moment, then took a deep breath. "Much to do before this evening's festivities." He snapped his fingers. "Take them!" he said.

Another snap of his fingers released Brianna from the compulsion to be still and her knees gave way. Two men took her arms, dragging her toward the back of the warehouse.

"No! Leave me with Evan, please!"

She fought them as best she could, but Copper's compulsion had sapped her muscles of strength. Over her shoulder she watched, dismayed, as two other men came to claim Evan, taking him away in the opposite direction.

She was unceremoniously shoved into a small room containing a chair and an empty desk, the door locked behind the men as they left. She was a prisoner of a madman, about to kill an innocent man she'd never met.

*And there's nothing I can do to stop it.*

## Chapter Twenty-Seven

Evan thought he had a chance to challenge Copper, when Brianna noticed him awake. But before he could take action, the lunatic's attention span faded. He suddenly was bored with them both.

It was hard to mask his reaction as the two hulking lackeys took Brianna away, but he knew his only chance would come if they thought he'd surrendered to the will of the all-powerful Copper Delacroix.

*What a crock.*

He'd rather they'd been locked up together, too. Maybe he could devise a plan that made sense, some way to defuse this hold Copper had over them. Over him. All because of a stupid sandwich bonus card, from the sub shop where he'd taken his five-year-old niece Ashley for lunch on a Saturday.

He remembered after their sandwiches were done, how she'd sat, right up on her edge of the seat in the booth, kicking her legs back and forth as she'd taken the stickers and glued them to the card...

*Wait a minute.*

Evan replayed the scene again, and knew he'd remembered it correctly. It wasn't his saliva on the card at all. It was Ashley's.

This voodoo magic had all been a head game. He'd done it to himself.

*Well, now don't I feel like a complete idiot...*

The ring with Brianna's hair, now, was different.

If there was any reality to this voodoo stuff, then perhaps Copper did have dominion over her.

*If.*

Copper's casual explanation of his choice of Brianna to do his dirty work made Evan sick. How dare he take others' lives into his hands and play with them like they were toy dolls or plastic bricks to use for his own purposes and then discard?

Brianna had bought pretty heavily into the whole concept once Madame Masika had verified the meaning of the note. Frankly, they both had.

The confirmation by an independent third party that the note was a legitimate charge to them, a curse, even, which must be followed to save them, had seemed the tipping point.

*But what if Madame Masika wasn't an independent third party?*

Annoyed his legal analysis skills had waited to evidence themselves until this particular point, now that he was locked up, unable to take action, Evan tried to put aside his self-loathing for a few minutes and deal with the facts.

If the so-called "spiritual adviser" was a follower of Copper Delacroix, then everything she said, all those encouraging words could have been offered to suck them in further.

*And we bought it, because Brianna wanted to believe. Copper said she'd been granted her wish. What the hell did she want so badly that a wish was worth all this?*

What would he have wished for in the same circumstances?

He knew what he'd been thinking when she threw his coins into the fountain at the Spanish Plaza. He'd wanted her to notice him as a person, not just as some jerk from a rival law firm. What he'd received was the attention of a passionate woman who seemed like the answer to all his dreams, certainly something he'd been missing from his life so far.

Maybe they'd both been granted their wishes.

Now they had to save themselves from certain catastrophe in order to hope they might be together in the future.

What time did Rex come ashore? Sunset?

Evan glanced at the window, watching the light fade. *It wouldn't be long now.*

His cell phone, his wallet, his identification had been taken away from him with his clothing. He had nothing but this dandified pale suit and his not-inconsiderable intelligence. *Ought to be enough. Mamma didn't raise a fool.*

He executed imaginary scenarios in his head, imagining how he'd react in each. He'd scoured the room he'd been left in, too, hoping to find something, but had only come up with a six-inch pocket wrench.

Not exactly the weapon of champions, now, was it?

When they came to get him, he shambled forward as if he had no will of his own, meekly walking where they directed him.

*I should be able to pull this devoted-underling act off. After all, when Frank Dellenbach says jump, I ask how high, right? How much different can this be?*

He resolved to keep a close eye out for Brianna, and any opportunity to interpose himself between her and the fate Copper had chosen for her.

The two men took him to the back door of the warehouse and straight out into a black limousine that waited there. Brianna was already seated in the far back seat, staring straight ahead, her billowy crinolines taking up a huge chunk of the space.

Next to her was Copper, sitting tall and swollen with pride as if he'd worn Rex's crown on his own head. Evan sat across from Copper, and some broad-shouldered minion sat on Evan's left, across from Brianna. Brianna gave no sign she noticed Evan's presence.

He saw no sign she'd been injured in any way. As Copper had said, he needed her at this point. If any of his crazed followers had harmed her, putting a roadblock in the way of their priest's plans, surely the wrath of Damballah—or at least a ticked-off Copper—would have landed hard on their backs.

So they had one point moving in their favor.

The car took off smoothly. The windows were shaded so Evan couldn't see out, but then to appear concerned with anything wasn't in character at the moment. He tried not to demonstrate too much interest in his surroundings or what was going on around him. He was supposed to be along for the ride. Right? What had Copper said? "Insurance" that if Brianna failed to stay mesmerized for the main event, then she risked Evan's life in the process.

*Not if I can help it.*

He'd tried to imagine every possible permutation of what might unfold, even coming down to something as serious as knocking Brianna out, if he had to, to prevent the crime from taking place. The thought made his stomach turn.

After everything she'd been through, the last thing he wanted was to inflict pain on her.

But it was a damned sight better than a murder rap.

All that was left was the waiting. And a car ride that seemed interminable. Less than half a mile—what was taking so long?

Once they'd arrived, and the doors were opened, he could see why: the crush of people on the sidewalks, in the street, everywhere. The lackey opened Brianna's door, helping her from the car, checked to make sure she carried the white bag, and then took her arm.

Any thought Evan had of trying to make a break at the door ended when he saw the gun inside the lackey's suit jacket. The order might well have been given to terminate Brianna if the plan went awry. A glance at Copper and his slow nod confirmed his suspicion.

*Damn. Damn. And damn again. Impossible. Just impossible…*

"You and I will follow behind, Mr. Farrell. Come now."

Copper drew Evan alongside him. Evan concentrated on trying to walk as though he resisted every step—a lot harder to fake than the real thing. He desperately tried to keep tabs on Brianna, but the man walking with her seemed determined to push her through to the front of the crowd.

The scene was everything Evan had pictured about Mardi Gras, a capsule set of what he might have described to friends back home if he'd stayed anywhere else, even at the lowly Mom and Pop hotel he'd considered in Slidell.

On the upper level of the Spanish Plaza, a jazz quartet played Dixieland for all they were worth.

People with "geaux" cups—pronounced GO cups for some reason he didn't understand, maybe something French—elbowed their way through the crowd, wishing each other happy Lundi Gras and jockeying for position to see the King of Rex come ashore.

Everyone seemed happy and drunk and determined to have a good time. *If only they knew…*

"Soon, now," Copper muttered. "Soon now." He stopped in the middle of the crowd, looking out toward the river. "The boat, she comes. Soon I will have my revenge."

Evan's frustration increased to almost the point of explosion when Copper halted in the middle of a mass of people. Most of his calculations had involved at least being within arms' reach of Brianna. He could do nothing to help her or stop her from back here. This would not do at all.

What could he do to move things along, before the boat met the dock?

"Can't see it," he mumbled.

"What?" Copper snapped, irritated.

"Can't see from here. How will you know if she succeeds?"

"Don't you worry about that. When I see that great man fall, then Copper will have his satisfaction, yes he will."

"So many people," Evan stubbornly insisted, careful to hang his head. "You won't see his face, when he knows you've taken him down. That would be the sweetest revenge, wouldn't it?"

He held his breath, waiting to see if the gambit worked. Copper was silent for a long moment, then he seized Evan's arm, dragging him forward through the crowd.

Stumbling as he was yanked along, Evan gave small thanks for Copper's overreaching ego and tried to keep his balance as he bumped into dozens of people, most of whom didn't give him a hard time. Half of them were probably too numbed with alcohol to notice.

*I sure as hell wish I was.*

The one thing he needed to do was get to Brianna before that gun went off. He didn't care how it happened.

Copper came to an abrupt stop. Evan dared to look up, scouting the crowd around them for Brianna. They'd come close enough to see the area of Riverwalk where Rex would debark with his Queen, illuminated by floodlights.

TV cameras were set up nearby, their lenses trained on the spot where the boat had just come into view. Not fifty yards between him and the end of Brianna's world.

The horn on the boat blew as it arrived at the dock, and a cheer went up from the crowd.

He craned his neck to find her, and finally spotted her pink dress through a break in the sea of people around them. She and her escort moved relentlessly toward the dais at the end of the Spanish Plaza.

The mayor of the city, resplendent in a shiny green top hat and green, purple and gold sequined suit jacket, beamed with pleasure, honorary key to the city in his hand.

Several people came to the gangway of the ship, dressed in the fancy medieval style of Rex's captains and lieutenants, sounding the trumpet as the King crossed onto solid ground. The TV cameras focused on the smiling faces as the King and mayor exchanged greetings and the band broke into the official song of the King of Rex, *If Ever I Cease to Love*.

This was it.

She was close enough now that anything the lackey did might hamper her mission. Surely Copper wouldn't endanger that mission no matter what else happened. Evan had to take that risk in order to get close enough to save her.

He watched Copper for several seconds, seeing him fondle that ring, noting when his vigilant attention over Evan faded. He took a deep breath.

*This is it.*

He shoved Copper sideways as hard as he could and sprinted through the crowd, shoving his way toward the front without apology, heading for that pink dress.

Chapter Twenty-Eight

Copper had visited her in the locked room before they left the warehouse, and ever since then, Brianna had not been able to think quite straight. A buzz in her brain like a hum of static drowned out her thoughts.

She let Copper's minions seat her in the limousine, needing their help to get that horrendous skirt tucked into the car. A thought about how ridiculous old-style hoops skirts must have been came and went before she could really decide. Others got into the car, but she only noticed Copper.

*I have an important task to do for him. I have to protect Evan.*

That thought, and that one alone, was clear as a bell.

A white evening bag sat in her lap. It was important that she carry it with her at all times. Something in that bag would save Evan's life.

She hardly noticed the movement of the limousine as it drove them to the Plaza. Her head buzzed warmer and warmer with Copper's touch. All she had to do was what she'd been asked to do and then all the rewards she deserved would be given to her.

When they arrived, the Plaza was a blur of noise and color, partygoers in bright costumes like hers, others in Dr. Seuss striped hats or T-shirts that bragged where their wearers had been drinking themselves blind the night before.

Music played in the distance and the babble of voices threatened to overtake the buzz for a moment.

She was taken from the car. Someone walked with her, someone not Copper.

A dozen feet from the car, the noise in her head faded slightly. That clarity increased the farther she got from it, and from Copper.

She became much more aware of the crowd around her, the women in low-cut gowns, the old men in guayaberas, khaki shorts and black socks with their street shoes. Children romped around the plaza, playing in the water before the heat of the day faded.

She checked to make sure the bag was in her hand as the man hurried her along. Someone stepped on the hem of her dress, pulling her loose for a moment, making copious apologies her escort ignored. He just reaffixed his grip on her arm and started forward again.

*I'm at the Spanish Plaza. What's going on?*

Her mind's gears started latching into synch again. *I'm at the Spanish Plaza. The King of Rex comes to Riverwalk tonight, at the Spanish Plaza.*

She suddenly remembered what Copper had told her to do. Horrified, her feet stopped. She stood like a statue, Copper's lackey nearly losing his grip as he hurried onward.

"Evan?" she called. She turned in a quick circle and didn't see him. "Evan!"

Copper's servant clamped down harder. "Don't be worried about your man," he warned. "Copper have him back in the crowd where he be safe. For now."

He gave her a meaningful look and started forward again.

Hanging back as much as she was able, she mentally scrambled for a way out of her predicament. If Copper had Evan, she wasn't sure how to save him. The best she could hope for was to avoid killing this innocent man on the pier.

Copper's voice suddenly echoed in her head, a rhythmic chant.

*You must kill him. You must kill him. You must kill him.*

She couldn't shut it out. Like the drums, it eventually became part of her, taking over her pulse beat. It was all she could think about.

She saw the man who must be the mayor, surrounded by staff, a few police officers and others, all approaching the dock.

A trumpet sounded. At the top of the gangway, several men in bright costumes started down.

The man dragged her to the front of the crowd, causing some hard feelings in those displaced by their passage, but a hard look from him frightened those who complained into silence.

The man who must be Rex and his young queen paused at the top of the gangway, then came down to meet the mayor. They all shook hands, standing there in the open, laughing, as though it was perfectly safe.

*Why don't they know? Why don't they do something before it's too late?*

"You go on now." The man put one of his large hands in the center of her back and pushed her forward toward the meeting place. Confused, she looked over her shoulder at him, but he just gestured to her to move up. So she did, holding the white purse in both hands.

*Now, p'tit,* came the voice in her head. *Reach in*

*your bag and take out your tools.*

She opened the purse and wrapped her hand around the butt of the gun.

*Stop it. Stop!* she screamed silently, without effect.

She held the gun by her side, in the folds of her skirt. A signal would come to her, but it had not yet. She stood with death in her hand, ready to inflict it to a man that surely didn't deserve it.

*And yet if I don't, another man, equally innocent, will pay the price.*

She dropped the bag to the ground, no longer needing it to conceal the gun.

It was almost time.

The music played, a song that everyone in the crowd seemed to know. They sang the words together, or at least most of them, swaying, hanging on each other if they were too drunk to stand. It reminded her of New Year's Eve in downtown Pittsburgh, when everyone sang "Old Lang Syne" when the fireworks went off.

That was it.

The signal.

The fireworks.

When the fireworks went off, she was supposed to shoot.

Dread bubbling up in her, she prayed for intervention, even that a hurricane would suddenly descend upon the pier to postpone the pyrotechnic display.

Anything.

Anything at all.

A drunk could maul her. Heck, an earthquake. Anything but—

Suddenly there was a familiar muted thud, and a few seconds later, a glittery gold star burst outward overhead. *The fireworks! No!*

Her right hand, holding the gun, came up, pointed at the intended target. Her left came up to brace it, just the way her uncle had showed her when she was a teenager. A couple of shouts around her were drowned out by the next rocket igniting overhead, showering the sky with green and gold fizzles.

Her finger contracted on the trigger.

At the same moment, she felt a heavy body collide with her, grabbing her arm, twisting it in the direction of the river when it discharged. Her wrist jerked with the jarring recoil.

She looked up into the shocked eyes of Evan Farrell.

"Drop the gun."

He spoke quietly, as if he was trying not to draw anyone's attention.

Her body remained stiff. "I can't."

"Hey, she's got a gun!" someone screamed next to them.

"A gun!"

"A gun!" rippled through the crowd. Suddenly a small circle of space opened around them, leaving Evan and Brianna in the center, the clear targets.

"Well, you'd best hide it," he said. Determined, he took her arm and pointed the weapon toward the ground, tucking it again in the folds of her skirt.

Chaos reigned at the podium, as the dignitaries were rushed off to safety. The heavy footsteps of police ran toward them.

"I didn't hit him," she said.

"No, love. You didn't hit him." Evan stood with her, right beside her as the police approached, weapons drawn.

"Drop your weapon!" the closest one barked. "Drop it now and get down on the ground, both of you!"

The crowd around them babbled, intent on the action as if it were a reality show. Brianna wondered in some disconnected part of her mind whether they would call in to vote for her good behavior. The situation was so unreal.

Her fingers clenched on the gun and she couldn't put it down. She physically couldn't do it.

Worst of all, she knew they'd never believe her.

"Okay, it's okay!" Evan called out. "No more shooting's going on here." He stood between her and the officers.

"Sir, get your ass on the ground! Don't you make us shoot you!"

Evan licked his dry lips and gave her a smile. "It's an adventure, right?" he whispered.

He turned to the crowd and yelled out, "Copper Delacroix, you've failed. The King of Rex didn't die at her hand like you wanted, you weak little scum-sucking snake!"

The cops' attention jerked away for just a moment. The crowd dwindled between them and Copper, who stood some fifty feet away, his hand pointed at her.

"No. You have to do it," Cooper demanded. "You have to do it. Shoot him. You are compelled by Damballah. Shoot him!"

"You lose, Copper!"

Evan taunted him again, but by then, the police had

spread wide enough to handle all the troublemakers at once. The three behind Evan tackled him and Brianna, dropping them hard to the concrete, while several more went after Copper, who tried to escape into the crowd.

An officer finally wrestled the gun from her hand, nearly breaking her finger in the process. She lay there in her soiled finery, in tears, as they handcuffed her and marched her over to a police car, shoving her in the back. They cuffed Evan and shoved him in with her. Soon they took the ride down to the precinct house.

Her head hurt where it had hit the sidewalk, and her hand was already swollen. The handcuffs didn't help. She looked over at Evan. "You all right?"

"I'm great." A big bruise graced his left cheek, and his forehead was bleeding. "You still look beautiful."

She tried to look out the window to see whether Copper had been apprehended. "You think they got him?"

"I don't know. But you didn't hurt anyone, love. Hopefully it'll just be a little while, and this will all be straightened out."

Her comfort in his presence, whole and relatively unharmed, was short-lived. When they got to the station, they were separated. She was photographed, fingerprinted, and handed an inmate uniform to wear instead of the ridiculous skirt, now muddy and torn. The guard only surface-searched her—the booking officer didn't have time for anything more invasive, as there was a steady stream of occupants for the station holding cells.

"What am I being charged with?" she asked several people in sequence. "Listen, I know my rights. You have to tell me what the charges are."

The jail guard, a heavy-set black woman, looked her up and down. "Listen, Tinkerbell, everybody here know their rights, you know? We just doin' our job. Don't make it hard. Just move along."

Miserable time passed, she wasn't sure how much. At one point she caught sight of a clock that read eleven p.m. Then they shoved her in a cell with a dozen other temporary inmates and left her to brood in hell.

## Chapter Twenty-Nine

Evan never knew exactly what piece of luck he managed to pull out of thin air, but something made him remember the name Lambeau—the officer he'd talked to earlier about his suspicions of Copper's iniquity.

He loudly demanded to see Sergeant Lambeau and didn't stop, despite threats from the others on the wing to knock off the noise.

Finally a large black officer lumbered into the men's holding area. "Which wonna you guys is Farrell?"

Evan leaped up, practically hanging on the bars. He didn't recognize the ranking marks on the officer's sleeve, but the nametag read *Lambeau.* "Me! I'm Farrell."

As soon as he did it, several others mimicked him, calling out, "Me! I'm Farrell! I'm Farrell!" The last one yelled out, "I'm Spartacus!" which set all the drunks laughing.

Lambeau eyed Evan for a long moment, then let him out of the cell.

"Come on. We want to talk to you."

Practically trembling with relief at his success, Evan followed him to an interrogation room. It looked pretty much the same as everyone he'd ever been in, right down to the large mirror/window he knew was two way. He didn't care. He was glad to be out of the raucous holding cell and wanted to get the hell out of this place.

And take Brianna with him.

"Did you get him?" Evan asked Lambeau. "Did they get Copper Delacroix?"

The sergeant sat down heavily across from him. "What do you know about Delacroix?"

Evan patiently told the whole story as best he could remember it, reiterating that he'd already told him about the strange note and the missing wallet when they'd talked before.

"So you're telling me that after all that bullshit, you and her dragged yourselves out into that swamp and drank chicken blood and all that stupid crap? Are you idiots?"

"No chicken blood." Evan frowned, hoping like hell it really hadn't been.

He shuddered, thinking about it. "We went out there trying to get some more information about this whole scenario that's actually come to pass. Brianna heard Delacroix make that threat two days ago—"

Lambeau glared at him. "Which you neglected to tell me about when you were worried about your damn wallet!"

"Right. I couldn't even get you excited about a note that was all about death and blood and whatever. So some "maybe" overheard threat that might be about someone would have gotten immediate response. Is that what you're saying?"

The sergeant growled and looked down at the table.

"Besides, something happened once we got out there. I'm telling you, we were compelled. I don't know what the hell it was. We just…did what he said. Like we didn't have a choice. That's how we ended up in his warehouse tonight."

"And where was that again?"

Evan described the place on Julia Street the best he could, and Lambeau nodded, seeming satisfied.

"So your girlfriend was supposed to shoot DeArment?"

Evan nodded fervently. "Copper set her up. They took all our stuff—I'm sure you'll find it there, if you send a team with a warrant. But she didn't actually shoot anyone. I made sure of it. I mean, maybe some carp in the river. No one else, right?

His desperation must have been clear, because the expression on Lambeau's face warmed a few degrees.

"I can see where you'd think that, but it's not our call." He took a deep breath in and looked over his paperwork. "Brass has decided to cut *you* loose. Go on home. Have a drink."

"And Brianna?"

The sergeant shrugged. "They haven't decided what to do about her. I mean we got reckless discharge of a firearm for sure, even if they don't get her for attempted homicide."

"Now look! This wasn't her fault! She had no *mens rea*—you can't prove her intent under any circumstances."

"Oh, that's right. Under all those sissy clothes, you're a lawyer." That brought Lambeau a chuckle.

Evan's eyes narrowed, a slow burn creeping through him. "Can I stay and wait for her?"

Lambeau shook his head. "Too many people around as it is. You hang out too long and they'll cite you for loitering." He shrugged. "Anyway, you want a phone call, you can make one at the desk."

He left the room and some subordinate trooped in to walk Evan to the desk. He asked for a phone book, since he had no cell with his numbers in it. Finally he dialed the Worleys' and got a worried Terri on the line.

"Evan, my God!" she cried. "Where are you? Where is Brianna? Are the two of you all right? We saw it all on television!"

"We're okay. At least I think so. What did they say on the news?"

"That she'd tried to shoot Edwin DeArment! Please tell me that's not really what happened."

"Not really—"

"This has to do with that Copper Delacroix, doesn't it? I told you nothing good would come of him. Nothing at all!"

"I've got to agree with you there." His body ached from the rough treatment it had endured so far that evening, Evan stretched and groaned. "Hey, could I trouble you to come pick me up at the police station?"

\*\*\*\*

An hour later, he was back in the heart of their little B&B family, showered, in his own clothes and a cold beer in his hand, his mind set on determining what he could do for Brianna. The other visitors kept a wide berth, hardly making eye contact as if they would "catch" demonic possession or something.

"So what are you going to do?" Hank asked. He seemed torn between bemused shame that his guests were shooting up the town, and pride that they'd become some sort of folk heroes.

"I don't know. No one there would tell me

anything. I guess we'll get her a lawyer in the morning. I just feel bad she's got to stay there tonight. It's not fair."

"No, it's not. It's outrageous," Terri agreed. She plied him with little snacks and treats and the promise of ice packs and bandages until they all went to bed in the wee hours, having debated the issue of what to do for Brianna, but having no idea what might really help her.

Evan in particular felt guilty leaving her in that place. He didn't sleep till nearly dawn, brainstorming scenarios to bust her out of jail and get her on that plane home with him by Wednesday night.

He'd even change his flight so they could fly home together. If he could get her back in his arms, he wouldn't let her go.

If only he could come up with the right solution.

\*\*\*\*

He never anticipated the solution that actually arrived.

Terri burst into his room and dragged him downstairs to see the morning news report. "Hurry!" she urged when he nearly stumbled down the stairs. "Hank, turn it to the FOX station. They'll have the local news five minutes later."

They all huddled around the screen, waiting for the local car dealer commercial to pass before the announcer came back on, his face somber. The graphic behind his head read "Mysterious death."

"New Orleans jail officials report that an inmate died while in police custody last night," the newscaster said.

Evan's first thought, even through the muddled

layers of waking, was that they meant Brianna. "No way," he said. His heart began to race, his knees weak, and he leaned on the nearest chair.

"No, no, listen," Terri ordered.

"Local businessman Copper Delacroix was found dead in his cell this morning, the apparent victim of poison. Officials are not yet sure how the poison was administered, as the inmate was searched before he went into the cell. Investigation continues. In other news, today's parades are—"

Hank switched off the sound. "I bet his momma did him in for embarrassing the family."

Evan did sit down then, hard, in the nearest chair.

"Do you think that gets Brianna off the hook?"

"It just might," Terri said. "Let me give our family lawyer a call and see what he can find out."

It took some persuading to motivate the man to work on a city holiday, but Terri eventually convinced him to look into things. Police found all of Evan and Brianna's personal possessions in Copper's warehouse, just as Evan had said.

Intake interviews showed Evan and Brianna corroborated each other's stories, while Copper only raved about how DeArment had done him wrong, so why hadn't anyone arrested *him* or taken any action against *him?*

"Somehow, they pieced together a confession out of that. So they're cutting your girl loose. Come down and pick her up."

Evan wasted no time jumping in his car to go retrieve her, carrying some of her own clothing down for her to change into, instead of whatever the jail had given her. He waited anxiously for her to come out front, hoping nothing worse had befallen her in city custody overnight.

When he saw her, her expression was blank, dark circles under her eyes. She didn't smile. All he wanted to do was take her in his arms, but something in the way she carried herself felt like a startled porcupine. He thought better of it.

He opened her door, then once she was in, hurrying around to his side. Her expression didn't change. He had to say something to lighten the moment, or his heart would break. "Some experience, huh?"

Her jaw set, she just shook her head.

"You heard about Copper?"

"Yes. Everyone heard about Copper." She gave him a sidewise glance. "Someone said snakes were crawling around the male detention area. But we didn't see anything like that."

He glanced at her, seeing an odd expression in her eyes. "I bet that would have been something to witness."

She nodded.

"You sure you're all right, Bri?"

"I don't know. I don't even know what's up and down right now." Her hands twisted nervously in her lap.

He felt bad for her, but tried not to let it flip over into outright pity. She was a strong woman. She'd recover, he was sure of it.

"I'll bet. What you need is a nice hot bath, and a pretty dress, and some of Terri's super-coffee. I think you'll feel more like yourself. You want to try that?"

"Just take me home, Evan."

She leaned her head back on the seat and closed

her eyes.

So he did. He paced anxiously while she took three showers before she was convinced she was clean again. She retreated to her room, and he offered to bring her anything she wanted to eat and drink, but she wanted nothing.

Even Terri tried to cheer her up, but came out, defeated.

"I'm so worried about her," Terri confessed to Evan. "Maybe after y'all get back home, safe away from all this, things'll go back to the way they were before."

She hurried downstairs to tend to the other guests, never realizing Evan felt her words like a splash into icy water. He wondered whether that's what would happen, now that Copper's dark machinations had ceased once and for all. Would they really go back to the way they were before? Lawyers on opposite sides of causes, battling all day in court, never to experience the sweetness of the love they'd had, and the love they'd made?

He didn't think he could stand that.

As far as the outside world was concerned, Brianna might have no long-term effects from this weekend. In the end, all the charges had been dismissed. Her license was safe. Once she left the city of New Orleans, she'd be good to go.

*But what we felt for each other, that can't have been just part of this bad dream. Can't some good come out of this? Just one thing?*

He hesitated in front of her door, hand raised to knock, but he couldn't do it. The fact that she'd shut him out seemed to make it clear that she didn't want him.

He went back to his own room to mope, packing up his laundry into a plastic bag, then shoving it into his suitcase. Hank had offered him a stiff drink, downstairs, but he hadn't been interested. All he wanted to do was find out what was going on in Brianna's head.

*But I'm afraid to find out. More afraid than I even was down on the Spanish Plaza. If I can't have her in my life...*

No.

*Wait a minute.*

If all their involvement was a figment of Copper's imagination, then why did Evan still feel the way he did?

He'd been physically attracted to Brianna from the moment he saw her. Their early sparring just piqued his interest, and as the days developed into nightmare, she'd proved herself to be strong, courageous and willing to engage in even the worst circumstances if the end result was the greater good. These were certainly fine qualities in a legal partner, but even better in a life partner. He wanted her. He wanted this lovely, intelligent, caring woman all for himself.

He still did.

If those feelings were real and true for Evan, why wouldn't they be still true for Brianna, too?

He marched out of his room and over to her door, knocking boldly. "Brianna, open up!"

Several long seconds passed, maybe half a minute or more, before the door opened. Brianna stood just behind it, peering around its edge. Her face was tear-streaked, without makeup, her hair lightly rumpled. "What do you want?" she asked, barely above a whisper.

Even didn't hesitate. "Baby, I want you. I want you now, and next week, and next month, and for as long as you'll have me."

The expression on her face read something between astonishment and immense relief.

"I thought….I thought…"

She turned away, but she didn't close the door. He stepped in and closed it behind him before she could lock him out again.

"You thought what?"

It was all he could do not to embrace her, to reassure her, but she was still putting off those "stay-clear" vibes.

"I thought this was all something Copper generated." She stood facing the mirror, her colorful print blouse in stark contrast to the pale flash of her face.

"Evan, you have no blame in any of this. You tried to warn me against it. You did everything—anything—that could have been expected under the circumstances. I should be getting down on my knees to beg your forgiveness for all I put you through—"

That broke him. He couldn't listen to any more. He reached for her and cut off anything further with a kiss.

She held back at first, but then she slowly warmed to him. Not the fiery explosion she'd been the day before, but hints of that passion shone through in the way her fingers smoothed along his skin, and how she pressed against him.

That's all it took, was a kiss.

When they broke apart, she studied him, voice shaky as she spoke.

"It's real," she said. "It's really real."

"What is?"

"This love. I was afraid it was all a part of Copper's plan, that compulsion, and once he was gone, it would be too. That's what happened, that night, you know."

She pulled away from him.

"When Copper died, I knew the minute it happened. It was like a weight lifted from my mind, and I was free."

She took a shuddery breath, then sat on the edge of her bed. "Everyone started talking about it, right away, passing the news from cell to cell. Rumors flew that Mama Delacroix had killed her son with her own magic as retribution for the public humiliation they'd suffered. I didn't care. I just didn't care. As long as he was gone."

Evan didn't understand, but he didn't want to push her. Perhaps it really happened just as she said. If Copper's magic could make other people come to harm, then it seemed fair that he was punished through the same means.

"When you didn't speak to me on the way home, I thought…" He couldn't tell her he thought it was over. That hurt too much.

"You thought my feelings for you were gone." She spoke matter-of-factly, staring down at her hands in her lap. "Just like Copper was gone."

"Yes."

"Never," she said, looking up at him with complete trust. "Through all of the nightmare, I believed in you. I knew somehow you would find a way to keep me safe. And you did. If what we feel is real, and I believe it is now, then I don't intend to let you go at all. Ever."

He took her into his arms again. "You've got a deal, woman."

He didn't know how long they stood there, comforting each other, but finally, his stomach gave off a loud growl. The interruption actually made her giggle.

"I'm keeping you from your dinner," she said.

"You know, everyone's really worried about you. Why don't we both go downstairs and get something to eat? We can try to relax a little. It's our last night, after all." The thought of leaving New Orleans both made him sad and gave him hope. What a vacation they'd had! Not anything like either of them had planned. *And they were lucky they'd survived...*

She agreed to mingle with the other tourists, now returning from their final day of Mardi Gras hoopla, petered out after a week of collecting purple, green and gold swag. The guests unanimously agreed to pitch in for a pizza dinner, so their hosts could relax and no one had to cook.

Mrs. Nielssen brought her collection out to the back deck to sort through. Her pile of pretties had grown, like Godzilla, until it was a mountain of plastic cups, doubloons, strands of beads, both fancy and plain—completely out of control. She finally stuffed it into a large black trash bag.

"That is incredible," Evan said, thinking of the perhaps three sets of beads he had upstairs. "How are you going to get that on the plane?"

"Oh, sonny, we drove down. It's a pretty straight shot down Interstate 55."

"That's her second bag," Terri interjected. "She's promised to share with half the neighborhood when she gets back."

Mrs. Nielssen gestured to Brianna, who was ensconced in a turquoise-cushioned Adirondack chair with a tall pink drink in her hand. Lit by the torches that burned along the perimeter of the deck, she seemed to be enjoying a tropical paradise.

"Honey, you missed out on a whole lot of the parades, with all these shenanigans, are you sure you wouldn't like some?"

Brianna shook her head, her expression somber. "You're very kind, really. But I'm sure I have enough to remind me of this visit." Her hand unconsciously went to the lump on the side of her head, a souvenir from her encounter with the police.

She leaned back and took a long sip of her drink. Evan wasn't sure exactly what it was, but Hank had poured several kinds of liquor into it. Terri had encouraged him, saying Brianna "needed to relax a little." Evan wholeheartedly agreed.

He caught her watching him, and she raised her glass with a little smile. She'd been through a lot.

*Plenty of worse things in the world than appearing before Judge Stevens...although I'm not sure I would have thought so before this week.*

Everything they'd experienced together—it was a trial by fire, and they'd come through the flames. Her feelings were more than just those of two people burnt together in the crucible of a crisis, and he wanted to believe her. Once that pressure was removed, would the attachment last?

*Here's my wish, spirits of New Orleans....let her love me, too.*

A puff of smoke came from several of the burning

torches, all at once, without any cause he could see.

"What was that?" asked Mr. Nielssen, bent nearly double trying to carry one of his wife's bags.

Hank got up to adjust the wicks. "Dunno. Looks fine to me. Maybe just a gust of wind." He shrugged and returned inside, mumbling about leftover *etouffee*.

Evan knew, though. He'd seen that happen before, out in the swamp, when Copper had placed "wishes" in that little boat. They'd vanished in the same kind of puff of smoke.

Maybe there was something to this magic, after all.

\*\*\*\*

Exhausted from her ordeal, Brianna kept thinking she should go to bed early, but she couldn't separate herself from the others. After the night she'd spent in jail with some truly depraved souls (and a whole lot of loud, happy drunks), her faith in people was deeply shaken.

Copper Delacroix had stolen her blind trust, catching her up in it like a fisherman's net, ready to sink her to the bottom of the ocean…and she'd let him.

She felt unworthy. At least, sitting here among familiar faces gave her a small safe haven where no one bad could touch her.

*And I have Evan.*

His eyes hardly left her all evening, his furrowed brow, the worried chewing of his lip. Was there something else he knew that she didn't? Something remaining in the trail of terror? Or could they truly put it behind them once and for all?

As the night grew late, the revelry in the neighborhood seemed to ratchet up a notch, the music louder, the parties more raucous, but she remained in her chair, letting the pleasant, relaxed sensation flow through her.

The other tourist couples went off to bed, two by two, and finally Terri and Hank, once assured there was nothing else they could do for her, followed. Evan took the seat next to her, stifling a yawn.

He reached over and took her hand. The burning lamps reflected like liquid emotion in his eyes. "Are you all right? Really?"

"I think I am. Thanks to you."

She smiled, thinking—*yes, thinking, as in logically moving from one thought to the next, rather than just accepting what was in front of her*—that considering the madness she'd entered into, she'd come out pretty well. A night in jail hadn't left any permanent scars, and when she'd come out, Evan was there, waiting for her.

He believed in her.

In her heart, she knew she believed in him, too.

It was a great way to begin.

They sat in companionable silence, watching the clear skies full of stars till she started yawning, too. When she would have apologized, he shushed her in the most pleasant way possible.

"We both are a little short on shut-eye. The best thing we could do for ourselves is head upstairs." His arm slipped around her and he helped her to her feet. "Come on, you're half asleep. Let me tuck you in."

A little wobbly on her feet, she was grateful for the arm of support around her as they locked up and went upstairs, but it wasn't the booze talking when she invited him into her room for the night.

"Are you sure, Brianna? I don't want to pressure you, not after all this."

She drew him inside. "It's no pressure. Now that I trust we really have feelings about each other, not something conjured by voodoo magic, I want to be with you.

"But I've got to get out of these clothes."

She grabbed her nightgown and slipped past him to the bathroom.

When she was ready, picturing his face, remembering his smell, she didn't experience that instant heat that had driven her the last time they'd been together, but it was a different feeling, more like a fire's warm embers than a flame. Touching him would reassure her and protect her, allowing her to finally rest.

Of all the things she could have collected to bring home from New Orleans, she had found the best souvenir ever, and he waited for her in her room.

Her heart skipping a couple of beats as she contemplated what might happen next, she quietly traversed the few steps back to her room, closing the door. But a glance at her bed threw them all awry and made her smile. Evan lay under the sheets, sound asleep.

*Poor thing, he must have been exhausted, too.*

Feeling all maternal and protective, she slipped in beside him, pulling the coverlets over them both. He shifted as she touched him, spooning up behind, his arms around her. Then he gently snored in her ear.

Brianna thought it was the sweetest sound in the world, and she let that soft noise and the feeling of safety all around her put her to sleep at last.

## Chapter Thirty

The airport was overcrowded, all the tourists heading home once again, many with the dark mark in the center of their forehead that meant they had been absolved of all their Mardi Gras sins by a church visit on Ash Wednesday morning.

Evan and Brianna, on the other hand, had slept till nearly noon, finally catching up on well-deserved rest. They'd kept their bags with them from the time they arrived at the airport until they boarded the plane, Brianna determined not to give anyone else a shot at destroying her peaceful exit from the city.

"I'm glad you could change your flight," Brianna said. "It wouldn't have been the same flying home alone."

Evan smiled. "I was happy to do it. I couldn't imagine having even those couple of hours out of touch with you." He shrugged. "Besides, you'd probably find some way to get into trouble."

Her feathers immediately ruffled, but she knew he was teasing. She made herself relax into her coach seat, glancing out the window with a wistful look at the bright sunshine. It certainly wouldn't be like that when they arrived back in Pittsburgh.

"So, when are you going to give Frank the bad news?"

"Probably at the end of the week."

"So soon?"

Her analytical mind clicked into gear. "We don't have office space yet, and no client list, and…Not even a secretary. I don't want the one I have at my office. She's such a noodle head! I mean, there's no office supplies, or anything. Or a desk. Or chairs. Or—"

He slid into the seat next to her. "I'm not rushing him, just warning him. We have plenty of time to do this right. Besides, I thought we agreed you were going to learn to lighten up a little."

She mock-glared at him. "This is my lightened phase, dear. Get used to it."

He leaned over to kiss her cheek. "I intend to get very accustomed to this phase and any other phase you have to hand out, Bri. I'm not worried about how you'll cope at all. The woman I love is someone I know is brave enough to take a leap off a cliff without always measuring her parachute to the millimeter. I've seen her do it."

*The woman I love…*

His words filled her with warmth like the tropical sunshine out the window. The smile that came to her lips was a clear expression of delight, finally unclouded by the voodoo curse hanging over their heads.

Evan had shown her more ways to security than collecting as much money as she could. In his arms, she knew she could withstand anything life had to throw at her.

She knew, too, he wouldn't hold her back from trying to meet any challenge she chose to go after.

*Perhaps we have many, many more adventures in our future. I can't wait to find out.*

## A word about the author...

Alana Lorens is the author of the Pittsburgh Lady Lawyer series, of which Voodoo Dreams is the third volume. By day she's a novelist and family law attorney, and by night she's mother to some special needs children on the autism spectrum and a science-fiction addict.

Her website is
http://alanalorens.com,
and you can Like her on Facebook at
https://www.facebook.com/AlanaLorens
Find her at Goodreads, too!

Thank you for purchasing
this publication of The Wild Rose Press, Inc.
For other wonderful stories of romance,
please visit our on-line bookstore at
www.thewildrosepress.com.

For questions or more information
contact us at
info@thewildrosepress.com.

The Wild Rose Press, Inc.
www.thewildrosepress.com

To visit with authors of
The Wild Rose Press, Inc.
join our yahoo loop at
http://groups.yahoo.com/group/thewildrosepress/